WITCHMASTER

WITCHMASTER

ISBN-13: 978-1-61317-190-5 (ebook)

ISBN 13: 978-1-83557-010-4 (print)

Editor: K.B. Spangler

Cover Design: Tara O'Shea

Cover Art: Aleksandar Sotirovski

For Fiadh all over again
(sorry it took so long)

WITCHMASTER

THE GUILDMASTER SAGA

BOOK V

C.E. MURPHY

A MIZKIT PRODUCTION

Rasim al Ilialio was orphaned at birth, victim of the Great Fire that tore the powerful delta city of Ilyara apart. Now age thirteen, he holds his place in the Seamasters' Guild by dint of quick thinking and sheer stubbornness. Possessed of little magic but a sharp mind, Rasim's greatest talent seems to be finding trouble—or perhaps escaping it just in time.

When a second, less devastating fire sweeps through Ilyara, Rasim's merchant friend Kisia finds evidence that the second fire was set on purpose. With Kisia at his side, Rasim brings the evidence to his Guildmaster, Isidri, an ancient and incredibly skilled sea witch. Isidri not only accepts their evidence as true, but also accepts Kisia into the Guild when she petitions to join—despite the fact that it's well-known that the Ilyaran guilds are peopled only by orphans, and that no one in Ilyaran history has ever learned magic after age ten.

No one is more surprised than Rasim when he and

Kisia earn a place on the fleet's flagship, the *Wafiya*. Rasim's rival, the powerful young apprentice Desimi, also joins them as they're sent North for a daring mission. But when a sea serpent attacks, apparently killing Kisia, Rasim is separated from the fleet.

He's rescued by Donnin, a pirate queen struggling to take her Island home back from the ambitious Lord Roscord. Rasim makes a bargain with her: if she'll sail him to the Northlands where his fleet is meant to be, he'll try to convince his people to help her regain her home.

But the Ilyaran fleet is nowhere to be found in the Northern city of Hongrunn. Instead, he learns that Hongrunn's water supply has been growing fouler for almost thirteen years—beginning when the Great Fire swept Ilyara. Rasim suspects the two things are somehow related.

The Northern princess, Inga, agrees to help Donnin's people. She sends her brother Lorens with Rasim, but things go wrong when Lord Roscord captures Rasim. To his shock, the *Wafiya* arrives to rescue him. Kisia is alive, and convinced that despite Rasim's weak magic, he saved her during the serpent attack. Roscord disappears, and Lady Donnin regains her lands.

Reunited with the *Wafiya*, Rasim returns to Ilyara only to discover that the Seamasters' Guild, accused of treachery, has been disbanded. He, Kisia, and Desimi are all arrested, and barely escape to find that Lord Roscord has made his way to Ilyara and poisoned the Ilyaran king, Taishm, against the Seamasters. In a climactic battle, Roscord is slain by Prince Lorens of the Northlands as Desimi masters tremendous magic to save Taishm's life.

The three apprentices are recognized as friends to the throne, with Desimi in particular earning the king's regard. Rasim, having been at the center of an international incident, is sent to study with the Sunmasters, who have long been the diplomatic support to the Ilyaran throne.

Weeks pass. Guildmaster Isidri, who had held off Roscord's fleet with a massive use of magic, regains some, but not all, of her strength. In a ceremony attended by not only the guild, but members of all the other guilds and King Taishm, Isidri passes the leadership of the Seamasters' Guild to Asindo, formerly captain of the *Wafiya*. She also elevates Rasim, Desimi, and Kisia to journeyman status before the king announces the creation of the King's Guild, which he hopes will allow apprentices and journeymen from all the guilds to learn magic from each other.

During the ceremony, Isidri mentions that when she was young, the guilds used to come and go from the palace as advisors and diplomats, depending on the particular magical strengths of the reigning monarch. The Sunmasters, however, have now held sway for nearly a hundred years, so long that almost no one remembers that it was ever different. Rasim is outraged that they've taken advantage of being in power for so long.

Taishm sends all the members of his newly formed King's Guild to the Northlands to help fix Hongrunn's water supply. The new captain of the *Wafiya*, Nasira, despises Rasim, and trouble follows him the whole journey. An afternoon of trying to practice sunmastery ends up with every rope on the ship going up in flames. The ship is put in to shore at a bleak little island, and the crew searches for something to use as rope.

Rasim is attacked by his crewmate Missio, who resents the fact that he was assigned to the *Wafiya* instead of her adoptive brother, who was killed in the sea serpent attack a few months earlier. But his near-miss with death leads Rasim to the wreckage of the *Sinaz*, another Ilyaran ship thought lost during the serpent attack. They realize its surviving crew was taken by slavers, and Nasira swears she'll find and rescue them.

A second attempt is made on Rasim's life: he, Kisia, and the Stonemaster journeymen who sailed north with them are all thrown overboard. Kisia, believing strongly in Rasim's witchery, tells him to save them; when he somehow summons the magic to do so, he and Kisia are also granted a visit from Siliaria, the sea goddess herself. In the wake of that visit, Rasim comes fully into his powers as a Seamaster.

After making landfall, the journeymen are captured. Telun and the extremely powerful Milu are sold into slavery: their stone witchery is too valuable to waste, while Kisia and Rasim are sent to the mines. Rasim tentatively tries to use stonemastery, but isn't entirely sure if it works. With help from others slaving in the mines, they escape and follow Telun and Milu, only to fight a tremendous magical beast, a stone snake which they manage to subdue.

When they're reunited with the rest of the crew in Hongrunn, they go with them to help purify the salt-poisoned waters, but a terrible trap has been set to prevent that. Almost half the *Wafiya's* crew are killed, and the Northern princess Inga barely escapes with her life. In the aftermath of that disaster, Rasim slips away and, using the stone witchery he can't even sense himself working, secretly sculpts a memorial to the dead. Having confirmed he can use the magic, he plans to tell no one as he returns to Hongrunn.

The Hongrunn harbor freezes solid while the Ilyarans mourn their dead. Desimi and Kisia take a little time to relax while Rasim worries. As they challenge each other to tests of magical skill, an unknown faction sets slavers upon the rest of the *Wafiya's* crew. Rasim barely succeeds in saving Sesin, a sea witch with a talent for healing, and has to reveal his talent for stonemastery to do so.

The attack by the slavers comes with a vast outpouring of sea witchery, far beyond what anyone on the crew can manage except perhaps Desimi, who isn't even there. Rasim discovers it's his former crewmate Missio, who has been given an incredibly powerful drug that allows her to use a huge amount of magic at once—and pays for the effort with her life. Rasim acquires a little of the drug and uses it to break the Ilyaran ships free of the frozen harbor…and wakes up three days later, exhausted and barely functional.

Captain Nasira has sailed the *Wafiya* to the mouth

of the River Moran, upon which the city of Moran, the largest slaving city on the continent, sits. Rasim concocts a plan to trick the Moranese into believing Nasira has chosen to enslave her crew, which works surprisingly well—until Lady Amdria of the Moranese Council requests a 'gift' of one of Nasira's crew, and the captain chooses Rasim.

He's given mindkiller, a drug meant to prevent witches from using their magic except under direct order. Once drugged, he's thrown into a gladiator arena and partnered with Agnet, a huge Northern woman with exceptional fighting skills, and a young man from the Shenryalan plains, far to the west. Neither Rasim nor the Shenryalan boy, Bayar, are warriors. Agnet keeps them alive while Rasim tries to work his way around the mindkiller by not using *sea witchery*: nobody ever told him not to use stonemastery! It doesn't work very well, though: he has no feel for stone witchery at all.

Cast into the arena to fight another enslaved Ilyaran, Rasim is forced to try using sky witchery. It succeeds, but the vicious battle summons a glasswing, an extraordinary dragonfly-like beast of solid air, which is destroyed in their fight. Rasim escapes the arena in the aftermath, almost starting a slave rebellion, but it falters and he's dragged back to be executed.

At the last moment, the remainder of the *Wafiya*'s free crew—including Desimi and Kisia—storms the arena and saves him, as well as Bayar, who proves to be not just Shenryalan, but a prince of Shenryal. He requests an escort home, but as the Ilyarans make their escape, freeing slaves along the way, a formerly enslaved stone witch destroys the city of Moran. The *Wafiya* flees, leaving devastation behind.

They've barely reached Shenryal when a dragon appears. Rasim draws it away from his friends, but is then swept away *by* it. Unexpected rescue comes from Shenryalan riders, who immediately bring him to their shaman, Oyun. The old woman declares Rasim 'unbalanced,' and takes him on a spirit journey that teaches him to use the final Ilyaran magic, sun witchery, in order to restore his balance. By the time his friends catch up, Rasim has discovered that several people he knows, including the Stonemaster journeymen Telun and Milu, are being held captive by the Shenryalans, who distrust outsiders and are preparing for war in hopes of bringing their missing prince, Bayar, home.

Bayar's kidnapping is, to Rasim's quick mind, the final piece in a continent-wide conspiracy that he believes was meant to destabilize the centers of power: Ilyara suffered the Great Fire; the eastern Islands spent over a decade under an internal power struggle; Hongrunn's northern water supply was poisoned; and finally, the heir apparent to the Shenryalan clans was kidnapped. But Rasim realizes the kidnapping—and a later attempt at poisoning that nearly kills both Bayar and Kisia—were not orchestrated by outsiders, but instead by Shenryalans searching for personal power, and willing to work with Northerners to achieve it.

When a Shenryalan earth witch is accused, she runs...and Desimi, in an act of desperation, works earth witchery himself to stop her. She accuses Prince

Lorens of having helped her learn earth magic, and when Rasim tries to find the Northern prince to see if it's true, he discovers Lorens has fled. The *Wafiya*'s crew decides it's time to leave, although first Kisia is adopted by Bayar's mother as a 'heart-daughter,' for her part in helping to save the Shenryalan prince's life. The Shenryalan cavalry also promises to ride to Ilyara to help protect the city from the approaching Moranese army.

Once they're on the sea again, Rasim figures out how to teach Desimi air witchery, and, realizing that the Ilyaran fleet is half destroyed, suggests to Captain Nasira that they sail to the Islands to ask Lady Donnin for help before going home. Nasira reluctantly agrees, but before they reach the Islands, the *Wafiya* is attacked by Northern ships carrying witches who work with lightning.

The *Wafiya* itself is destroyed in the attack, leaving the crew alive but devastated. On Nasira's orders, Rasim and Desimi work a huge piece of air witchery, calling a glasswing to them on the open sea, and, with Kisia, fly back to Ilyara to warn their beloved home city of what awaits them…

CHAPTER ONE

Kisia smelled the desert first.

They were still impossibly far from the Ilyaran basin, Rasim thought. Even at the height they skimmed through the sky, far higher than any ship's mast could reach, the world below them was only ocean, with no land masses shadowing the horizon. But when Kisia exclaimed that she could smell the desert, Rasim straightened on the glasswing's back and took a deep breath, trying to catch the dry flat scent of sun-baked sand.

Maybe he could. Maybe a prevailing wind coming off the desert carried Ilyaran sand up to where three Seamaster journeymen clung to the glittering spine of a fragile creature made of elemental air.

Glasswings lived in the sky, as real as a gust of wind, and most of the time, as hard to see. They were drawn to magic—Rasim was discovering a lot of terri-fying things were drawn to magic—and when they incorporated into something visible, they were beautiful. Huge, dragonfly-like wings fluttered against the air as long, sinuous bodies caught the light in a thousand colorful prisms.

There wasn't really room for three teenagers to fit on one's back, but Rasim, Kisia and Desimi had been desperately hanging on for days now. They hadn't had much to drink, had eaten even less, and none of them wanted to talk about what eliminating bodily waste entailed.

It was not, overall, a journey Rasim wanted to repeat. It was, though, much faster than even the swiftest Ilyaran ship, and time was of desperate essence. "I still don't smell it," he said on a dry throat. "But I hope you're right."

Kisia sniffed. "Well, I guess I just smell better than you do."

Desimi, who rode at the front because he was biggest and the glasswing seemed to be able to carry him most easily directly between its wings, looked back at the other two with a guffaw swept away by the wind. "None of us smell very good right now, Kees!"

The short-haired girl was squished in the middle between the two boys, but still managed to elbow Desimi's torso. "That's not what I meant!"

"She probably still *does* smell better than we do," Rasim said through a grin. They were all unwashed and stinky, but thirteen-year-old boys somehow *did* seem to smell worse than fourteen-year-old girls.

"The glasswing doesn't have to fly us all the way to Ilyara," Kisia said fervently. "Just to the river delta. It can dump us in, for all I care, as long as I get to wash."

"Soon," Rasim promised.

"You have no idea if it'll be soon or not," Desimi muttered, but aside from brief bouts of conversation like this, none of them had the energy to talk a lot, much less bicker. The glasswing's natural tendency was to fade back into the air, dissolving into something largely untouchable. Either Rasim or Desimi had to keep up a continuous use of sky witchery, the magic that allowed certain Ilyarans to control wind and air, to keep the glasswing beneath them.

Before a few months ago, neither of the boys, both raised in the water-magic-using Seamasters Guild, had been able to command sky witchery at all. Now, between the glasswing's lightning-fast wingbeats and the tailwind they maintained, the trio had made impossibly good time in their race home.

"I can smell the sand," Kisia said again, defiantly. Rasim, who didn't really doubt her, straightened up a little more to see if a deeper breath would help him smell what she did.

Instead, for a heartbeat, he was shocked breathless at the expanse of ocean below them, at the curve of the earth, and the sheer emptiness of the world from this height. That shock had hit them all more than once as they flew. Although he knew he wouldn't see anything, Rasim twisted around, searching for the continents and islands he knew were out there.

He had flown this high—or almost—once before, on the back of an enraged red dragon. Then, though, it had been across the Shenryalan steppes, far to the west of where they now flew. The steppes had been surrounded on all sides by mountains, making the plains like the bottom of a vast bowl. The rest of the world had been invisible beyond the mountainous boundaries. Even that had been impossibly huge, but it didn't compare to the ocean's endless width. The clouds seemed small, compared to the ocean, and their shadows flickered across the rolling water like mirages.

Sunset had begun scattering through the clouds and water alike, streaks of red and gold playing with the shadows and dancing over the ocean's surface. During the nights, they kept an eye on the stars to navigate. Now Rasim glanced upward, wondering if there were enough of them out yet to tell them where they were, but only one or two shone palely in the fading blue sky. He'd hoped they wouldn't be stuck on the glasswing another night, but wasn't sure Kisia's nose would lead them to land soon enough.

"There." Desimi spoke with his gaze on the south-western horizon. "Land ho. Kisia was right."

Kisia sniffed again, this time indignantly. "Of course I was right."

Rasim grinned and leaned around her, looking toward where Desimi had indicated. The faintest smudge discolored the ocean, although within minutes —hardly any time, compared to how long a ship took— visible greenery spilled across the fast-approaching land mass. Just as fast, that greenery faded to desert, touching the coast here and there. Mostly, though, the desert ran deep into the continent, such an unbroken expanse of pale sand that all three journeymen fell silent in awe.

"I knew the desert was big," Desimi whispered as the sand, now below them, went blue with rising moonlight. "I just didn't know it was...*this* big."

Rasim nodded silently. They were more or less following the continent's coast now, riding gusts of unexpected warmer air that rose from the land below. The vast delta their home city sat on opened onto the sea, so they didn't have to fly into the desert. Still, seeing it spreading endlessly beneath them was somehow a shock.

They had all grown up knowing that the patch of deep vegetation that Ilyara had developed in turned to desert where the river's waters couldn't reach. They had all sailed the Ilyaran Sea, and had seen the desert stretching out beside them on that journey.

It was different, seeing its breadth from the sky. Seeing how it stretched so far into the continent that the southerly border couldn't be seen, or really even imagined. Like the ocean, Rasim thought. Once the *Wafiya*, the now-fallen Ilyaran flagship, left the sight of land, the rest of the world faded away. The desert was like that. Once its borders were breached, there was really nothing else. But he knew the sea in a way that he didn't know the endless sandy dunes. "Do you think the Stonemasters know how big it is? I mean..." He faded off, not sure how to put what he meant in words.

"You mean like, do they spend as much time studying it and traveling it and learning it as we do the ocean? Probably." Desimi sounded so thoughtful it was almost critical.

Given that Desimi hardly ever thought at all, Rasim

decided he shouldn't object to the critical tone. Especially when the bigger boy, still gazing out at the desert spilling off to their left, added, "I'm beginning to see why the king wants a guild of witches who study all the magics. We'd be studying the landscape, too, wouldn't we? Learning about how everything works together. I know the desert is *there*," he said impatiently. "I know how to live for a little while in it, but I didn't even know how *big* it was."

Kisia twisted her head around to give Rasim a brief, big-eyed glance. He widened his own eyes in turn, a silent exchange of surprise and agreement in those two quick looks. Desimi had been born with an extraordinary talent for water witchery, the kind of power that practically guaranteed him a ship of his own and a crew to command. He had always been arrogant and obnoxious in his power, showing very little inclination to even learn how to be a good captain, never mind think beyond the Seamasters Guild and consider the rest of Ilyara. Hearing frustration in his voice about things he didn't know was simply astonishing.

And neither Rasim nor Kisia were going to say a single word out loud to express their amazement, because Desimi was bigger than both of them put together and would probably push them off the glasswing if they had the nerve to mention they were amazed he was using his brain. Rasim grinned into Kisia's shoulder at the idea, and took his gaze from the endless desert on their left to watch the dark blue Ilyaran Sea stretching below them on their right.

Another continent lay farther yet to the right, still so far away that even from the glasswing's back, Rasim couldn't see it across the sea's white-capped breadth. He wished he knew what was happening at its heart, where the slaver city of Moran had crumbled under a rebellion he'd accidentally started. But he and the others had been far away from any standard trade routes that might bring news for weeks now. The best they could do was hurry on to Ilyara learn what they could, and share what they knew with the Ilyaran king.

He'd been running through thoughts like that for days, ever since they had flown away from the wrecked *Wafiya*. He had no more answers now than he ever had, and eventually his circling thoughts spiraled into silence. For a while he slept as much as he could on the uncomfortable, dragonfly-like back. Desimi woke him in the middle of the night to take over the air witchery that kept the glasswing's attention, and Rasim watched the black water below gradually turn grey as dawn chased them. After what felt like hours of glazed watching, he finally realized he'd been staring blankly down at rich green foliage for a while.

"We're home!" The excitement in his voice woke the other two. "The delta is ahead of us!"

"Oh, thank Siliaria," Kisia breathed. "Let's go home."

"Let's land," Desimi said at almost the same time. His shoulders stiffened as Rasim and Kisia both said, "Land?" as if he'd started speaking another language.

"We're exhausted. All of us. And we don't know what's going on in Ilyara. If it's bad…"

Kisia's sigh matched Rasim's own. "Then we should be rested before we go try to fix it."

A sudden laugh rose in Rasim's throat and he tried to choke it off. It ended up being an awful snort of a sound instead, one that first startled, then amused the other two enough that they were all abruptly giggling with hysterical weariness. Kisia, after a startled heartbeat, grinned. "Because of *course* three unwashed journeymen who haven't heard the news in six weeks will just sweep in and fix anything that four Guildmasters, their guilds, and a king can't handle, right?"

A new whoop of laughter broke from Rasim's chest while Desimi simply bent forward over the glasswing and howled his disbelief against the beast's glittering thorax. Kisia, feeble with her own laughter, pounded on his back. "Get this thing to bring us to the ground before we fall off from laughing too hard."

Rasim thought it was more likely they'd lose control of the witchery that kept it solid and all plummet to their deaths, but that didn't seem like the right thing to say. Instead, wiping tears of laughter from his eyes, he sent the wind around then on a slow arc toward the ground, and after several minutes, they finally tumbled off the glasswing's back onto soft, rich, delta earth.

The glasswing leaped back into the air, back hunched, then flexing, stretching itself like the weight off its shoulders was a tremendous relief. Leaves and dust sprayed with the rapid flutter of its wings, and it darted in a small circle above them, obviously pleased to be unencumbered again. Rasim called, "Thank you," to the translucent creature, and it flexed one more time before rushing higher into the sky. All the witchery he and Desimi had been holding to keep it with them faded, and between one blink and the next, the extraordinary beast disappeared, once again no more visible than the wind.

Both boys collapsed into the dirt, leaving Kisia standing above them with an air of exasperation. "Fine, fine, *I'll* get fish and fruit and water. Don't mind me, doing all the work here." At Rasim's croak of protest, she laughed. "No, I'm kidding. I'll look for all of it. You two have been using witchery for days on end. Sleep. I'll be back in a while."

Rasim said, "No, I'll help," and the next thing he knew, a stack of deliciously-cooked white fish lay wrapped in leaves within a small stone cairn that Kisia had clearly built. He made a guilty sound at the effort she'd put in while the boys slept, but kept it quiet so the others wouldn't waken, although they both did before he was done eating. None of them spoke much as they ate. Without discussing it, they went into the water together to swim up the Ilyaran delta as secretively as possible. Witchery gave them the air they needed, and the speed: it wasn't long before they surfaced in the harbor, barely rising above eye level in the water like a trio of curious seals.

For a few seconds none of them really understood what they were seeing, and then Desimi gave a choked sound that echoed the feeling in Rasim's heart.

The Ilyaran harbor was filled with ships, every single one of them burned to the water-line.

CHAPTER TWO

Instantly, without speaking, all three journeymen submerged again. They always carried enough air under water to speak, but this time all of them made larger bubbles around themselves than usual, as if they all expected to have a lot to say. Except no one spoke after all: instead they frowned worriedly around the harbor from under water, comparing what they'd seen on the surface with what lay below.

Nothing had been scuttled: there were no ships on the harbor floor, just the burned hulls bobbing too high in the water without the rest of the ships to weigh them down. Rasim had spent weeks trying to anticipate the worst disasters that could have befallen Ilyara. Moran could have, somehow, moved more quickly than expected and an army could have descended upon the unprepared city. Perhaps Prince Lorens of the Northlands, who had been acting against them for all the time Rasim had known him, had sailed to Ilyara even more quickly than the journeymen could fly on the glasswing. Maybe the pirate captain and lady of the Islands, Donnin, had brought her army to Ilyara, although she was, at least in theory, an ally.

All of those things were possible, but none of them seemed very likely. Which left only one probable explanation for the burned ships at the harbor's surface: Ilyara faced trouble from within.

He didn't—couldn't—know for sure, but he suspected the Sunmasters' Guild of treachery. Like many other sea witches, he had only recently learned that once, the four magic-using Ilyaran guilds had rotated through the palace as advisors and teachers to the royal family. In his lifetime, though, only the Sunmasters had been the royal diplomats, counselors, and tutors. They had come to power nearly a hundred years ago, when Isidri, once Guildmaster to the Seamasters, had been a girl…and they had never let it go. There were reasons for that, even good reasons, but the fact remained that one guild had rooted itself where four used to pass through.

By itself, that was predictable, maybe, but not necessarily *evil*, Rasim thought. Wrong, but not evil.

But almost fourteen years ago, Ilyara had been stricken by a great fire, one that the Sunmasters had failed to subdue. There were reasons for that, too: the king, who usually guided major works of magic within the city, had been away from Ilyara at the time, and the guild had been unable to organize without that guidance.

Unless, of course, they had *chosen* not to, rather than been unable to.

"Rasi." Desimi spoke in a low voice, dragging Rasim out of his thoughts. "Are we going to stay at the bottom of the harbor forever?"

He took a sharp breath and shook his head. "We should go in through the shipyards," he said in an equally low voice. The other two nodded, and as if by agreement, used only the very minimum witchery necessary to swim deep, as close to the harbor's bottom as they could manage. Given the state of the boats above, Rasim didn't really think anybody was searching the harbor for new arrivals, but Ilyaran waters were notoriously clear. Depth at least offered a measure of obscurity, and Rasim, heart hammering with worried anticipation, was afraid they could use every bit of protection they could get.

The shipyards backed up to the guildhall, a protected segment of the harbor that let shipwrights work year round and still return to the hall easily at night. The journeymen swam through them together, toward a ladder worked into the sea walls, and scrambled out with the ease of long habit.

For the first moments above the surface, all Rasim could think about was the heat and the noise. It had been months since they'd been in Ilyara's humid delta heat. Rasim had thought the Shenryalan steppes were cold, but now, for the first time, he thought Ilyara was hot.

Desimi, just behind him climbing up the ladder, exhaled in surprise, too. "It's hot."

Kisia, ahead of them both, snorted quietly under all

the distant sound. "This isn't hot. Try baking with the ovens roaring in mid-summer. *That's* hot."

"This is hot too," Rasim breathed. For a moment, he wished he'd come out of the water wet, but sea witches really only got wet if they meant to. He took the last steps up to the shipyard's docks, wiped his hand across his forehead, and frowned around at the shipyards in confusion.

There were no shipwrights at work. It looked like there hadn't been for weeks, maybe months. Rasim could see ships in the same stage of completion they'd been when they had left almost half a year ago. But beyond the shipyard there was shouting, cries of anger and pain, orders being called, and beyond *that*, a roar that seemed to run through the whole of Ilyara. Kisia whispered, "What is going *on*?" not as if she expected an answer, but as if she couldn't keep the words in.

"Nothing good." Desimi took a few steps forward, then paused to look back at the other two. "Well, come on. We're not going to learn anything standing here."

"I'm not sure I want to know what's going on," Rasim said lowly.

The big journeyman gave him a dark grin. "Me either, but we didn't come this far to run away now, did we?"

"Nasira was right," Rasim said as he and Kisia joined the bigger boy. "The three of us together are determined to get in trouble."

"Did she say that?" Kisia sounded oddly pleased.

"Something like it." The shipyard was separated from

the main hall grounds by a gated wall, mostly to keep very young apprentices from doing themselves harm on the building site, and Rasim thought he was prepared for whatever he would see when he pushed the gate open.

He was wrong.

Whatever he had imagined for their return to Ilyara, the guildhall wracked by chaos wasn't it. People lay in temporary beds and stretchers all over the huge open grounds, while Seamaster-clad healers moved between them with grim expressions. The temperature dropped noticeably as the journeymen stepped between the shipyard and the main grounds, with unexpected shadows providing relief from the heat. Rasim's gaze went upward to find tremendous canvases pulled taut between the hall and its outer walls, dramatically reducing the sunlight that fell on injured and dying Ilyarans.

Desimi whispered, "Siliaria's *tears*. What…?"

"They're at war," Kisia said just as quietly. "Ilyara is at war."

Rasim's voice cracked. "With *who*?"

"Everyone's brown, like us," Desimi said after a few grim seconds. "Either they're not healing foreign soldiers in the guildhall, or…"

"Or we're fighting ourselves," Kisia whispered. "Ilyarans are killing each other. Rasim." She hiccuped his name, fear carried in it. "Rasim, do you think the Sunmasters…?"

Even Rasim barely knew how to finish that question. He could hardly imagine that the Sunmasters—or anyone—might have actually tried to overthrow King

Taishm, but obviously something terrible was happening. "If they did, at least we're not letting them win without a fight."

Kisia, gazing at the injured and dying ahead of them, said, "Is that a good thing?" as they edged into the makeshift hospital. No one had noticed them yet, and Rasim wasn't sure anyone would. There were so many people, so many injured, and so many sea witches struggling to help them. The healers' arm of the Seamasters had never been large, and was obviously taxed far past its limits. Sea witches who Rasim knew had never healed anyone were among those trying to help, but there'd been a reason Master Usia had been so pleased to discover that the fourth-year journeyman Sesin had a talent for healing. It just wasn't common, even among seamasters.

"There's pressure around his heart." Kisia had stopped beside a too-pale Ilyaran, who lay with his eyes crushed shut and sweat pouring off his body. "I know how to squeeze a heart. I don't know if I know how to…" Witchery flowed, cautious and gentle as she tried to figure out what was wrong inside the man and offer him some relief. "It's hard," she said in a tight voice. "The heart is in a sac of water, did you know that? And there's too much water around his, and there's nowhere to pull it out from. I don't know how."

"Diffuse it." Desimi crouched beside them, his hands spread but no power washing from him. "The body is full of liquid, Kees. If you can tell the difference between the heart sac and the rest of the blood, you can thin it out until it's back in his blood. I can't do it. Sesin tried to explain it to me when you were poisoned, but all I could do was slow the blood in your body a little. Just take your time."

"But how do you know?" Kisia's voice broke with fear. "What if I make it worse?"

"I don't think you can." The man spoke, every word breathy and difficult to hear. "Two witches have looked at me already and gone on because they couldn't even tell what was wrong. If you can tell…at least try. Your goddess and I…" He ran out of breath and lay gasping a few long moments before he managed to whisper, "We'll both forgive you, if it doesn't work. Try."

Tears spilled down Kisia's cheeks as she put her hand on his chest very lightly. For a long time she and Desimi stayed crouched where they were, with Rasim standing over them, his fists clenched. He could just barely feel the subtle witchery she worked, and couldn't feel the difference between the different fluids she was trying to move in the man's body at all. Desimi looked up at him once, a question in his eyes, and Rasim shook his head. Desimi mouthed, "Me either," and looked back down at the man and the work Kisia was trying to do.

Little by little, the man's breathing got easier, and his color began to return. Kisia kept her head bent, eyes closed, until a faint smile broke over his face and he had the strength to lift a hand and capture her wrist. "Thank you, Healer."

New tears flooded Kisia's face and she smiled blindly at the man as she rose. "I'm not, though."

"Enough of one for me," he whispered. "My name is

Darrak. Find me in the clothier's quarters when this war has ended, and I'll make you a gown in thanks."

"Darrak," Kisia echoed with a nod. "I'll come see you." She lurched with exhaustion, and Desimi put an arm around her waist, guiding her away.

"I could never have done that," he said in a low voice. "The guild doesn't know how lucky it was when you joined it, Kisia."

Kisia gave a wet laugh and buried her face in his shoulder as they moved toward the guildhall. Even with the pause to help—and Rasim thought they might have stood at Darrak's side for hours—they hadn't yet been noticed. Everyone was too focused on their jobs to realize a trio of journeymen who had been long gone were back again. Rasim saw many witches he knew, but a slow knot of dread began to form in his gut as he searched for two faces in particular, and couldn't find them.

The main doors swung open and for a moment the plaza outside the guildhall was visible. People lined it, keeping a peaceful gauntlet to bring the injured through, but beyond them, a fight surged. Even in the few seconds Rasim watched, it seemed clear it wasn't a constant pitched battle, but he could see barricades farther down the street, and angry voices rose above clashes of metal and wood.

Then a raft of injured people were swept in, and the doors closed behind them again. Witches rushed to meet the newcomers. Rasim and the others fought the tide, pushing toward the guildhall's largest building. They still hadn't been noticed, not in a meaningful way.

As they slipped inside the main hall, Rasim thought they might never be, because it was filled with beds and injured people, too. Even without a healer's sense, he understood almost immediately that these people were in greater danger than the ones outside. It was cooler in here, less stressful for hurt bodies, but given some of the injuries he'd seen outdoors, he was afraid to see what *worse* meant.

A thin, crisp voice sailed over the sounds of agony, and knee-buckling relief nearly stopped Rasim in his tracks. All three of the journeymen turned toward that voice, and after a few seconds, as if she felt the weight of their gazes, Isidri al Ilialio, leader of the Seamasters' Guild for fifty years and only recently retired, raised her head and looked toward them.

Her ancient face was a network of wrinkles beneath white hair pulled back in a waist-length, wrist-thick braid. The symbol of her Guildmaster status, the green ribbon threaded through the braid, had never been removed; she would be honorary Guildmaster until she died, even if the position itself was now held by Asindo, former captain of the *Wafiya*.

Rasim's throat tightened and his eyes went hot with unshed tears. Isidri wore guild colors, though they were far from clean. No one's were, in the sick room, but seeing Isidri as spattered and mucky as everyone else brought home the seriousness of the situation more than even the outside hospital had.

Genuine joy shone in the old woman's face, despite the circumstances. She gestured, and all three of them hurried through the temporary hospital to her side.

Isidri managed to pull them into single embrace, and Rasim lost all hope of not crying. Even Desimi was wiping his eyes as the old woman let them go and studied them hard, as if no one else was there. She pronounced, "You've grown," and when Rasim put a hand on top of his head like he was measuring himself, snorted. "Not like that. Although that too, lad. You may find some height in you yet. I'm glad to have you home, Journeymen. All of you."

"We're glad to be home,." Rasim whispered. "And glad to see you, Guildmaster Isidri."

"Ah, you weren't worried about me, were you, lad? It takes more than a frozen harbor to put me down." She tossed a frown toward the outside world, adding, "And more than a war, as well. Asindo is out there, fighting fires. Where have you been? Where's Nasira? Arrat? Usia and Stonemaster Lusa? Where," she said, her old voice deepening dangerously, "is the crew of my *ship*? Where's my ship, for that matter?"

The *Wafiya* hadn't technically been hers for decades, but Rasim wasn't about to correct her. Especially with sickness and guilt rising in his belly as he struggled to find the easiest, or at least fastest, answers to impossibly difficult questions. "Guildmaster, the... we lost the *Wafiya*."

Isidri's dark skin went ashy enough that Rasim put his hand out to support her. To his relief, he got smacked for his efforts. Isidri made a sharp gesture with one hand and led the journeymen away to a quiet corner. "What happened?"

Kisia and Desimi exchanged glances, then fell back

half a step, leaving Rasim to tell the story. He gave them both desperate looks, but Kisia widened her eyes and Desimi shrugged like *he* wasn't going to get involved in this. "Prince Lorens betrayed us," Rasim finally said, after trying a dozen times to find a place to start. "The North has lightning witches and they broke the *Wafiya's* keel. The crew survived, but…before that, there was an awful accident in the Northlands and so many people died. Stonemaster Lusa died."

Isidri had an iron grip on the walking stick she'd used since the harbor attack most of a year earlier. "We heard of the accident. Healer Usia?"

Rasim whispered, "I haven't seen him since the slavers attacked in Hongrunn," as if that would answer her question in any meaningful way.

The ancient Guildmaster seemed to age even more as she stared at him, all too clearly working her way through questions that she perhaps already had answers to, or maybe discounted as not important.

Or maybe not, because the one she asked couldn't possibly matter. "Why are you yellow-haired, Rasim?"

Rasim said, "I tried to disguise myself in Moran after starting a slave rebellion," in a small voice

"Mother of every fish in the sea," Isidri said so mildly that Rasim felt like his skin had been scraped across a barnacle-covered keel. "I see you haven't changed at all, Journeyman."

"Oh," Desimi said almost brightly, "I don't know, I think he's gotten worse."

"Nooo!" Rasim actually howled the word, although

he had enough sense to keep it quiet. "You're the one who's gotten worse! Nasira said so!"

"Stop." Isidri's voice cut across both of theirs. "Stop, and let me summon Asindo, and then you can tell us everything."

CHAPTER THREE

Rasim hadn't been in the Guildmaster's office since Asindo had been elevated to the job. It felt like a mix of Isidri's old office and Asindo's cabin on the *Wafiya*. A big desk had been pushed against one wall and had a huge piece of paper spread across it, pinned at the corners by paperweights that Rasim recognized from the ship. The walls held carefully-drawn maps whose copies were familiar to any sea witch. A few shelves held mementos of Asindo's years as a captain, from shaped pieces of driftwood to compasses and a colored glass dolphin. There were half a dozen chairs flung across the room's floor with enough space between them to make them private without being so far apart as to make conversation difficult.

Isidri perched in the one that had been hers for decades, and glowered the journeymen into silent stillness until a deeply weary-looking Asindo came in with a worried, "Tiss said you needed me, Isidri, what's—"

He stopped hard when he saw the journeymen. After a heartbeat of shocked staring he crossed to them, dropped to his knees, and hauled all three of them into a hug. The stout Guildmaster had never been a tall man, but he was strong, and Kisia squeaked in happy protest as his embrace squeezed them all.

It was a long moment before Asindo let them go, and his eyes were bright when he did. He wiped them, then heaved himself to his feet. "We're glad to have you home, journeymen. But how did you get here without us knowing? Where's the *Wafiya?*"

"We lost her, Guildmaster." Saying it a second time was no easier, and watching disbelief and horror drain color from Asindo's face sickened Rasim's stomach. "I'm sorry," he said helplessly. "I'm sorry, but it's also almost the last part of the story, so can I…can we start at the beginning?"

Asindo pulled a hand over his bearded face, studying the three of them, then nodded. "Go on, lad. Tell us your tale."

After another fumbling start, it felt like Rasim talked for hours. At some point, Asindo called for food. Desimi and Kisia interrupted more than the Guildmasters did, adding details that Rasim had glossed over. The only time Isidri broke in was when Kisia blurted, "But you skipped the part when we talked to Siliaria!" and the old Guildmaster's feathery white eyebrows shot up.

"You spoke with the *sea goddess?*"

Rasim slumped. "If Kisia hadn't been there, no one would believe me. Nobody really does anyway."

Isidri, in a peculiar and gentle voice, said, "I do."

Even Asindo looked at Isidri then, although she only said, "Go on," to the journeymen. After a moment of trying to remember where he'd left off, Rasim went on, trying to stick to only the most important parts of the story. It turned out they all felt important. He paused when plates of rice, fish, and bread were brought, along with tankards of fruit juice that they guzzled gratefully. Almost full, he found half a boiled egg hidden in his rice, and ate it greedily with some extra bread before wiping his hands and face.

Recounting it all, watching the Guildmasters' faces as every awful moment was explained, made Rasim wonder if it had all been even worse than he remembered. It had been terrible at the time, but it seemed almost worse talking about it. He had the sudden uncomfortable sense that it was all looming over him like an ill-maintained sail that would fall when he least expected it. His ability to tell the story faltered, and after a concerned peek at him, Kisia summarized the rest with, "So Rasim is a witchmaster now. He can use all the witcheries, the way Taishm wanted. So can Desimi."

"I can't either." Desimi's correction was surprisingly mild, for him. "I can use sky and earth witchery, though."

"*Earth* witchery? Not stonemastery?" Isidri's voice rose.

"The Shenryalans use earth magic, and it was important," Desimi said like it explained everything.

"See," Rasim hissed at him. "See, this is how it

happens! That's how I end up in trouble all the time! It's important, so I do something, and—" He spread his hands as if an explosion was happening.

The Guildmasters sat a moment, absorbing everything the journeymen had told them. Eventually, Isidri sighed. "Well. You've told us your story. I suppose we should tell you what's happened here."

"We're guessing the Sunmasters took over," Kisia said in a low voice. "But not how or why or what happened to Taishm, or how the people are taking it, although…" She waved toward the outside world. "It didn't look like they were taking it very well."

"No one has seen the king in weeks," Asindo said wearily. "Guildmaster Jhikara of the Skymasters threw in with the Sunmasters. Luthan of the Stonemasters remained steadfast, but with the guilds two and two against each other…" He sighed as if words were too difficult, which, having just told the story of their last several months, Rasim understood.

Isidri picked up. "I suspect with the formation of the King's Guild, the Sunmasters felt they were losing their sway in the palace, and took steps to re-establish their hold."

Rasim's thoughts flew ahead, taking his mouth with them, so he only knew what he was thinking as he spoke. "No, it wasn't just the King's Guild. I bet they'd felt that way since King Laishn married Annaken. Everybody knows the royal bloodline was getting weaker and more dependent on the Sunmasters, which is why he married a Northerner, isn't it? Maybe not for stronger witchery, because the Northerners don't have any—"

Desimi and Kisia both made noises of disagreement, and Rasim pulled a face at them. "You know what I mean. Didn't have any that we knew about. The point is that Laishn married outside of Ilyara and they had their first baby fast, right? And if they'd had a lot of kids that could have risked the Sunmasters' hold on the palace. So I don't think the Sunmasters *started* with thinking the King's Guild was a risk. I think it went back farther than that, and the idea of creating a King's Guild made it worse."

Asindo exhaled. "Rasim may be right. He—"

Desimi muttered, "He usually is," sourly, which silenced everyone again.

Isidri and Asindo both sat back, watching the journeymen until all three of them squirmed uncomfortably. Asindo, dryly, said, "If it wouldn't inconvenience you for me to continue, Desimi...?"

Desimi set his jaw, then, in a low but defiant voice, spoke. "No. I have something to say. The Sunmasters must have thought they would take power without a fight. Because I don't believe they'd go to this much trouble to get into power and then let Moran or the Islands just come and take over. So maybe they're less prepared for the outside war than they should be, because they've got an inside one to deal with." He shot a quick glance at Rasim, but kept talking to the Guildmasters, each word careful, as if he was thinking it through while he spoke. Like Rasim did all the time, just more slowly. "We thought they'd be preparing

Ilyara for war against the Moranese, but if they can't even unite the city…"

Rasim finally saw where he was going, and felt cold spill through him as Desimi said, "Then we'll be overrun, won't we? We *will* lose the oncoming war, because we're fighting ourselves."

Admiration sketched itself over Isidri's face before she nodded. "You've become more thoughtful, Desimi. That's good. The three of you will be formidable, when you become masters."

"Me?" Kisia looked up in surprise. "I haven't done anything."

"Nothing except bludgeon your way into a guild and be adopted into a Shenryalan clan at fourteen," Isidri said dryly. "Do permit an old woman her suppositions, Kisia. Perhaps even imagine your elders have some experience in judging the potential in young people."

Kisia ducked her head and put her hand over her tattooed shoulder. "Sorry, Guildmaster."

"We're still ahead of the Moranese army, right?" Rasim asked. "We left the *Wafiya* behind because we thought we could be here faster, to at least warn you. They're not here yet, are they?" A pang went through him as he thought of the flagship, and he saw the same hurt in the rest of them, but they let it pass, because for the moment there was little else they could do.

Asindo rose and beckoned them across the office to the desk that had been shoved aside. The broad sheet of paper pinned to it was a map that showed the entire world that Rasim knew, its bottom border close to

Ilyara, with the Ilialio River disappearing off the page as it flowed deeper into the Ilyaran continent. Another continent lay above the Ilyaran Sea, a broad, mountainous land bridge connecting the two. Those mountains spilled to Ilyara's west, leading up toward Shenryal. At the top of the map, the Northlands were a long jagged peninsula that stretched east. Looking at it, Rasim could see how the eastern archipelago that made up the Islands might almost be a continuation of that narrow, mountain-ridden peninsula.

Well west of the Ilyaran desert, and just south of Shenryal, the mountains lowered into a broad pass marked with a wide river. Kisia tapped that pass. "This is where Bayar said the Shenryalan cavalry would come through. And this…" She slid her fingertip back to the east, finding a pass on the western edge of the land bridge. "This is where he said the Moranese would likely come. It's the safest route."

"But this is faster and dumps them almost on top of us." Rasim poked a higher, narrow pass in the mountains, closer to the bridge's eastern side.

"There's three days of desert on a sturdy camel between us and that pass," Asindo replied. "I wouldn't call that 'on top of us,' Rasim."

Rasim sighed. "I guess. Do we know where they are?"

Asindo shook his head. "I assume Taishm did, but unless Isidri is holding out on me, the Seamasters don't have spies in Moran."

"An oversight I propose we correct," Isidri said dryly.

"That's why I said we need to work with the Skymasters," Rasim said impatiently. "Why we need to build outposts at regular intervals, so they can pass messages to each other on the wind and we can send this kind of information quickly!"

Both the Guildmasters stared at him, making him realize these particular adults hadn't heard his suggestion before. Asindo made a sound of incredulity, and Isidri exhaled explosively. "A fine idea. Pity we never thought of it before. Never mind the lad becoming a witchmaster. He ought to be an administrator."

"All I want to be is a sea witch!"

"But it's not all you are." The old Guildmaster turned her attention on him and Rasim suddenly felt like a fish hauled from the water for examination. "You're exactly what Taishm hoped you would be, Rasim. And Desimi is only a few steps behind you."

"I told you," Kisia said. "I told you you'd end up in the palace one way or another."

Rasim wanted badly to argue, but instead set his teeth and said, "Not if we don't save the palace from the Sunmasters and the Moranese first. Bayar's people are expecting the Ilyarans to have a united front, Guildmasters. We either have to stop the in-fighting here or warn the Shenryalans that they're riding toward a disaster."

"An invading army concentrates the mind wonderfully," Isidri said. "We'll try to impress the urgency on the other guildmasters. Luthan will listen. Jhikara…"

"She might," Asindo said. "Even Sunmaster Pydasho

might, because Desimi is right. He can't want to give up Ilyaran witchery to the Moranese."

"He'll want us to bend a knee to him, or to his guild, at least," Isidri said with sharp warning. "Aye, there's a greater threat, an outside threat, but he won't accept a truce for the time it takes to turn them away. He'll want us to bend a knee, and I wouldn't want to be the one left explaining that to Taishm, when he's restored."

"If he's alive to be restored," Asindo replied gently. "And you wouldn't be, Isidri. The long habit suits you, but I wear the Guildmaster's colors now."

Startlement akin to offense flew across the old Guildmaster's face, although she didn't argue. She might have, Rasim thought. She might have, except he opened his mouth and another fully formed terrible idea came out. "It won't matter. It won't matter who explains it to him, because you'll both have the truth on your side. The truth is that if you have to, you'll agree to Guildmaster Pydasho's terms in order to unite Ilyara, and in the meantime, we're going to find King Taishm."

CHAPTER FOUR

Desimi put his face in his hands, then lifted it again with the calm expression of someone who had already accepted his fate. Kisia, though, grinned viciously. "Because nobody even knows we're here, right? We can't be missed, because we're not even here."

"How?" Asindo asked mildly. "*How*, Rasim, do you intend to just go out and find the king? Assuming the king is alive to be found?"

"Oh, he'll figure it out along the way," Desimi said before Rasim could think of anything. "He always does."

Rasim made a feeble gesture of agreement, but Asindo's gaze remained critical. "I know you've navigated rough waters with a hope and a prayer this last year, lad, but you're proposing finding one man in a city of a hundred thousand, assuming—"

"Assuming he's alive at all, yes," Rasim snapped. Asindo's eyebrows shot up and heat rushed Rasim's face. "I'm sorry, Guildmaster. But we have to assume he's alive, don't we? And…" He kept looking at Asindo, but he didn't really see him anymore as his thoughts tangled and ran into each other, searching for a clear path. He spoke slowly, hoping the words would find their way if he just kept talking. "Did you say no one has seen him for weeks? Captain, if *I* were the Sunmasters and *I'd* captured the king, I would fill him up with heartbreak and parade him around like he supported our coup. I'd use him as a figurehead to rally the people to my cause. I wouldn't keep him hidden away."

At the corner of his unfocused vision, he saw Isidri raise a hand to pinch the bridge of her nose. "Is that a fact, Journeyman. Is that what you would do."

"Well, yes! And if he was dead, I'd parade *that* around, and claim my enemies killed him and rally people to my cause that way!"

"Never mind the King's Guild," Isidri said to Asindo. "Never mind administration. Your journeyman should be a spymaster, or imprisoned. Siliaria's tits, child!"

With something resembling amused dignity, Asindo said, "The boy was raised to journeyman on your watch, Guildmaster," and Isidri shot him a purse-mouthed glower that made him chuckle.

Rasim's ears went hot again, this time in offense. "I'm not saying I'd do any of that! But if I was the bad guy, it's what I'd do!"

"Thank Siliaria you aren't the bad guy," Isidri said with real affection. "Nothing could stand against you. So you believe Taishm is alive," she said more softly, with a thread in her voice that Rasim thought might be hope.

"And probably not under Sunmaster control," Rasim said eagerly, then drooped. "Or maybe dead and not under Sunmaster control, but either way…"

"Let's hope for the former. Asi asks a good question, though. How do you expect to find one man in a city of a hundred thousand?"

Desimi mumbled, "Asi," with a grin that Rasim and Kisia shared before the Guildmaster lifted his heavy eyebrows in warning. Rasim, trying to think instead of smile, asked, "Is the King's Guard on the Sunmasters' side, or are they loyal?" and found not smiling was easy, after all.

Isidri reached for the tea the journeymen hadn't finished, poured herself a cup, and examined Rasim over its rim. "Do you expect to rope Commander Yalonta into your schemes, Journeyman? I suspect your last encounter with her didn't leave any particular affection for you in her heart."

"I don't think she'll help, no, not necessarily." Rasim rubbed his face. "I just wondered if the guards might know anywhere Taishm liked to go that other people didn't know about. Although I guess they'd have looked there already, wouldn't they. I don't know," he finally said to the Guildmasters. There was an itch of an idea at the back of his mind, but he couldn't bring it to life. "I don't know how I'll find him, but if he's out there to find, I will."

"And what will you do when you find him?" Asindo asked.

Rasim spread his hands with a weak smile. "Restore him to the throne, unite Ilyara, repel the Moranese army, and retire from adventuring?"

A burst of laughter rose around him. "You won't," Kisia said with confidence, despite her grin. "You're in for a lot more adventures. I know it. If nothing else, Spiritmaster Oyun wants you to go back to Shenryal to study with her."

Asindo and Isidri chorused, "She *what?*" and Rasim raised his hands defensively.

"It doesn't matter right now. And that won't be an *adventure,*" he told Kisia fiercely. "It'll just be... expanding my horizons."

Kisia tossed her head like she still wore her hair long, a knowing smirk in her eyes. "I'll bet you anything your horizons are going to end up way more expanded than you think. I bet you're—"

"—going to get us all in trouble," Desimi muttered. "And I think if we're going to start searching Ilyara secretly we should probably go. Somebody's going to notice the Guildmasters have been missing for hours already and they'll want to know why."

Both Guildmasters got that expression again, the slightly surprised one edged with tension that adults got so often when Rasim started making observations. After a few seconds, Isidri's eyebrows flickered upward. "I'm beginning to think we should send all our new journeymen into the world to slay monsters and argue politics, Asi. Desimi's gotten *thoughtful.*"

Desimi, very firmly, said, "I haven't slayed any

monsters and I almost got us killed the first time I said something political. Don't do that."

Isidri, in a tone of pure fascination, said, "Do tell," but Desimi clamped his lips together, and the other two journeymen, wide-eyed, shook their heads.

Asindo exhaled a rueful breath. "What was that you were saying about the three of them being formidable together, Isidri?" The adults let it go, though, as the new Guildmaster gestured around his office. "We can offer you some food and water to take with you, but not as much as I'd like. We need nearly everything here, for the injured."

"We'll be all right," Rasim said with more confidence than he felt.

That confidence melted away as Isidri's ancient gaze hardened. "You haven't seen the city, lad. It's worse than you imagine."

Kisia's voice went small. "My family?"

"I don't know. There's been a lot of fighting in the streets, and your parents' bakery is in a popular area."

Rasim slid his hand into Kisia's like a promise they would check on her family, although he didn't say that aloud because he was sure the Guildmasters would tell them not to. She gave him a weak but grateful smile, and he thought maybe she'd understood his unspoken promise. As if to distract the Guildmasters from what they hadn't said, Kisia suggested, "We should go out the way we came in, through the shipyards and then upstream to the river garden. There are lots of places there where kids can play in the water even if they're not sea witches."

"I've never been there," Rasim said in some surprise.

Kisia shrugged. "Well, I have, and I can navigate the city from there. Even in the dark, if it comes to it."

"There's a curfew now," Asindo warned. "Be careful after dark."

Desimi breathed, "Right. Because we were going to be so reckless in daylight."

There was a momentary silence in which the Guildmasters looked at him. Isidri rose and went out the door, leaving Asindo to continue giving Desimi a level look that made the big journeyman squirm. Eventually, Asindo said, "I've always been impressed with Rasim's ability to not rise to your bait, Journeyman, but now I wonder at it indeed."

Desimi hunched his broad shoulders and stared at the floor, muttering a barely-audible, "Sorry."

"I didn't hear you, Journeyman."

The big journeyman straightened and met Asindo's eyes. "I said, I'm sorry, Guildmaster."

"Mmm." Asindo nodded, and Desimi's shoulders dropped again, this time more in relief than guilt. Rasim pulled his gaze from the two of them, trying not to stare, and found himself studying the maps behind Asindo's desk.

"Guildmaster?"

"Aye, lad?"

"Could I—" Rasim pointed at one of the maps on the wall, with Ilyara left of center and edges of the Moranese and Shenryalan continents filling the upper half. "Can I take this with me, please? I want…"

Asindo was already taking the map down, dropping

the pins that kept it in place into a glass bowl on his desk. It folded as it fell, the embroidered cloth a common enough type of map on Ilyaran ships, where ink could run from the damp. "Looking to understand where your friends will come from, are you? I've a map of the city, too, if you need that."

Rasim nodded and folded the world map carefully to tuck into his belt. "Thank you. And—" He glanced quickly at Kisia, who nodded. "That might not be a bad idea. There's a lot of Ilyara I don't know."

The Guildmaster nodded and took another map from a desk drawer. This one was drawn on thin leather, almost as supple as the cloth, and gave a bird's eye view of the city that spread across both banks of the Ilialio. He knew the part of the city they were in: the Seamasters' guildhall, right on the harbor, and he knew his way eastward toward the palace and the Sunmasters' hall. The Stonemasters' hall, where he'd never been, lay on the other side of the river, closer to the desert's edge, and the Skymasters' hall stood on a rise almost as high as the one the palace occupied, but on the western side along with the Stonemasters. Now that he understood sky witchery a little, he understood why the wind witches liked their tall hill.

There was so much of the city he didn't know, though. More than he'd realized, really, although Kisia was smiling over his shoulder at the map like it showed her an old, familiar friend. "You know a lot more of Ilyara than I do, don't you," he said, startled.

"Guild apprentices and younger journeymen keep to themselves, mostly," she pointed out. "It's the upper journeymen and masters who work in the city to keep it clean and everything. But the merchants and traders and all the rest of us, we're always out there together rubbing shoulders."

The door opened and they all looked up as Isidri returned, carrying satchels packed with food, and tunics and trousers so worn that any hint of Seamaster color had long since faded from them. "You won't quite look like merchants, with your hair so short, but it's better than being immediately identifiable as Seamaster journeymen."

It took a few minutes to change into the nondescript clothing, and when they were ready, the former Guildmaster surprised them by pulling them all into a hug and releasing them with a brisk smile. "Don't die, children. I'm old, and don't want to go to Siliaria's arms with that on my conscience."

Desimi muttered, "Thanks for the vote of confidence," in a tone that Rasim agreed with, and the three of them slipped out of the guildhall in search of their king.

CHAPTER FIVE

They didn't stop to help anyone this time, although Kisia's face showed an agony of indecision. Rasim whispered, "We can help everyone, if we stop what's going on," and her expression steadied. She nodded, and the three of them slipped out the way they'd come, through the shipyards and into the harbor waters.

Although it seemed to Rasim like there were a thousand things to talk about, none of them spoke for a long time as they swam upriver. Maybe there was *too* much to discuss, and nobody could even figure out where to start. When they eventually reached a shallower part of the river than Rasim had ever been in, a surprised noise escaped him, and Kisia gave him a quick smile. "Thought it was all deep, did you?"

"We usually sail out," he admitted. "Not upriver. There are ships that do, of course, but..."

"Not the fleet," Desimi muttered. "Not the sea-sailing ships. They're—" He made a sound. "Their draft is too deep. I knew that. I just didn't *know* it."

"Like with the desert," Rasim said. For some reason that made Desimi pinch a frown, but he nodded.

"Well, now you do, and we're almost to the gardens." Kisia glanced upward, toward the surface, then sucked her teeth. "Should we stay in the water until it gets dark?"

"Depends on whether there's anybody playing in the river, I think," Rasim said. "If there is, we can probably come out safely, but if not, we'd better wait."

"And then what?" Kisia sounded very controlled, and Rasim thought he knew why.

"Then we'll go see your family. The king has been missing for weeks. A couple more hours to make sure your family is all right isn't going to make a difference."

Relief swept her face, and no one else said anything until the green shadows fell over them in the depths. Rasim looked up to see trees, wobbly with water and distance, bending low over the river, and stretched his witchery a little to feel the shape of the river. Most of the Ilialio was well contained within the city. Stone witches had shaped its original banks into walls long ago to minimize the effect of seasonal flooding. Through the gardens, though, where the river ran shallow, there were steps and pools built in on both sides, giving everyone easy access to a long span of recreational riverfront. Disturbances in the water told him people were bathing and playing long before he could see anyone. He wondered how people *could* be playing, with what was going on in the city.

He gave a sudden half-laughing groan. "We're going to have to get wet. What are we going to do about the supplies and the map?"

"What?" Desimi sounded like Rasim had suggested pulling out half his teeth. "Get wet? Why?"

Kisia cackled. "Because only sea witches could stay dry if they were swimming, and we're not supposed to draw attention to ourselves. There's an overhang up there. Put the things that have to stay dry in that, and we'll get them on our way out."

Rasim took the shoulder-packs and deposited them beneath the low-hanging branches of a tree by the river bank, and joined the other two again in time to hear Desimi mutter, "Ugh. I *hate* being a spy." A minute later they surfaced in the garden shallows, water streaming down Desimi's sullen expression as he hissed, "My *clothes* are all wet."

"It's hot," Kisia told him airily. "They'll dry fast." She cupped a handful of water and spattered him with it, earning an outraged howl from a journeyman who would normally use witchery to protect himself. Kisia cackled again and splashed him harder, then shrieked loudly as Rasim ducked under the water and yanked her feet out from under her. Desimi was laughing when he surfaced, and Kisia bobbled up again with a look of betrayed outrage. "I thought you were on my side!"

"I don't think there are any sides in a water fight," Rasim said happily. Kisia pushed a wave at him with both hands, just enough to make him bounce back a little if he didn't use witchery to steady himself. For a few minutes they took turns ganging up on each other and messing around like they hadn't spent months scared out of their minds, and Rasim suddenly understood why there were people playing, after all. Finally, gasping with tired laughter, they dragged themselves to the shore and collapsed there together. Rasim, breathless, said, "It's a lot more work to play in the water without witchery. I didn't know that, even if I wasn't much of a witch."

"I did." Kisia's voice was soft, not that Rasim himself had spoken loudly. "A year ago you weren't much of a witch, and I was a baker's daughter. Now…"

"You're still a baker's daughter," Rasim said thoughtfully. "At least, in a way the rest of us aren't. You chose Siliaria and the sea, this whole life. The rest of us were—" He faltered, because 'born to it' wasn't exactly right.

"Stuck with it," Desimi offered, then shrugged as the other two looked at him. "We were. The river saved us during the fire, and the same thing happened to us that happened to all the other orphans found in the river. We were raised by the Seamasters. We didn't have a choice."

"Would you have chosen something else?" Kisia asked, still very softly.

A crease of concentration appeared between Desimi's eyebrows again, so deep that Kisia reached over and pressed her fingers against it to wipe it away. It wrinkled up again as soon as she moved her hand, but not as deeply this time, Rasim thought. "I don't know," Desimi finally said. "Not very long ago I would've said yes. Just to *have* a choice. But a lot's changed. I've…"

He curled his hand around the necklace King Taishm had given him, and Rasim, despite lying on the ground, managed to knock his shoulder against Desimi's. "You've gotten thoughtful." He grinned. "Formidable."

Desimi snorted. "I was always formidable."

Rasim and Kisia both laughed, mostly because it was true. "Even I'd heard people say you were the strongest apprentice since Isidri," Kisia said.

"But strength isn't everything." Desimi said it grudgingly, like it was a lesson he'd taken a long, long time to learn. "And I'm not sure I would've ever known that if I hadn't ended up…" He waved his hand, clearly meaning 'in the Guild,' but Rasim also thought he meant the endless, exhausting adventures they'd been on over the past year. "I'd be somebody else," Desimi muttered. "If the river hadn't saved me, I'd be somebody else, and maybe that person never would've figured some stuff out."

"Imagine if you'd been put into one of the Sunmasters' temples to avoid the fire," Kisia said almost wonderingly. "We don't even know if you can use sun witchery. You might have been like Rasim, not much of a witch, inside the Sunmasters' Guild."

"Imagine if *he'd* been put into one of the temples," Desimi muttered. "The Shenryalan spiritmaster said he's a natural sun witch."

Rasim jolted and pushed up on his elbows to stare at the other boy. "I never thought of that."

Sly delight spread across Desimi's face. "Mark one on the wall for me. I thought of something before Rasim did."

"I…" Rasim tried to imagine what it might have been like to be raised in the Sunmasters' Guild, supported in the magic the old Shenryalan shaman had said was his inborn talent. Tried to imagine being as naturally gifted within his guild as Desimi was, only quicker of thought. Assuming, of course, that he hadn't learned to think quickly because his magic was so weak that he needed some other kind of advantage.

If he had been a quick thinker, and also powerful… after a long moment, Rasim shook his head. "I'm not sure I would have liked that me very much. What if that me thought the Sunmasters were right to try to do all of this? Take over the city, install themselves on the throne…?"

Kisia's eyes popped. "Oh, but I think you'd be surprised at how comfortable you'd find the throne."

Rasim laughed. "I've seen the throne, Kisia. It doesn't look very comfortable at all."

"No, I know, but I mean, look at what Taishm is trying to do. He's trying to find apprentices and jour-neymen who can use all the Ilyaran magics. Who *else* can use them all, besides you?"

"Well, Desimi," Rasim pointed out. "And Telun has a talent for sky witchery even if he was found by the Stonemasters. And—"

"Yes, but the *king* can," Kisia said impatiently.

"Not very well," Desimi pointed out. "The whole city knows the royal family's weaker than it used to be.

The whole *continent* knows, or they wouldn't be trying to take over Ilyara in the first place!"

Kisia blurted, "But—" and gave up as Rasim, exasperated, said, "I still say King Taishm has a lot more power than anybody thinks he does. Didn't you feel his witchery, Desi? When he used air witchery to tell the Seamasters to fight, when the harbor was frozen?"

Desimi eyed him. "Feel it? No, but I heard it. It was loud," he conceded. "But a royal family's 'not very good' could be a lot better than the rest of us's." He squinted. "Is that a word?"

"If you used it and we understood you, and we did, it's a word." Rasim bunched his hand in his tunic, then got to his feet. "My front is mostly dry. If we stay in the sunshine while we walk, our backsides will probably dry off pretty fast too."

"You didn't dry your back?" Desimi got up, his own backside dry. When Rasim made a sound of astonished protest, the bigger boy spread his hands and shrugged. "I figured people wouldn't see it!"

"Oh, he's definitely getting smarter," Kisia said with a laugh. "Good thing, too. The sun is going down and it'll be cold soon."

Rasim muttered and, now that the idea had been put into his head, slowly stripped the water from the back of his tunic and trousers. Once dry, he and the others ducked beneath the tree where their supplies were, got them, and finally joined a growing crowd of people leaving the riverbank.

It took longer than he expected to make their way through the city back toward the Seamasters' guildhall and Kisia's bakery. Partly it was because he didn't know Ilyara well from that direction. More of it, though, was that streets were blockaded, and worried-looking people glanced over their shoulders as they hurried toward the safety of their homes as sunset came on. That wasn't the Ilyara he knew, and when he glanced at his companions, he could see the same discomfort in their eyes.

There were guards on the streets, which wasn't all that unusual; many of them wore the colors of the King's Guard, whose job was to break up crowds before they became mobs, as much as it was to guard the king himself. But there were many others armored in the golds and whites of the Sunmasters' Guild. Rasim had never seen *any* guild colors or symbols on armor before. Among the Sunmasters were a few Stonemasters in similar uniforms, and wearing expressions of threat.

By the time they reached the street Kisia's family lived on, there were hardly any people out. That bothered Rasim as much as anything else: Ilyara was a huge city, and while it fell quiet late at night, its people were rarely done with their days at sunset. Normally sun witches tended the torches that lit the streets, but tonight, they were dark save for the light from two half-moons, and filled only with the last straying townsfolk rushing home.

Kisia, a few steps ahead of him, stopped abruptly with a swallowed hiss of sound, and stepped into the shadow of a doorway. The boys crowded in with her, and she dropped her voice to almost nothing. "There are guards at our bakery."

Rasim breathed, "What?" as Desimi leaned out of the doorway just a little, looking over their heads toward the bakery at the corner. He stayed quiet for a few long moments, then pulled himself back into the shadows, his bared teeth a flash of lightness in the faint moonlight.

"She's right. Sunmasters. I can tell because they're in white. It almost glows in the dark."

"Why would they be protecting our bakery?" Kisia kept her voice low, but fear rose in it.

"They're not protecting it." The answer came before Rasim thought through its implications, but when he did, he knew he was right. "They're looking for you. For us."

"Nobody even knows we're here!"

"No," Rasim whispered, "but if they think there's any chance of us coming back, wouldn't you put lookouts in the places you'd expect us to go? They can't get into the Seamasters' guildhall, but for all they know, neither can we. This would be the first safe place we'd go, wouldn't it? It *is* the first safe place we've gone, after leaving the guild."

Kisia's eyes were huge with anguish in the dimness. "But my family!"

"We wouldn't be doing them any favors to show up on their doorstep now," Desimi said said quietly. "It'd just pull them into our mess."

"Can't you—" Kisia broke off her protest, obviously

wanting to try some kind of witchery to get them into the bakery, and equally clearly not having any idea what kind of magic that would take. Her shoulders slumped and Rasim could see the shadows as she buried her face in her hands for a few long moments. "All right," she said, muffled, before lifting her head. "All right, fine, we're just going to have to find Taishm and end this thing so I can make sure my family is safe. I saw you earlier, Rasim. You looked like you had an idea. What's the plan?"

Rasim took a deep breath, turning his attention to Desimi. "You said you didn't feel it, when Taishm used his witchery? Do you feel it when anyone else does?"

Desimi scowled at him in the moonlit darkness, his entire presence suddenly somehow annoyed. "I don't even know what you're talking about, Sunburn."

The bigger boy hadn't used the not-very-good insult in days, and for some reason it made Rasim smile. "I feel it when someone uses magic. Like there's a weight in the air. You don't feel that?" He glanced at Kisia, who also shook her head. "Huh. I always could. I wonder if it's because I was concentrating so hard to try to use witchery at all."

"Or because you were meant to use a different kind and it made you sensitive to everything," Kisia suggested in a whisper. "What's the *point*, Rasim?"

"I know what Taishm's witchery feels like," Rasim replied, feeling rather triumphant. "I think I can use it to track him, if he's in the city and using it at all."

Even in the faint evening light, his friends both looked impressed. Desimi, a smile starting to pull at the corner of his mouth, said, "Go on, then," out loud.

The words echoed surprisingly in the quiet street, and a guard at Kisia's family bakery turned their way. Rasim's heart seized with panic, and he was afraid the expression showed on his face despite the distance and bad lighting. It must have, because suspicion colored the guard's voice. "Hey! You! What are you kids doing out at night? Come here!"

Desimi's eyes bugged, and Kisia, squeaking with alarm, called, "No, nothing, we're fine, sorry, thank you, just going home now!" She grabbed both boys by the hands and started walking away from the guard. Rasim found himself counting the steps under his breath, *one, two, three, four*, like if they could get a certain number of steps away, if they could get around a corner, it would all be fine.

"I said come here!" The guard came after them in a rush of heavy footsteps.

They bolted.

CHAPTER SIX

They weren't far from the Seamasters' guildhall, but Kisia knew the streets heading away from it better. She pulled ahead of the boys, leading them around corners, down alleys, and through archways that were unfamiliar to Rasim in the darkness. Maybe they'd be unfamiliar in the daytime, too, but now they seemed as foreign and frightening as Moran had, with potential danger all around. The guards didn't exactly keep up: instead, new ones were warned with shouts carried by sky witchery, until almost every turn seemed to have a threat lurking around it. Sweat dripped into Rasim's eyes and he wiped it away, gasping for air and wishing sky witchery could help him breathe more easily.

An idea hit him and he managed to snarl, "Siliaria's *teeth*," despite his breathlessness. Desimi, beside him, gasped, "What?" and Rasim hissed, "Sky witchery," at him, as if one phrase would explain everything.

Kisia spared a moment to glower over her shoulder

at them as she darted around another corner, and for what felt like the tenth time, nearly ran straight into another Sunmaster-garbed guard. The man drew breath to shout that he'd sighted them, and Rasim wove air magic, muffling the man's voice in a flutter of light-weight witchery.

Under other circumstances, the man's befuddled expression would have been funny. He forgot to even try to grab them, instead trying to shout again, utter confusion filling his features as his shout was as effective as yelling into a pillow. Desimi clapped Rasim on the shoulder so hard it sent the smaller boy staggering, but at least they were able to race past the guard, deeper into Ilyara's city center. Rasim felt a surge of triumph as he muted more guards and their path suddenly seemed clearer.

Then a hand snaked out of the darkness and grabbed him, fingers tight over his mouth, and the stone itself opened beneath his feet, dropping him into a cellar. Just ahead of him, Desimi yelled in shock as the ground opened and seized him too. Kisia fell, but didn't shout until she hit the floor, eight or ten feet below the stone street closing over their heads.

A man hissed, "Shh! It's me! Taishm!" as Rasim's captor released him. He lurched away, staggering toward where Kisia's voice rang out in the darkness: "*Taishm? The king?*"

A flicker of sun witchery lit the cellar under the city streets, illuminating three Seamaster journeymen doing their best to cling to one another without knowing where exactly they all were, and Taishm al

Ilyara, looking rather worse for the wear. He was usually a thinly handsome man, but now wore a scraggly beard that didn't much suit him, and his normally tidy hair was chaotically long and loose. A mark, not quite a scar, bruised his cheekbone. He looked both older and wearier than he had the last time Rasim had seen him, and he agreed, "Taishm," a little wryly. "The king, although perhaps not at my most regal. Dare I—"

His question was cut off by the three of them surging forward together to hug him. His calling of sun witchery momentarily blinked into darkness, and his breath sounded rough and startled as he carefully returned the embrace. The light didn't return until the journeymen fell back again, and in the gentle firelight, Taishm brushed his hand across his eyes before smiling crookedly at them. "Thank you. I think I needed a welcome like that more than I knew. Gods, I'm glad to see you children, but…dare I ask why you're being chased through the streets?"

Rasim exchanged glances with the other two, then, trying to stick to the most important bits, said, "We were looking for you."

"Ah." Taishm's eyebrows rose a little. "That would do it, yes."

"How did you find us? Why did you rescue us?" Desimi demanded. "Are you all right? What's going on in Ilyara? The Guildmasters told us some of it, but how could you let the Sunmasters have so much power? Wh—"

Taishm lifted a palm, stopping Desimi's flow of

questions, and his eyebrows rose higher. "You're beginning to sound like Rasim, King's Man."

Desimi clutched the necklace Taishm had given him and tried, Rasim thought, to blush. He was too dark-skinned for that to work, but his expression suggested he was both mortified and proud. Rasim grinned, but didn't say anything as Taishm examined the journeymen one by one and decided which questions to answer. "I knew Rasim was there. I recognized the feel of his witchery. And where he is, you two tend to be."

Rasim's voice broke on a surprised squeak. "That's how I was going to find you! If you were using it at all, I thought I could hone in on you!"

A smile colored Taishm's response. "It worked."

"Sort of," Kisia said, the thoughtful words echoing quietly off the stone walls. "But opposite. What happened in the palace? Isidri and Asindo didn't know the details, but you must have been right there."

"I'll explain what I can, but..." Taishm glanced upward. "I suspect they'll start searching the cellars soon. First, tell me: was the journey to the North successful?" He sounded strained, and surprise lurched through Rasim again. The Guildmasters hadn't know much of what had happened over the past months, but somehow he'd imagined the king would be better informed.

"How long have you been out of touch? The Guildmasters said weeks, but I don't know how fast news travels—"

Kisia muttered, "Without those Skymaster waystations," and Rasim shrugged agreement.

Taishm said, "Skymaster waystations?" in a tone that didn't expect an answer, and crushed any chance of one by adding, "Nearly two months."

"Two months ago…" Rasim fell silent, trying to remember where they'd been, two months earlier. "We were almost leaving Moran, by then."

"Moran?" The king's voice sharpened in confusion. "What were you doing in Moran?"

Both Desimi and Kisia glanced back at Rasim, who groaned. "I'll tell you in a minute, but if you've been hiding for two months, you *must* have heard some of what happened in Hongrunn. It doesn't take that long for news to travel!"

Desimi's mortification changed to exasperation. "No, but who would get the news first, in Ilyara?"

Rasim frowned in confusion, then scowled even more deeply as he understood Desimi's point. "Nasira's right. You're getting cleverer." He paused, and deliberately said, "Is that a word?"

Desimi's exasperated look faded into a grin, and Kisia smiled, very briefly. "It is if we understood what it meant. Desimi's right, though. You get most of your information through the Sunmasters, don't you?" She lifted her chin at the king, as if he could see her from behind.

Taishm, through gritted teeth, said, "I do."

"So they knew before you did," Desimi said, almost gently. "They knew what had happened in Hongrunn, and they turned on you, didn't they? How did you escape?"

"There are passages through the palace. Shortcuts

from one place to another. Mostly the servants use them, but there are a few the royal family keeps to themselves. I suppose there are Sunmasters who know about them, but my cousin and I used to play in them, when we were children. We snuck out more times than I could count, and I knew them well. One goes down to the river, and from there, I went beneath the city. Now what happened in Hongrunn that caused my closest advisors, diplomats, and *friends*," the word was said with a snarl, "to turn on me?"

The other two journeymen cast wide-eyed looks back at Rasim, who exhaled heavily, then plunged, again, into the shortest explanation he could manage of the last few months. Taishm's shoulders rose higher and higher as Rasim talked, although he didn't interrupt, not even when Rasim confessed to inadvertently instigating the destruction of an entire city. Finally, looking exhausted, the king moved to lean on a barrel that the owners of the cellar seemed to have long-since abandoned. "If I understood all of that correctly, you're telling me I have a navy and two armies, one of which is friendly, bearing down on my city, which is itself overcome by strife and rebellion? And I am personally besieged by the very people who were meant to protect and advise me, although that isn't news to me. It is only…"

He pushed his hands through his hair and fell silent, eyes closed as he took in everything they'd told him. "I knew Jhikara didn't like me," he said mildly after a few minutes. "I never understood it, given that if I have any particular talent in witchery, it lies in skymastery. I thought the Sky Guild's leader might be a little fond of me because of that. But Pydasho of the Sunmasters had seemed a friend to me, and to Laishn before me. What do they *want*?" He opened his eyes to focus on Rasim, who let out a high-pitched laugh.

"I don't know, your majesty. Power, obviously, but I don't know Guildmasters Jhikara or Pydasho at all, so I don't know what they might specifically want."

Taishm laughed, a bark of sound that echoed off the stone walls. "Which, of course, you *would* know if you'd met them personally."

"That's not what I meant!"

"It's kind of what you suggested, though," Kisia said. Rasim elbowed her. Taishm sighed heavily, dropping his head back again, and leaned in silence long enough to have the three journeymen casting uncomfortable looks at one another. Then he extended his hand, palm up, although he didn't yet open his eyes.

"The things you were given in Shenryal. I'd like to see them, please."

Kisia said, "Er," and covered her tattooed shoulder with the other hand. "I can't exactly put this in your hands."

"No," Taishm said dryly, "but you could come over, and let me see it. Journeyman." The emphasis on the final word said that he'd noticed that she didn't address him by his title.

A faint wince of guilt crossed Kisia's face as she did what she'd been told. The king examined the beautiful, twisting black lines of the horse tattoo on her shoulder, then examined her, too, from up close, with a pursed mouth and drawn-down eyebrows. "What is it you object to about calling me 'your majesty,' Journeyman? You use the Guildmasters' titles easily enough."

Kisia dragged in a deep breath, said, "They earned it," and fell silent again.

Taishm's eyebrows reversed their course, shooting upward, and he chuckled quietly. "And I was born to mine? You don't like that?"

"I was born to be a baker." Kisia's voice was unusually tight, so tight that Rasim thought she was barely holding back anger. "Don't get me wrong, I like baking and I'm good at it, but if anyone looked at where I came from, they'd say that was all I was meant to be, and all I could be. I don't like that. And if Guildmaster Isidri was anybody else, it's still probably all I'd ever be. Maybe a King's Guard, if I wanted to fight, but nothing that would much change where I belonged in society. Even in Ilyara, which other places call Golden, there isn't much room to *move*. So, no. I don't like that you get to be a king who learns all the magic in the world, and I get to be a baker's daughter except through the grace of a Guildmaster and the goddess of the sea. I think you're probably a pretty good person. But you're a person, Taishm, and you haven't *earned* the right to have me call you *majesty*."

The title was spoken so sharply that Rasim saw Taishm's chin lift again as he took the brunt it, like a cut. "I wonder," he said after a long moment, "whether that's what Jhikara and Pydasho think of me, too." He nodded, dismissing her. Even though it obviously *was* a dismissal and Kisia had just been protesting his authority to dismiss her, she still returned to the boys with her chest heaving like she'd run a race. The king said, "Desimi," and the big journeyman scrambled to show Taishm the colorful, beautiful silk strips that Bikat of the Horse Clans had given him.

Rasim hadn't seen them in weeks. They'd been tucked into Desimi's voyaging pouch, wrapped around the carving of the goddess Siliaria that all sea witches carried with them. He'd forgotten how vibrant their colors were, although they were now wrinkly from being stuffed in a small bag for weeks on end. Taishm had a genuinely peculiar expression as he smoothed the soft pieces of cloth across his palms, examining the weave and the gleam of the silk. "A very generous gift," he finally said. "I've rarely seen their like. Thank you for showing them to me." He returned them, examining the big journeyman thoughtfully as Desimi re-wrapped the silk around Siliaria's icon and tucked it all back into his pouch.

By then Rasim was already on his feet, offering the horsehair braid that old Oyun, the spiritmaster, had given him. "An invitation into Shenryal," Taishm said very softly. "There aren't many of these issued, Rasim. Treasure it."

"I will. I do. But I want to use it, too." Rasim mashed his mouth shut. He hadn't meant to say that, or even known he'd wanted to, until it was out in the world.

To his relief, Taishm laughed. "Yes, of course you do. I don't know how this all will end, Journeyman, but if it ends well, I'll have you trained to your *teeth* to behave yourself before you ever again enter foreign lands as Ilyara's representative."

"I don't mean to cause trouble!"

"I know you don't." Taishm dismissed him, too, sending him back to the opposite wall with a brief gesture. Rasim retreated feeling like he'd narrowly escaped disaster, although with the way Taishm studied the three of them, he wasn't actually sure he *had* escaped.

That uncertainty turned to conviction as Taishm smiled roughly and said, "Well. Since you're here, I may as well have you cause trouble for *me*."

CHAPTER SEVEN

A flare of hope rushed through Rasim's chest. "What can we do? I promise, your majesty, all I want to do is help. I don't know how three journeymen can restore you to the throne, bu—"

Taishm's laugh interrupted him. "You don't aim low, do you, Rasim?"

Rasim blinked. "Well, isn't that what we need to do? We have to do something to stop the Sunmasters, and bringing you back to rally the people would work better than anything else, wouldn't it? And once we've dealt with them, if we're lucky, we'll still have time to prepare before the Moranese arrive. Hopefully Bayar's people will be here before then," he said more worriedly. "I borrowed a map from Guildmaster Asindo, and I'm afraid…" He pulled the embroidered map out and spread it on the floor.

Taishm, eyebrows quirked with curiosity, crouched to examine it with him as Rasim drew a finger over a small, high pass in the land bridge that connected

Ilyara's continent to the northerly one. "I'm afraid the Moranese are going to come through here. It cuts days off their route."

"It would, but there's a much safer pass here." Taishm brushed his own fingertip over the lower, wider pass near the western edge of the land bridge. "The high pass will be full of rotted snow, and no one would bring an army through it at this time of year."

"But it's closer," Rasim insisted. "So what if they did?"

"Then they'd be risking so many of their people that we'd only be fighting half their army when they crossed the desert and got to us. The western pass follows a river, Rasim. It goes underground at the edge of the desert, but there are oases all along its route, until it reaches the Ilialio." He traced a path on the cloth, marking where spots of green bloomed in the sand-colored threads. "Anyone invading Ilyara from the north or west would take that route. If I were leading an army north, I'd follow it myself. Often time is less important than the health of the troops, if you want to win a war."

Rasim, remembering the awful destruction of stone witchery ripping the Moranese river walls out of place, shook his head dubiously. "Their whole city fell, Taishm. If it was me, I'd take the fastest route and use the element of surprise."

"If their whole city fell," the king pointed out, "then there may be less of an army than you fear, Rasim. But," he said more briskly, "those are logistics, and not your concern. You've done your part. All of you have.

I'd like to send you back to the guildhall, where you'll be safe."

A sound of protest rose in Kisia's throat. "After all this? I don't think so! You said we could cause trouble!"

Taishm gave her a dour look. "Somehow I'm quite certain you would succeed in causing trouble within the safety of the guildhall walls. But I said I'd like to, not that I would. Not when I have two—two?" He cocked a curious eyebrow at Kisia, but had to finish the question before any of them knew what he meant. "At least two journeymen in front of me who did what I hoped they would: learned multiple magics."

"Oh." Kisia waved a dismissive hand. "Just two. I'm not meant for anyone other than Siliaria."

"That's what I used to think," Rasim said quietly, but Kisia turned a surprisingly brilliant smile on him.

"I know, but your story is different from mine. You should have been a sun witch from the beginning, and you're everything now so it's all balanced out. Me, I was supposed to be a baker's daughter, and I *chose* the sea, and then Siliaria chose me. She called me sister, Rasim." Kisia's eyes shone before she turned to the king. "I tried. I did try. I studied with Sunmaster Endat and with Rasim while he and Desimi figured out how to teach Desimi sky witchery, and I even tried stone witchery with Telun and Milu while they were learning Shenryalan magic from the old spiritmaster. But only Siliaria's song sings in my heart, and that's all I need. I swear it. I'll be a master sea witch one day, but I'm not meant for your King's Guild, Taishm. I'm me, and I choose my own path."

Taishm gazed at her a moment, then shook his head like he was trying to disguise how his mouth twitched with humor. "Gods defend anyone who gets in your way, Kisia al Ilialio. If anyone in the royal family had had your determination and clarity of purpose in the past hundred years, we might not be in this mess right now."

"Maybe not *this* mess, but Rasim's here, so we'd definitely be in *some* kind of mess."

"Hey!"

"It's not like she's wrong," Desimi said cheerfully. "Mess follows you."

"It does not!"

Even Taishm grinned. "Then that suggests you create it, Rasim."

Rasim tucked his chin in horror, shoulders hunching. "I don't mean to!"

"In this case," Taishm said with satisfaction, "I *want* you to. Rasim, you were doing something up there. It's how I tracked you."

"Muffling the guards? I used air witchery to make the air not carry a voice, instead of carrying it."

"Can you do that to the witches themselves? Block their magic?"

"I..." Rasim closed his eyes like he could see the inside of his head, trying to work out how he might accomplish what the king was asking. After a minute, though, he shook his head and met Taishm's gaze again. "No, I don't think so. I wasn't blocking their magic at all. They were sun witches. I just kept them from shouting."

Taishm's brows drew down thoughtfully. "Can you wrest control of someone's witchery from them?"

Rasim and Desimi exchanged glances. "We've been trading magic back and forth to keep control of the glasswings, but that's been—" Desimi hesitated, looking for the word, and Rasim said, "Cooperative. I'm not trying to stop Desi from using it when we do that. I'm just letting him take over. Or taking over from him. Why, what are you thinking?"

"I was hoping you might be able to thwart sun and sky magic," Taishm said. "Muffle it, as you said. Quench flame, perhaps, and at least prevent sky witches from speaking with one another. It may be too much to ask, and it's dangerous. I should be sending you back to your guildhall and safety, but..."

Rasim shrugged. "There's a fight already going on in Ilyara, and a war coming. There isn't much safety, your majesty."

The king nodded. "So anything you could do to weaken their witchery, and by extension, their hold over the city, would be of great value to me."

Rasim's head began to hurt from concentration as he tried to think it through. "We can probably stop them from talking to each other as easily, at least if they're nearby. And if there's fire around, I can put it out, but I don't think I can cut off their witchery. Can you?" He lifted his gaze to the king, suddenly hopeful, but Taishm shook his head.

"I never even thought to muffle a conversation, much less try block someone's magic. It would require practice, at least, and I don't think we have time."

"You can put fires out unless they're using that sticky fire that doesn't *go* out," Kisia said as if she'd been thinking things through. For a moment everyone was silent, remembering the strange, thick oily substance that had been used to ensure that the Great Fire—and the smaller one just under a year ago—were almost impossible to extinguish. The air felt thick and heavy to Rasim, like the very memory of the stuff was pressing down on him.

After a moment, though, Kisia shrugged. "But I guess those have to be set, and most sunmasters can't conjure fire from the air the way you and Taishm can. They'll just be drawing it from the torches and hearths around them. I can pull water and put those out, at least, and I could fight another water witch, but if I have to do that, we're in extra trouble anyway. So if Desimi can muffle people talking to each other, and Rasim and I can put out fires, we can at least cause *some* trouble for the rebel guilds. And besides." She flashed a sudden bright grin. "Rasim just naturally causes trouble wherever he goes, so if you set us loose, Taishm, I bet we can make a mess of things for you."

"I don't mean to." Rasim pressed the heels of his hands against his eyes, trying to push his headache away. "I wonder if we could stay here tonight and try to practice cutting witchery off. I know," he said to what felt like three people blinking at him in confusion. "No one said anything about sleeping. It's just the air is so heavy with magic, and my head hurts, and—" He dropped his hands suddenly, eyes wide as he looked around the cellar. "We're not using any witchery."

"Well." Taishm gestured gently, indicating the fire working he maintained for light.

"No," Rasim said urgently, "no, not enough to make the air keep feeling heavy like this."

"It's not witchery," Kisia said. "My head hurts and the air feels wrong to me, too." As she spoke, Taishm's flame flickered and nearly went out. He made a sound of surprise, reigniting it, but it shivered weakly even though Rasim could now feel the effort the king was putting into keeping the witchery alive.

Rasim stared at it, trying to think through an aching thickness in his skull. Desimi said, "Sleeping here sounds good, really," and for the first time, sat on the cellar floor.

"No." Rasim sounded faint to his own ears, and didn't know if he'd just spoken weakly, or if the air was somehow too thin to carry his voice. Then, more strongly, he said, "No!" again, and took a step or two toward the cellar door, putting himself between it and the king. "There's someone here. Near. Using sky witchery, making the air...go away. Desimi, can you...I need you to..." He couldn't think clearly. His head pounded with every heartbeat, and all his ideas seemed to be dribbling down, like rain following the mortar on bricks. They were too slippery to hold as they drained away, and his head hurt *so much*.

"No," Taishm said, "but *I* can." The king's voice carried in a way Rasim's hadn't, thunderous anger in it. All at once, a surge of light, dancing, *powerful* sky witchery spilled through the cellar room, wiping out the air-thinning magic that someone had been working.

A voice in the near distance, quiet only because of the thick stone walls, shouted in triumph, and other voices took up the cry. Rasim strained his ears, then, feeling stupid, cast witchery to see if he could bring their words to himself. "We've got him," he echoed, half aloud. "The king is near. Oh, Siliaria's *teeth*, they've found Taishm because of us!"

"It's fine, Rasim." Taishm was calm with acceptance when Rasim whipped to face him. "It's all right. They were going to find me sooner or later, and this way, at least, you three can still help the city by doing as I've asked. I'll surrender myself so they never even know you were here."

"They already know," Kisia said acerbically. "They chased us all over half of Ilyara. You shouldn't give yourself up for us, your majesty. They'll use you, or kill you, if they get their hands on you." She stepped up beside Rasim, helping to blockade the door. Desimi, who was considerably bigger than both of them, joined them, and Rasim thought they made a reasonable barricade. He had an idea working its way through his aching head, and tried to gather stone witchery. He wished he could feel stone magic coming to life, so he had some sense of whether he might succeed.

Taishm's smile turned to a crooked grin as he met Kisia's eyes. "I thought you didn't much like the position I hold."

"I don't, but that doesn't mean I can't recognize the importance of it," she snapped. "If you fall, Ilyara won't know what to do with itself, and since we've got a war coming, I'd rather the city was all working together!"

"If I survive this," Taishm told her, almost cheerfully, "I'm going to appoint you as a counselor, Journeyman Kisia. I don't think I've ever had anybody give me their opinions as straight-forwardly as you have. Now move, children," he said more gently. "If I walk out of this room now, they'll have no reason to come in, and you'll be safe."

"Or we could not." Desimi, belligerent as a young bull, braced himself like he'd actually tackle the king if necessary.

Taishm breathed a quiet laugh. "Desimi, it is *very* important to me that you not be captured. You're journeymen. I'm an adult, and the king. Step aside."

"We really can't do that, your majesty." Rasim was almost, *almost* positive his witchery was ready, although he flinched horribly when there was a huge, angry hammering on the cellar door. He glanced over his shoulder, watching the door bulge as something large and solid hit it, then looked back at Taishm. "I'm very, very sorry about this."

Dangerous concern darkened Taishm's eyes. "Sorry about *what*, Journeyman?"

Rasim wrinkled up his face, squeaked, "About this," and magicked a hole in the stone beneath Taishm's feet as the door behind them began to shatter.

CHAPTER EIGHT

The light from Taishm's witchery went out as he fell with a yelp of surprise. For just long enough, the cellar room was dark. Rasim hastily shaped the stone floor closed again, then whirled to face the door as it burst open. In the first flickers of brightness from the torches carried by Sun Guild guards, he caught glimpses of Desimi and Kisia's appalled faces. A giggle built in his throat and he tried to bite it back, which became easier as the room flooded with angry sun and sky witches.

In a heartbeat, the three journeymen were surrounded. They moved unconsciously to stand shoulder to shoulder and back to back, three faces of a defensive triangle. It felt strong, even if Rasim didn't imagine they could take on a dozen or so witches. One of them, a woman in Sun Guild colors, snapped, "Where is he?"

Rasim rolled his eyes wildly, looking around the small, dark cellar room. "We're all right here."

"The king," she snarled. "Where is Taishm?"

"I have no idea." That was even mostly true. Rasim knew where he'd *sent* the king. He was also certain that in the few seconds that had passed, Taishm was no longer in exactly the same place. "Aren't you Sunmasters supposed to keep an eye on him?"

Desimi elbowed Rasim's ribs hard. Rasim tried not to grunt, and tried not to laugh, either. Not that it was really *funny*, but he was scared and everything seemed a little funny right then. Apparently, though, Desimi didn't think taunting the Sunmasters was all that amusing.

To be fair, Desimi was probably right, which made Rasim think, again, that the bigger boy was getting more clever, and that seemed funny too. He coughed on a giggle and struggled to say, "I'm sorry. We really don't know where he is. We were just out late and got…lost?"

"In the cellars?" A sneer of disdain smeared across the guard's face. "How stupid do you think I am, boy?"

This time Kisia elbowed him before he could even speak. Vaguely offended, Rasim kicked a foot back into the little triangle between their bodies, hoping to catch somebody's ankle, but only scuffed his sole along the floor. He didn't *answer*, though, partly because he wasn't quite that stupid himself, and mostly because, despite getting called clever a lot, he couldn't actually think of a response that wouldn't get him cuffed.

"Never mind," another woman said from the cellar hall. "Taishm isn't in there, and interrogating teenagers in cellars at the fourth bell of the morning isn't my idea of fun. Bring them. We'll let Yalonta deal with them."

"We weren't doing anything wrong," Kisia said grumpily, and in a cadence Rasim had never heard from her. "It's only that me ma doesn't like me hanging out with the likes of these two so I was trying to get away with it and it got too late to get home safely."

The woman in the hall stepped entered, thin amusement stretched across her face. She wore skymaster colors, the intricately braided hair that sky witches often favored, and an air of casual authority that the sun-garbed guard didn't have. "And who's your mother, girl? I should deliver you home safely to her, instead of leaving you with the likes of these two."

Rasim couldn't really see Kisia's face, but her tone was as disdainful as the woman's. "Well, I wouldn't be telling *you* that, would I? You'd drag me home to her and it's me in trouble either way! C'mere now." Her voice changed to wheedling. "They're only my b—my friends, you know what it's like. Give us a break, will you? Weren't you ever young and dumb?"

"Your boyfriends, are they?" The woman's amusement sounded more real this time, although Rasim felt his face get hot and Desimi coughed. "You like all sorts, then, girl. The big lad and the little one. I'd admire you if I believed a word of it, but *someone* in this room was using sky witchery, and none of you are skymaster apprentices. Take them to Commander Yalonta. We'll find out the truth soon enough."

Kisia muttered, "It was worth a shot," as the guards

jostled them out of the room, and a little to Rasim's surprise, the Skymaster laughed.

"It was, and if I was a softer or stupider woman, it would have worked."

"Who *are* you?" Rasim blurted.

The woman's eyebrows rose and she lifted a hand, slowing their procession. "Guildmaster Jhikara, of course. Who are *you*?"

Rasim tripped over his own feet and nearly over his own tongue, stunned to find a Guildmaster in the cellars beneath Ilyara, and desperate to not tell her any more than absolutely necessary. Then, with a second shock, he realized he should have recognized Jhikara: she had been at the ceremony, months ago, that had seen Isidri step down as Guildmaster of the Sea Guild.

The same ceremony where Rasim, Desimi, and Kisia had been raised up to journeymen, and announced as the first members of the King's Guild.

He was suddenly certain that Jhikara knew exactly who they were, and was enjoying watching them squirm. Something in his expression must have given him away, because she laughed a second time, a bright thin sound that echoed sharply off the cellar walls. "He sees through me," she announced to no one in particu-lar. "Tell me, Journeyman, did it work? Did you learn other witcheries, so that although you're *not* a skymaster apprentice, you still command the air? Or *was* Taishm in there with you, and rescued himself with stone shaping as he left you all behind? Take them," she said again, and this time stepped back to allow them passage through the narrow halls.

For a little while, Rasim was mostly concerned with not stepping on Desimi's heels. He'd known that a tremendous number of Ilyaran homes and businesses had cellars shaped into the bedrock. He hadn't realized how many of them were linked with the skinny hallways, hardly wide enough for Desimi's broad shoulders to fit through. They bumped along for several long minutes before taking an equally narrow set of stairs upward into a tailor's shop. Even in the relative darkness, the clothes in it were clearly fine, suggesting that between running across Ilyara and then walking beneath it, they'd traveled very close to the palace.

A moment later they were on the street, and Rasim was wondering why he hadn't used stone witchery to trap their captors' feet so they could run away. The answer, though, was the same as ever: he had no sense of the stone, and couldn't feel the magic working. He needed to be still and concentrate in order to successfully shape stone, and it didn't seem likely the witches surrounding them would offer him that opportunity.

Kisia, a step behind him, stumbled hard enough to crash against Rasim's spine. He staggered too, turning to catch her so they wouldn't both go down, and in the impact she hissed, "Taishm?" so quietly that only he could hear her.

He breathed, "Sewers," in response, and her eyes bugged comically as she lurched back to her feet and irritably threw off the hands of guards trying to help. Or perhaps trying to separate them, Rasim thought, as if they could devise some brilliant plot in the few seconds they had to speak unheard.

He *could* create a bubble in which they could converse privately, using sky witchery to keep their words from spilling to unfriendly ears, except there was a master sky witch there. Not just a master: *the* master, the *Guildmaster*, whose magical talent would be matched by her political skill. She'd probably work such a subtle witchery that she'd be able to hear everything they said without Rasim even knowing she was listening in.

He wondered if she'd already done that somehow, and used a magic like that to locate them. For a moment he swallowed the question, but then it occurred to him he probably wouldn't get another chance to ask. "How did you find us?"

Jhikara, who was tall, had strode ahead several paces, but now slowed to answer, as if she thought this was all highly entertaining. "You started using skymastery, and your grasp on it is incredibly disruptive. Really, Journeyman, you need training if you're going to be a skymaster. Assuming you live that long, anyway. Once I felt the disturbances in the air flow that you were creating by muffling the guards chasing you, it was easy enough to track the eddies and currents you left in the air as you ran."

Rasim's jaw dropped in admiring astonishment. "You can *do* that?"

"I can," Jhikara said with a subtle note in her voice in that indicated not many others could. "And then they vanished, Journeyman. Between one step and the next, the very placement you took up in the air itself vanished, leaving only an upward rush of breeze. That meant you went down, and swiftly. The only way for that to happen was if you fell somewhere out of the city's air flow. There are no gaping potholes in Ilyaran streets, so someone with stone-shaping magic almost certainly had to open the street beneath your feet, which left the cellars as the most likely place to find you. We simply began to search them around where you'd disappeared."

An embarrassingly large grin spread across Rasim's face. "That's amazing. Most people wouldn't think of that. I probably would, b—"

Jhikara threw her head back, her thin laugh bursting with genuine humor as they approached the palace. "Do you *often* liken yourself to Guildmasters, Journeyman? How incredibly bold of you."

Heat scored Rasim's cheekbones, but he didn't lose much of his delighted grin. "No, I mean, yes, I kind of do, but mostly I don't meet people who think that fast. That was really *clever* of you."

"*Rasim!*" Kisia, behind him, kicked his ankle. "She's the bad guy!"

"No, I know, but, I mean—"

"Goddess's breath," Desimi said in disgust. "He's got a crush on the Guildmaster."

"I do *not!*"

The other two journeymen, in tandem, said, "Uh-*huh*," in tones of such disbelief that this time Rasim's whole face heated up.

"It's just that it's *clever*," he muttered, and to his utter horror, Jhikara stepped close enough to knock her shoulder against his. She smelled nice, fresh, like the wind, with a little spicy something in her perfume, or in the oil for her hair. Rasim's whole chest got hotter, until he thought he might burst into flame, just like calling sun witchery.

"It is clever," she said cheerfully, "and I appreciate a journeyman who appreciates *that*. I assume Taishm worked the stone witchery."

All at once the heat in Rasim's body turned from embarrassment to anger. He glared up at Jhikara. "I'm not *that* easy to manipulate."

Pure delight sparkled in her dark eyes. "How unexpected and wonderful. The thing is, Rasim, either Taishm was there, or one of you has stone witchery as well, and both are magnificently valuable things to know."

Rasim's stomach dropped as he realized that was true, and dropped farther as Jhikara, almost whirling with enthusiasm, announced, "This is so *exciting*," to the night in general. They had nearly reached the palace now: the streets were broad and well-lit, with guards lining the stairs that led to the palace grounds. "I cannot *wait* to see what Yalonta gets out of you three."

He dared a glance at Desimi and Kisia, who had identical expressions of stoic anger, and mumbled, "Is that what it's like when I think of something faster than anybody else?"

They both hissed, "*Yes*," and Rasim shrank into himself. "I'm sorry."

"Don't worry," Jhikara said, still cheerfully as they climbed the steps. "You're the most interesting thing that's happened to the Skymasters' Guild in years. I'll put in a petition on your behalf."

Rasim croaked, "A petition?"

"Oh, yes," Jhikara promised as the guards swept them all into the palace. "A petition to spare you from death."

CHAPTER NINE

"Spare us from *death*?" Desimi squawked. "Why would somebody kill us?"

"Oh, there's a long line of people who'd like to see you dead," Jhikara assured him. "Less you specifically than Rasim. He seems to be the one who instigates most of the trouble. Most of it," she added, eyebrows drawing down thoughtfully. "I have the impression the baker's girl led something of a rebellion in Moran. Stormed their sporting arena and freed a shocking number of slaves." She smiled brightly at Desimi. "But aside from the company you keep, you don't personally seem to be a problem. You might live through this, if you cooperate."

"Her name," Desimi said in a low, dangerous voice, "is Kisia al Ilialio, and she's a lot truer to the guilds and Ilyara than *you* are, traitor."

Jhikara gave Kisia a quick, wicked little smile. "So eager to leap to your defense. They *are* your boyfriends, aren't they? How charming."

Kisia rolled her eyes so hard the darks disappeared for a moment, but didn't otherwise respond. They were being ushered through the palace's unfriendly halls as Jhikara teased them. Their footsteps echoed off bare walls, and there was little light, as if even the torches had been extinguished to mourn the disappearance of the king.

Except that wasn't it at all, Rasim thought. The people now occupying the palace had driven the king out. If it was dark, they had chosen to keep it that way, like a warning of the future they planned: Golden Ilyara plunged into chaos, warfare, and cruelty. "Why did you side with the Sunmasters?" he asked softly, not really expecting an answer.

"Because I'm clever," Jhikara said with a faint smile. "I can see how the world is changing around us. Ilyara has carefully hoarded its magic a long time, while the rest of the world has grown more and more envious. They were always going to move against us. It was only a matter of when, and how controlled it was. I want to come out of it alive, Rasim. The costs are high, but standing against Pydasho is even more expensive."

"You're wrong."

"I'm not." A touch of air magic swirled, light and easy as she pitched her voice elsewhere, letting her power carry it. "We lost Taishm, but we found an unexpected bounty instead. The Seamaster journeymen who have been causing trouble all over the continent were with him. We've got them now."

Rasim was certain she was letting them hear her half of the conversation, because the other half was muted, for her ears only. She chuckled, though, shrugging with graceful ease. "He abandoned them once. I don't imagine he'll come slinking into the palace to trade himself for them. I'll—" She paused, eyebrows rising, and glanced at the journeymen before shrugging again. "Very well. We'll be there shortly."

Her witchery faded, but a thread of relief swam through Rasim's belly. As long as the rebels believed Taishm had saved himself instead of them, the king's odds of remaining free seemed higher. Rasim just hoped Taishm *wouldn't* decide that turning himself in to keep them safe was a good idea. The thread of relief in his gut suddenly turned to a sinking feeling. He was pretty sure Jhikara and Pydasho wouldn't free them even if the king *did* turn himself in, so he *really* hoped Taishm wouldn't make that mistake.

"Taishm isn't stupid enough to trade himself for us when he knows you're not going to let us go anyway," Kisia said.

Rasim shot a wild grin over his shoulder at her. "That's what I was just thinking."

"Why wouldn't they let us go?" Desimi demanded. "We're not as important as a king."

"The king," Jhikara murmured, "didn't actually stomp across the continent leaving chaos and war behind him, so I'm not entirely sure that's true."

"Mostly I sailed," Rasim said in a small voice. Kisia snorted, Desimi glared, and Jhikara laughed again.

"I like you. What a shame the river found you, instead of the winds outside the city. Pydasho—ah, but no, here we are." She stepped aside, letting their Sun guard escort lead them into what had once been the throne room.

Rasim supposed it still was, but when he'd been there before, the throne had been the dominant feature, with rows of people mostly on foot to stand and face the king. It still sat at the far end, but it was covered with black cloth that made it little more than a shadow, a memory, of what once had been. There were an unexpected number of tables in the enormous room now, covered in maps, paperwork, and food. There was lighting at the near end, where they'd entered, and the Sun Guild's leader, Pydasho, leaned heavily over one of the tables, examining its contents with a scowl.

"Things must not be going well," Rasim said before he thought about it. "Otherwise you'd both be asleep right now."

Pydasho lifted his head and sent a look like a line of fire directly into Rasim's eyes. He shivered, but it was too late, of course: he'd already *said* the thing, and there was no taking it back.

Jhikara, though, all but bounced on her toes and actually stepped close enough to knock her shoulder against his, like she was another journeyman and not a master thirty years his senior. "You see, you *are* clever, lad. It looks bad, doesn't it? The problem—"

"Is that you talk too much, Jhikara." Pydasho had a deep, resonant voice that would carry across a battle-field even without a sky witch to help. "You're mistaken, Journeyman. Everything is going to plan."

"Really?" Desimi asked with a bright note in his

voice. "Losing the king right away, was that part of your plan?"

Rasim's attempt at holding back a grin failed until Pydasho straightened. He'd seen the Guildmaster before, but he hadn't *seen* him, Rasim decided. He hadn't noticed that Pydasho was huge, a broad-shouldered barrel of a man who looked like he didn't need witchery to obliterate someone. He could just squeeze Rasim's skull in his hands, and his brain would pop out the top of his head. His tunic was sleeveless, showing off thickly muscled arms, and his hair, like all sun witches', was cropped short. Journeyman-short by Seamaster standards: a tightly cropped cut indicated the transition from apprentice to journeyman. Regrowing it traced the next years of study, until they'd earned the braid and the bands of a master.

Sun witches, Rasim supposed, needed to be more concerned about not setting their hair on fire, which was easier if it was kept very short. Although Guildmaster Pydasho didn't look like he'd ever worried about anything burning him in his life. He was so solidly built, Rasim thought flame would take one look at him and give up trying.

He and Jhikara couldn't have been more different. She was slim and rather soft-looking, now that Rasim could see her better. She looked like someone who would be swept aside, if thrown against Pydasho.

Somehow Rasim was very certain that was not actually true, but she *looked* it. And she did step aside, easy and light as the breeze, as the enormous Sunmaster leader paced toward them between the tables. His angry rumble sounded like the deepest part of a huge fire, not crackling so much as roaring with a constant background strength. "No. Losing Taishm was not part of the plan. Guiding a king toward making the right choices for Ilyara *was*, but you," and the big man spat the word almost literally, making the journeymen flinch back to avoid his saliva, *"you* put different ideas into his head. We almost had him. With the Islands lord and Lorens and the uprising last year, we almost had him, and you—"

Kisia took a step back as Pydasho advanced on them, and Rasim couldn't blame her. He held his ground mostly because he, at least, could use sun witchery. If the Guildmaster attacked, Rasim wanted to be between him and both Kisia and Desimi.

Because, looking at the deep, angry lines in the big Guildmaster's face, Rasim thought he might. He'd lost control of his speech for a few seconds, spluttering with dislike and temper. Desimi, who was considerably bigger than Rasim, but also only thirteen and nowhere near Pydasho's size, edged in front of Kisia, standing at Rasim's side to scowl viciously up at the Guildmaster. Rasim sort of wished he hadn't—it would be easier to protect him from sun witchery if he was *behind* Rasim —but was also incredibly grateful that his powerful, grumpy friend was fully on his side.

"I didn't put any ideas into his head," Rasim said into the Guildmaster's momentary spluttering silence. "I'd only talked to him twice. Once he told me to take the day off."

Behind him, Kisia giggled, a high sound of terrified

humor. Rasim had to try hard not to shoot a panicked grin over his shoulder at her. Pydasho's gaze snapped her way, and Rasim, sharply, said, "But what was *supposed* to happen?" to draw the Guildmaster's attention back to him. There was a light of something uncomfortable and familiar in Pydasho's eyes when he focused on Rasim again. A bright, heated spark, something that seemed to be a little beyond reason or rationality. Rasim had seen it somewhere before, but couldn't place where, not right then with the Guildmaster growling at him.

"Lord Roscord was meant to attack Taishm," he snarled. "Betray him. Prove that despite their friendship, the world outside Ilyara wasn't trustworthy and we had to ready ourselves for more attacks. But it went wrong because of you!"

"I didn't—no, never mind that. What did *Roscord* think was going to happen? Because there's no way he expected to end up dead. I talked to him enough to know he had bigger plans than that." Rasim's gaze darted to the darkened throne at the far end of the room. "You wouldn't have promised him the Ilyaran throne. He might have wanted it, but it's too far from the Islands, where he was consolidating power, and besides, you wouldn't have wanted to give that away when you can have it for yourself."

Kisia, close enough to feel the warmth of her body, made a tiny sound, maybe an objection. Rasim was thinking, though, that skipping-through-ideas speed that meant he barely touched on them before he'd caught enough of their shape to move on. It only took a breath to consider what little he knew about the rich-voiced Islands warlord, and looked back up at Pydasho. "You promised him witches, didn't you? Ilyaran witches to help him conquer and hold the Islands. That was an easy promise to make, because you always meant for him to end up dead. Probably the guards were supposed to kill him, or even Taishm himself. But then he ran, and if he'd survived, he would have told Taishm the whole plan, so Lorens had to kill him."

Jhikara's thin laughter spiraled upward as she clapped her hands together. "I told you he was clever!"

"Did you send witches north to train Lorens's people?" Rasim, despite himself, was genuinely fascinated. "I know they used to have magic in the Northlands, but everyone there said it had been lost a long time ago. Did you help them find it again?" He waited a heartbeat, then, gambling on an impulse, added, "That was a really good idea, if it was yours."

Pydasho flinched, as if the compliment was an attack he didn't know how to counter. The irrational spark in his gaze faded a little, or at least changed as he slid from defensive toward curious. Rasim barreled ahead before the Guildmaster had a chance to speak. "Because you're right, you know. The world is changing. And it should, shouldn't it? And since Ilyara has so *much* witchery, and has for so long, it only makes sense that we should—"

"Be the first among equals at a table of magic-using nations!" Pydasho roared triumphantly. "If only your Guildmaster understood that! If only our idiot king grasped it!"

Rasim said, "Er," and Desimi stepped on his foot, like Rasim was too dumb to know he shouldn't disagree with Pydasho. He had obviously *not* been going to say 'first among equals,' although he could almost see how the Sunmaster got there. Almost. *He* had been going to say help other nations to re-ignite their witchery and make their societies more equal and fair, abolishing slavery and using magic to ease daily life. It was so close to Pydasho's vision, and also so very far away. "You're, uh, it's a, uh…" He took a deep breath, trying to steady himself, then managed a weak smile at the Guildmaster. "You made allies, obviously. Prince Lorens."

For a moment, darkness actually swam in Rasim's eyes, a dizzy wave threatening to pull him down. He'd been unsure where Lorens's loyalties lay for months, but the Northern prince's betrayal had still been a sickening blow. The memory of the *Wafiya*'s keel cracking, that terrible sound on an empty sea, would stay with Rasim for the rest of his life.

It took everything he had to throw off those memories and keep talking in as inviting a tone as he could manage. "Lady Amdria in Moran. A lot of the Moranese council, I think? They wanted what you could provide. Witches. The knowledge of witchery itself. How was it supposed to go?" he asked again, carefully. "How *is* it supposed to go now?"

Jhikara, her voice light and warning, murmured, "Pydasho," but she didn't look surprised when the Guildmaster ignored her. Neither was Rasim, honestly. He didn't dare look at her himself, because he was certain she understood what he was trying to do.

Pydasho, who should have understood, but either didn't, or didn't care, growled again. "It's all fallen apart, thanks to you. The Moranese were our allies! I had them in the palm of my hand, and now—"

"I'm sorry." Rasim's voice quavered more than he wished it would. "They're going to come kill us all, aren't they? Because we destroyed their city. And they'll be here any minute. The eastern pass—"

"They won't come through the high pass," Pydasho said disdainfully. "I wish they would. A half competent stonemaster and a couple of apprentices could hold that pass for a week. What I need," he snarled, "is the Seamasters to help hold the *western* pass. The river there could slow them for months, if only your cursed guild would cooperate!"

"Then maybe you shouldn't have deposed the king." To his horror, Rasim realized he was the person who'd said that. Kisia groaned very quietly, but Jhikara laughed again.

The sound was nearly drowned out by Pydasho's roar of outrage. "He didn't see what I see! The world changing! The value of our witchery! The guild limitations are old, outdated ideas when we could be profiting from our power! Ilyara could rule the world, don't you see? It only takes *vision*!"

His eyes were bright with madness again, and Rasim abruptly realized where he'd seen that fanatic brilliance before. Missio, the sea witch who had died by Lorens's hand after he'd used her to work a magic far beyond her usual ability. Her eyes had burned the same way Pydasho's did, fevered with uncanny conviction.

But poor Missio had been misled and drugged. Rasim was nearly certain Pydasho's fervor was born from the absolute certainty that he was right. He thought that might be even more dangerous than a drug. It seemed like someone might be weaned off a drug. Rasim didn't know if it was possible to convince someone they were wrong, when their belief in their rightness was born of pure faith.

"Take them away." Pydasho was nearly panting with effort, like his frustration with those who saw the world differently was as physical as a long run. "Separate them. The witch cells beneath the palace."

Jhikara murmured, "Pydasho," again, and he roared, "Do not question me, Skymaster! Do as I say!"

The slim woman paused, all the dancing humor draining from her changeable expression. "I would remind you that I share the same rank you do, *Guildmaster*, and that you would do well to call me by it. Remember that fire cannot burn without air."

Pydasho said, "Guildmaster," through his teeth, then snapped at the guards who lingered in the room. "Take them away."

Without a word, a dozen Sun-clad guards surrounded them, and the last thing Rasim saw as they were escorted out was the amused twist of Jhikara's mouth.

CHAPTER TEN

"Well," Desimi said under his breath, a few steps outside of the throne room, "at least we're not dead."

"I don't unders—" Kisia lingered on the *s*, bugging her eyes at Rasim, who cautiously tested the air to see if Jhikara was holding witchery out of his ability to use it.

She wasn't. He hadn't expected her to be, not with the expression he'd seen on her face. He wove a little sky witchery, keeping their conversation to themselves, and nodded at Kisia, who hissed, "I don't understand why she didn't tell him you two could use more than one witchery! They can stick us in the cells down there, but they won't stop us from getting away because you can witch their barriers!"

"She tried." Desimi muttered that, although his gaze jerked to Rasim's for confirmation. "That's why she kept saying his name, right? But he ignored her."

Rasim nodded. "And she knows how to do something I'm really bad at."

Kisia and Desimi both blurted, "What?" and Rasim grinned crookedly at both of them.

"She knows how to shut up and let people make their own mistakes."

They stared at him a moment before Kisia cackled. "You're right. You're really bad at that. But doesn't she want what Pydasho wants?"

"She wants to win," Desimi said with a note of aggravated certainty. "It's not the same thing."

"It seems like the same thing," Kisia said dubiously, but Rasim shook his head after casting a quick glance at their guards. They mostly looked journeyman-age, not yet masters, and not dedicated enough to Pydasho's cause that they seemed to care that an unheard conversation was going on under their noses.

"Desi's right. Pydasho wants to rule Ilyara and dominate the world with magic. I think Jhikara just wants to come out on the winning side. I'm not sure which side that is matters all that much to her. If it means witches run the world, she's fine with that. If it means order is restored and she keeps her position, I think she's fine with that, too."

"*I* wouldn't let her keep her position, if I was Taishm!"

"Me either," Rasim admitted. "On the other hand, maybe she's hoping letting us go will be enough. We can escape, and maybe even update Taishm, because she's looking the other way."

"Siliaria's breath," Desimi said in disgust. "You still

have a crush on her, Sunburn."

Rasim's ears flamed. "I do not! I just think I under-stand what she's doing!"

"And you think it's great!"

"I think it's better than Pydasho knowing we've got multiple witcheries and cutting off our heads instead of locking us in cells we can get away from!"

Desimi looked like he wanted to argue with that even though it was obviously better to not be executed. Kisia interrupted his scowl by saying, "Do we have to wait until we're in the cells to escape? And should I have—" She took a deep, abrupt breath, and spoke as if she was almost ashamed of herself. "He wasn't threat-ening us, not really. If he had been, I might have… but there was a minute there when he was really angry that I thought it would probably be pretty easy to stop his heart, and I didn't. Should I have?" Her voice got even smaller. "It might have ended this whole thing right there?"

Rasim said, "No!" so sharply it broke through the witchery he'd woven and startled their guards into paying attention to them. A couple of them frowned as if they'd just realized their captives' mouths had been moving without them hearing the conversation, but Desimi distracted them by spinning on his heel and punching the nearest one in the stomach.

The sun witch's breath rushed out of him so hard that his eyes crossed. He dropped to his knees, not even able to wheeze, and Desimi whipped around to punch the next one almost as hard. He staggered back, breath-less and dazed, although he didn't fall. Desimi was on the third one, using his big fists like sledgehammers, almost before Rasim had time to blink.

Fast as it all was, one of their guards had the wit to draw breath and try to shout for help. Kisia threw herself against the woman, knocking them both into a wall, and between grunts of pain as they both went down, snapped, "Rasim! Shut them up!"

For a horrible instant he thought of the worst way to do that, by drawing all the air away from them so they choked and died. Then, shocked at himself, he took a much safer path and wove the same kind of witchery that had hushed their voices, but cast it over the whole group. A grim-faced young woman reached outward, toward the torches farther down then all, and fire leaped to her hands, whirling under her command. Rasim whispered, "Fire can't burn without air," and with a whisk of magic, sucked the air from around her flame.

Her expression was almost comical for the heartbeat or so before Kisia tackled her, too. Rasim shot a baffled glance toward the first woman Kisia had gone after, only to find her slumped woozily against the wall. He decided he didn't want to know how Kisia had gotten her that way.

They'd had about ten guards, and half of them were down already. One lifted his hands in surrender and sat, obviously not having any interest in being on the receiving end of Kisia or Desimi's violent tendencies. A few seconds later, the rest of them were out of the fight, too, and Rasim barely knew how any of it had happened.

Desimi, chest heaving with effort, said, "The problem is even if we had something to tie them up with, they'd burn through it as soon as we were out of reach."

"Not if we put all the torches nearby out." Kisia climbed to her feet from where she'd bested another sun witch, her face glowing with enthusiasm. "Hardly any sun witches can start fires of their own. They need the spark. I've got my witchery around their hearts right now," she went on quite cheerfully. "They can't exert themselves. So tie them up while Rasim goes and puts the torches out."

"I—right." Rasim could do it from there, but it was better to not let a cohort of Pydasho's people know that. "Are their clothes enough to tie them up with? We might have to tear—"

"Don't teach a sailor to tie knots, Sunburn." Desimi was already tearing cloth and binding wrists and ankles. "Go deal with the torches." He also wove a thin stream of air witchery, adding, "I'll keep them quiet," and took over the working that Rasim had begun.

That was almost effortless now, Rasim thought as he hurried down the hall to start putting torches out. The first time Desimi had transferred a magical working to him, it had nearly flattened Rasim. Of course, it had been a huge piece of witchery, and they'd both been exhausted at the time. But even when they'd figured out how to teach Desimi skymastery, the transition had been difficult.

But that had been before they'd worked together for days to keep so much witchery alive that a glasswing stayed solid beneath them as they flew across thousands of miles. Rasim didn't know if they could cast other witcheries back and forth as smoothly, but handing off lightweight air magic was easier than he could ever have imagined.

It only took a few minutes to extinguish the torches near enough for the Sun guards to use. Rasim returned to his friends, who had thoroughly tied up their former captors, and together the three of them slipped down the halls, whispering suggestions about how to escape the palace.

"There are secret passages," Rasim remembered. "Taishm said so. Maybe we could find one."

"How?" Desimi demanded. "I don't have stonemastery and yours is terrible!"

"Where are Taishm's rooms?" Kisia asked. "If we could get in there we could probably find the entrance to one of the passageways. But the palace complex is huge. I don't have any idea where the royal family actually lives."

Desimi guessed, "Behind the throne room," and Rasim swayed, closing his eyes a moment.

"No, that's what they want people to think. So if assassins—if anyone who wants to hurt the royal family—gets onto the palace grounds, they go in the wrong direction. I learned that when I was studying with the Sunmasters at the end of last year."

"That seems like a *really dumb* thing to tell a first-year apprentice," Desimi said incredulously. "Even one as old as you."

Kisia said, "Desimi!" sharply, but Rasim smiled a little as he forced his eyes open.

"No, he's right. Somebody mentioned it when they weren't supposed to, because they were mad about me being rushed through a lot of other diplomatic stuff. I wasn't supposed to overhear. The king's chambers are in the…" He hesitated, trying to orient himself to where the throne room was, then blinked. "They should just be a couple of corridors over, if we're where I think we are."

"Can your terrible stone magic open up one of these walls so we can go straight through?" Desimi asked.

"It would probably take longer to do that than to use the halls," Rasim said apologetically.

"Fine!" Kisia got them moving again, which was good, because Rasim didn't think he could convince himself to do much of anything that required a plan right then. Several minutes and more than one mis-turn later, they found a hall touched by the rising sun, and lined with both sculptures and fabrics to soften the ancient stone walls. Nothing else in the palace had been decorated like that, and Kisia snorted. "I'm not sure making the king's wing fancy when everything else is plain is a good way to convince anybody this isn't the direction assassins should go, but right now I don't care."

Desimi muttered, "It better not be a decoy," but they hurried down the hall and trying doors, hoping to find the king's chambers. Kisia kept twitching her gaze around, clearly looking for guards who weren't there. Rasim guessed if there was no king to protect, they didn't need to be there. And maybe if they were loyal enough to try, Pydasho had gotten rid of them.

"Here." Desimi pushed a surprisingly ordinary-looking door open onto an exceptionally beautifully appointed room that all of them thought must be Taishm's, even though they didn't discuss it. They slipped inside, and Desimi locked it behind them before whispering, "Can you search the walls for hollow spaces with stone witchery?"

"I can try."

"And if not," Kisia said, "where would you hide a secret passageway? In a closet? Under the desk?" She gestured for Desimi to check the closet while she went to the desk. A moment later, her voice strange, she said, "Rasim? Is this…what is this?"

He joined her at the desk, which was itself so beautiful—deeply polished red wood, carved along the edges with fantastical creatures that looked as though they'd risen from the wood, rather than been shaped by tools—that it took him a few moments to even look at the papers on top of it. But a chill ran over him, making the hairs on his arms rise as he sifted through them, then picked a few up, reading them in dismay before sinking into the desk's chair. "I think these are Guild-master Pydasho's papers."

"What?" Desimi, outraged, stopped looking for passageways and came over to the desk. "He really thinks he's going to be king, doesn't he?"

Rasim nodded, still looking through the papers, hands trembling and stomach lurching with every page he turned. "These are—Siliaria's fins, these are letters from—this one's signed by Lady Amdria!"

"The one who tried to have you executed in Moran?" Kisia reached for the letter and Rasim pulled it away, wanting to finish reading it.

"They're old plans," he said as he read. "At least, I think they're old. From before we destroyed Moran."

"*We* didn't destroy it," Desimi said fiercely. "*We* just made it a little wet. That Stonemaster destroyed it."

Rasim gave him a look, and Desimi pressed his lips together but made a gesture indicating he was right, no matter what Rasim thought. Rasim turned his attention back to the letter, flinching as he read it. "They were arranging an invasion. A way to threaten Ilyara and force Taishm to act. They *were* going to come through the high gap!"

"But not at the end of winter, I bet." Kisia reached for the letter. "This wasn't written that long ago. Before Cindu wrecked Moran, but…why would he encourage them to take the shorter passage? Why would he do this at all? Encourage them to invade Ilyara? How would that help him?"

Rasim wished he couldn't think of an answer, but one came to mind all too easily. "Because he thinks he can stop them in the pass. Or he thought he could. He thought he would have Taishm under his thumb and the Stonemasters on his side. He didn't imagine he wouldn't have full control over the city. We—*I*—changed the timeline too much."

He shuffled through more papers, every motion stiff

and slow and tired. "I think they'll still come through the gap, even if it's dangerous with the snow rotting in the mountains. We'll be overrun. And I don't know who we can tell, to ask for help. Even if we can find Taishm in time, he's not in charge of anything right now."

"What was Pydasho thinking?" Desimi interrupted, his forehead wrinkled in a frown. "He's got a snarl worse than a torn fishing net here, Sunburn, and I don't see any way it wasn't always a snarl. He's been working with Lorens a long time, right? Long enough to poison Hongrunn's water supply, anyway, and that had been going on most of our lives."

Rasim nodded like he was asking a question, and Desimi came over to push at the papers on Pydasho's desk, too, as if one of them might contain an answer. "So what was he thinking? Lure the Northern prince in, teach his followers witchery, and then what? Let him control the Northern witches while Pydasho rules the Ilyaran ones? And..." The bigger boy rubbed his temples, his expression suggesting thinking this much made his head hurt.

"Same thing with the Islands," Kisia said slowly. "If Pydasho always meant for Roscord to end up dead, what good does that do him? It doesn't leave him with any control in the Islands, and there aren't really any witches there to worry about. Except the girl you taught. Carla, was it?"

"Carley," Rasim said immediately, and Kisia gave him a sly grin that made his face heat up. He muttered, "If there aren't any witches there, *or* a ruling lord to organize them, it could make the Islands easy to conquer. And that's what Pydasho said he wanted, was to rule everybody with witchery. But Desimi's right about Lorens." He hesitated. "The Northlands are a long way away. Maybe Pydasho thought he needed a lieutenant up there. Someone he could control because he taught them magic and thinks he can take that away again."

"He can, with enough of the heartbreak drug," Kisia pointed out. "And that's a desert flower, not one of the Shenryalan plants. Pydasho has access to it."

"But what about Moran?" Desimi almost stomped his foot in frustration. "What was he *thinking*? The Shenryalans thought the Moranese had kidnapped Prince Bayar—"

Kisia said, "He's not really a prince," under her breath, but Desimi barreled on anyway, clearly trying to talk almost faster than he could think. Rasim knew exactly how that felt.

"—and so the Shenryalans were going to ride in and get vengeance for Bayar until we brought him back and found out it had been other Shenryalans who kidnapped him after Lorens told them to! If Pydasho was bargaining with Moran, offering them power or an easy route to invade Ilyara, why would he *also* set it up so the Shenryalans would declare war on them?"

"Because he never meant to give them any power!" Rasim actually staggered a couple of steps from the desk with the force of his answer, and gaped at Desimi, wide-eyed with astonished admiration. "That's why, but I couldn't figure it out until you asked all those questions together. He's trying to weaken *everybody*."

He stepped back to the desk, then, unable to find a map, took the embroidered one out of his tunic and spread it so he could skim his hands over the whole continent that it displayed. "Look, you're right, Desimi, those were the right questions to ask. Why kill Roscord? Because he'd been consolidating power in the Islands. Kill him and there's a leadership void. Either they'd start infighting, or just go back to being a bunch of little separate communities, easy to conquer."

Kisia's voice cracked on a giggle. "Only you brought what's her name, the pirate lady, back from the sea to lead the people."

"Donnin," Rasim said, and this time Kisia's grin, quick and bright, didn't make him blush. "So there wasn't a power void there after all. And in the North…" He ran his fingertips to the huge jagged peninsula that made up the Northlands. "Oh, see, maybe he's more clever than Jhikara thinks, after all. Because if he supports Lorens, Lorens will do his dirty work— maybe even try to kill his mother and sister—and either it'll work, or it'll start a civil war. Even if it doesn't start a war, there'll be a resistance to a new king who killed his family to take the throne. It leaves the North weak!"

"Ripe for conquering by the world's strongest witching nation," Desimi said almost triumphantly. "All right, that makes sense. But what about Moran and Shenryal?"

Rasim spread his hand across the space on the map where three continents collided. His heart beat so fast he felt sick, and his fingers were icy with excitement.

"Moran's strong. They've got a lot of enslaved witches, an army, and routes all over the continent for supplies. But the Shenryalan riders are *legendary*. If they're at war with each other, then Ilyara, under Pydasho's command, could choose one and force them to a war on two fronts, which would weaken either of them an awful lot. And by the time either of those wars was over, the one we hadn't picked a fight with would be a lot weaker and we could probably take them pretty easily. And then..." He opened his hands wide, covering as much of the map as he possibly could with them. "Then Pydasho has won."

Kisia gave another one of those high giggles. "Only you got involved and now both the Islands and Shenryal are our allies, and Moran is our enemy. That's *impressive*," she said. "You broke *everything*."

"I don't know how you always think through these things so fast." Desimi rubbed his temples again. "It makes my head hurt."

"You did some fast thinking there, though," Rasim said. "And besides, this one makes my head hurt, too."

"Why doesn't that make me feel any better?"

"Wait." Kisia looked toward the windows and the brightening sky. "Wait, Pydasho is staying in these rooms."

"Yeah, so?" Desimi dropped his hands, glaring at Kisia as if everything was her fault.

"So he's going to come *back* at some point, right?"

The door swept open as she spoke, and Pydasho spoke, low and dangerous. "Right."

CHAPTER ELEVEN

"Of all the stupid places to run." Pydasho closed the door behind him, the lock settling in place again with a terrifyingly loud click. Rasim hadn't heard it open, but they'd been talking so intensely he wasn't sure he'd have heard anything short of a dragon on the doorstep. "You might have left the palace, at least," the Guildmaster went on. "We might not have caught you, then. How long did you think it would take me to notice the guards hadn't returned? I don't know how you did it, but I will."

Rasim whispered, "Find the passageway, Desi," as softly as he could, and stepped in front of his friends for the second time that night, staring Pydasho down. "You still weren't wrong, Guildmaster. Ilyarans should share their magic. You're just going about it the wrong way. I think you can do better."

Pydasho snarled, dark and angry. "I'm not Isidri or Taishm, you arrogant young whelp. I see the world for what it is—"

Sudden disgust filled Rasim's chest and came out on the words he spoke. "You see it for what you're trying to make it. It can be so much better than that. I don't know if all Sunmasters are corrupted by power, or if that's just a poison you've swallowed, but it doesn't have to be us or them, Pydasho. We can make things better for everybody."

Neither Desimi nor Kisia had moved from behind him. Rasim desperately hoped that it meant Desimi was doing what Rasim had asked, in the most obvious and unlikely way possible. If not, they were going to have to go out the window, and he had no idea what was below it. He *did* know that sky witchery, for all its many uses, did not allow people to fly like birds, and he wasn't sure he could call a glasswing when he was facing down a sun witch. Stomach in knots, trying to buy Desimi some time, he said, "You were encouraging the Moranese to come through the high gap. So you could stop them, right? You were going to have stonemasters crush their army in the narrow gap so you could show the world how powerful Ilyara really is?"

Pydasho advanced a step. Rasim, who wanted to do anything else in the entire world, did too, because he was still the one with sun witchery, and he was already asking too much of Desimi. He could feel Kisia's own magic stirring, and hoped she wouldn't start to squeeze Pydasho's heart.

Mostly. Mostly he hoped that. And he wasn't very proud of it only being mostly, but his whole body was tight with terror and he thought he might throw up when Pydasho snarled again. "I can't believe a handful of *apprentices* ruined so many plans. You couldn't have made things worse if you'd been directed."

Kisia piped up with, "Journeymen!"

Pydasho's eyes bugged so far that a little of Rasim's dread faded into a near-giggle. He whispered, "We *were* apprentices at first," to Kisia, who made a dramatically dismissive sound. Rasim bit back another giggle, but suspicion glittered in the Sun Guildmaster's face.

"You *were* apprentices. Children who could be told what to do by a Guildmaster. Isidri!" he hissed. "That old witch has been pushing people around my entire life. *She* put you up to all of this, didn't she? I'll see her dead," he growled. "If it's the last thing I do, I'll see that witch dead."

Red rage rose in Rasim's vision. His hands clenched, and he thought the only reason he didn't call witchery was they all boiled inside him, eager to be used, and he couldn't think clearly enough to choose one. "Careful, Sunmaster." He barely recognized his own voice, distorted with fury as it was. "You're sailing dangerous seas."

He was only small, and a journeyman. Pydasho was a big man by anybody's standards, and a Guildmaster besides. None-the-less, the Guildmaster hesitated as if he was considering the possibility he might have gone too far. As if wondering whether Rasim, slight and young and aching with anger, might actually be a threat to him.

As if remembering that Rasim had somehow insti-gated chaos and danger across three continents, and might be able to do it again right now.

Before the Guildmaster could make a decision, Desimi, in a tone of faint astonishment, said, "Found it," and things started to happen very fast.

Kisia grabbed Rasim, nearly jerking him off his feet as she and Desimi went from a standstill into a full run. That was the excuse Pydasho needed: his sun witchery came on in a full attack, encircling the journeymen before they'd gone more than a few steps. Rasim, partly expecting it and also furiously glad to have an excuse, crushed the fire with his own witchery.

Glee shot through him at Pydasho's inarticulate roar of surprise. Kisia stumbled, so Rasim did too, but they made it a little farther across the room before flame washed toward them again.

The Guildmaster's second attack was *hotter* somehow, almost as hot as dragon fire. Rasim hadn't known that was even possible. He threw up a shield of air, sending the fire splitting around them, and setting the trappings on Taishm's bed aflame. Desimi yowled, "Siliaria's *fins*, Rasim, we need to get beneath that!"

A panicked laugh rose in Rasim's throat. "Why didn't you say so?"

"Because a bad guy could hear me?! Kisia, water, I can't—!"

Kisia howled, "There isn't any water!" as Desimi dragged her toward the bed. Rasim, trying to keep his feet under him and concentrate on witchery at the same time, convinced the fire to go out, although it felt as though it didn't want to: cloth burned so nicely.

Sun witchery, he decided, was *dangerous*. So was water magic, of course, but water's destructiveness didn't have a sense of delight about it. Fire felt like it *wanted* to burn and enjoyed the devastation it caused. Rasim shrieked as Pydasho grabbed his arm and hauled him the other way. Kisia lost her grip and yelled as she tried to get him back, but he shouted, "Go, go go go!" and she reluctantly retreated toward the no-longer burning bed.

For a few seconds Rasim hung limply in Pydasho's grasp, trying to prepare himself for another onslaught of fiery combat, but the Guildmaster seemed to have realized he wouldn't win that way. He held Rasim's upper arm in an iron grip, his expression both enraged and uncertain, like he didn't know what to do with Rasim now.

It would be strange, Rasim thought, to have spent your whole life responding to problems in one specific way, only to find that it didn't work anymore. It would be like him suddenly being unable to think quickly, even if sometimes he wished he didn't always think quite so fast. He had a thought now, but it would take time, so he said, "You aren't going to win," mostly to keep Pydasho from deciding what to do next.

Judging from the freshly rising anger in the Guildmaster's face, it worked. The big man didn't seem to think well when he was angry, and he was angry a lot. "I will win. I've spent a lifetime working toward the power of a throne. Laishn betrayed me," he said bitterly. "Married that Northerner and had a sea-strong witch whelp with her. Isidri is old enough to remember how things used to be. She would have pushed her way into the palace. I had to do something."

"You set the fire." Rasim's entire body ached with sorrow, and his upper arm, where Pydasho's hand knotted, hurt so badly he could hardly put the words together. "You started the Great Fire. You killed Queen Annaken and her baby. How can you even live with yourself?"

"*I had to*! Laishn could have stopped me, if he'd been in Ilyara! It was easy to convince the guild that without him to focus our power we couldn't contain the fire! Some of them tried anyway." The anger in Pydasho's eyes was overtaken by another kind of madness. "I dealt with them. There were so many dead, anyway. What was a few more?"

Sickness shuddered through Rasim, nearly disrupting the thin magic he was trying to work. "You're sick, Guildmaster. You have a sickness in your head or your heart or something. You need help, not power."

Pydasho's lip curled. "Without me, Ilyara is powerless against the world's greed. You'll see. You'll understand. I'll keep you alive long enough to watch me succeed, and then..."

His imagination failed him, which was just as well, as far as Rasim was concerned. He was ready, and didn't need any more threats. As casually as he could, he said, "I don't think so."

Brief surprise pinched Pydasho's eyebrows. "What?"

Rasim smiled. "Look down."

The Guildmaster did, and in the instant his grip loosened with confusion, Rasim twisted hard, breaking free and leaping out of Pydasho's reach.

And, despite the stone boots that had grown out of the floor to encase the Guildmaster's feet almost to his knees, Pydasho tried to lurch after him. Instead, stone bruised his shins and he shouted with pain as Rasim danced away, then dropped to hands and knees to scramble under the bed.

There was a trap door there, open now, but so smoothly set into the floor that no one would find it unless they knew it was there—or had stone witchery at their command. A narrow staircase began just beyond the doors, which fell inward. Rasim swung his feet around and dropped into the hole, scooted far enough down to close the doors above his head, and, effortfully, sealed them with witchery.

It was *completely* dark with the doors closed, as dark as the Northern mines where he and Kisia had briefly been forced to work. He waved his hand in front of his face, then put his palm against his nose, just to make sure he hadn't lost what he couldn't see.

Kisia's voice came out of the darkness, thin and frightened. "Rasim? Can you make some light? It's too dark. I can't breathe."

"Yeah, yes, hold on." Rasim, understanding how she felt about it being too dark to breathe, made himself take a very deep breath, trying to steady his heartbeat. He realized he was shaking, the near-escape scarier than he'd thought, and he'd thought it was bad enough already. It took a couple of tries to calm himself enough to ignite the internal ember of flame that Sunmaster Endat had spent weeks trying to teach him to find. Light finally sputtered to life, and all three of them made harsh little sounds of relief.

Desimi's was followed by a grimly desperate, "Help."

"Help, what?" Rasim bumped down the narrow stairs on his butt—there were a lot of them, as if an entire wall existed beneath the king's bed just to harbor the stairs—to a slightly broader passageway that ran two directions from the bottom of the stairs. Kisia was pressed against one wall.

Desimi's arm was stuck in the other.

Rasim stopped dead and stared.

"You can't blame him," Kisia whispered. "He found the passageway with stone witchery, or maybe earth sorcery, I'm not sure—"

"Stone," Desimi growled.

"—so when we got to the bottom of the stairs he started experimenting—"

"And it worked," Desimi snapped. "I sank my hand right into the wall. And then *you* started messing with stonemastery—"

"You felt that?" Rasim's voice shot up and broke with surprise.

"—and it felt weird and I panicked and the stupid wall closed around my arm and now I can't get it out again, so *help*!"

Rasim sucked his cheeks in so he wouldn't grin, then looked around for a torch. "I need to put the fire in something. I can't get you out and keep it going all at once and I'd rather see what I was doing, since I can't feel it. You *felt* my stone witchery? Why aren't there any torches down here?"

"Yes! No! I felt the stone moving up there and it felt weird and I panicked!"

"Because the royal family would be able to carry flame like you're doing right now," Kisia said, sounding furious as she stripped her tunic off and started tearing and knotting it into something to burn. "I'm never going adventuring without a backpack again."

"We *had* backpacks. Isidri gave them to us." Rasim stared around again, as if they might suddenly appear. "Where did we leave them?"

"In the cellar," Desimi said after a moment's thought, and with a sigh. "Where Jhikara found us. We forgot them there. And I'm hungry."

As if given permission, all three of their stomachs growled so loudly Rasim thought he actually heard them echoing off the passage walls. Kisia rubbed her belly and lifted a frayed end of her knotted-up tunic to Rasim so he could transfer his witchery to it. The fire burned a little brighter with something to consume, and Kisia held it up carefully while Rasim leaned on the wall next to Desimi's arm and sent his inert-feeling stone witchery into the rock.

It took a few minutes, as his stone witchery always did. Then, all at once, Desimi's arm was free. He yanked it out of the wall and shook it vigorously, then rubbed it like he was making sure it was all still there. Hairs stood up on his nape, but Rasim couldn't help grinning at him. "Stonemaster, huh? Or, I don't know, you got yourself stuck in stone, maybe we should start calling you Statue."

"That's a stupid nickname."

"Yeah." Rasim's grin grew. "Yeah, it is. *Statue*."

"You two are idiots," Kisia announced. "Can we get out of here before the fire goes out? I know it won't!" she snapped at Rasim. "Can we get out of here *anyway*?"

"Earth *and* stone witchery," Rasim said cheerfully to Desimi. "And air and water. Are you sure it wasn't you who set fire to the ropes on the *Wafiya*?"

"Yes!" Desimi hesitated, frowned, and hunched his shoulders. "Probably."

"You were mad at something when it happened," Kisia said. "I remember we were trying to get the fire to leap from the charcoals and you got mad. Probably at Rasim."

"I wasn't even there!" He had been, of course, but he had been up in the crow's nest, not down working with the other journeymen. A little guiltily, he added, "And I was mad too."

"See," Desimi muttered. "It was probably Rasim."

"Never mind. Which way should we go, and where will we find food? I'm hungry." Kisia whined the last word, and Rasim looked up and down the passage.

"Taishm said the passage he took leads to the river. Desimi, can you feel the Ilialio more strongly in one direction?"

Desimi eyed him. "Can't you?" Still, after a moment, he jerked his chin toward their left. "That way. If we can get to the river we can find food, and figure out what we're doing next."

"Oh, I know what we're doing," Rasim said as they

set off. Desimi gave him another wary look, but Kisia grinned with anticipation.

"We're going to find Taishm and bring him back to rally the city, right? We're going to lead the resistance against Pydasho?"

"Oh." Rasim slowed, suddenly uncertain. "That might be better than what I had planned. Maybe you two should go do that."

Desimi's expression grew even warier. "Why? What are *you* going to do?"

"I'm going to go close the Eastern Gap."

Silence met his determination before Desimi, incredulously, said, "You can't do that *alone!*"

"Well, you just got your arm stuck in a wall, so I don't know how much help *you'll* be, *Statue!*"

"You two certainly aren't going without *me*," Kisia said with a sniff. "So let's get some supplies and go, because we both already know we're not talking Rasim out of it, Desi."

"But how are we going to get out there? It's three days across the desert!"

"Camels," Rasim said with aplomb.

"We're going to steal supplies *and* camels?"

"*Borrow.* We'll pay them back when we have guild resources again," Kisia promised Desimi. "My parents would never forgive me, otherwise."

The bigger journeyman kept glowering in disbelief at Rasim. "Camels? Have you ever ridden a camel?"

"No, but it can't be as bad as a horse."

CHAPTER TWELVE

It was much worse than a horse.

Horses at least didn't moan and groan with effort when they got off the ground, and they were much shorter than camels. And, very importantly, horses didn't throw up on somebody if they got mad.

One of the camels they tried to steal—*borrow*—didn't wanted to come with them. Desimi pulled on its halter, trying to convince it, until it spat at him. He barely dodged, and all three journeymen stared in horror at the disgusting, stinking, thick black goo that the animal had ejected. "I knew they spat," Kisia whispered. "I didn't know they spat like *that*. I think that came all the way from its other end."

Desimi, gagging at the bilious stench, backed away from that camel, and the three of them together stared at the other huge, gangly animals in alarm bordering on fear. After a long time, Kisia said, "So, no camels."

"No camels." Rasim looked helplessly at the other two. "Horses?"

"*I*," Kisia hissed, "am not stealing—*borrowing*—desert horses. The people who breed them would take the price of them out of our backsides if we got caught, and they keep *guards*, Rasim."

"Well, then, how are we going to get t—" A gust of night-cool sandy breeze caught him, and Rasim lifted his gaze to the half-moons in the sky above. "Never mind. I'm not clever at all. In fact, I'm very stupid."

"Yeah, you are," Desimi said happily. "How come?"

"Because I just tried to steal camels instead of calling glasswings."

Desimi said, "Oh," and then, "Oh! Oh, yeah, that's a better idea. Faster. I bet it'll only take a few hours to get to the gap on one of those things."

Kisia shook her head, murmuring, "First he came up with a way to let skymasters talk over huge distances, and now he's going to revolutionize travel."

"Hah. Not unless an awful lot more people can call glasswings than I think can. Let's get some food," Rasim whispered. "Even if it's only a short flight, we might need to be there a while to get the gap closed."

"Not with me there," Desimi said self-importantly. "I can work stone now, too."

"You got your arm stuck in a wall, *Statue*," Kisia said. "Don't get above yourself."

Desimi's shoulders hunched, and he remained sullen as they *borrowed* food, tents, turbans, and clothes from a variety of vendors on their way out of the city. They even walked a couple miles out into the desert, not wanting to start a tremendous working of sky witchery too near to Jhikara, and he sulked his way through that, too. They called two this time, one for Kisia and Rasim, and one for Desimi alone. That improved his temper a little: he was enough bigger than the other two that he'd really been crowded, flying three on one glasswing. But his bad mood faded away entirely as they flew, because nobody, Rasim thought, could actually remain peevish on a glasswing's back. The stars were too close and too bright, and the translucent amber-hued wings of the desert-born creatures were far too beautiful to be angry around.

They had flown for so long across the ocean that Rasim was stunned when Desimi was right, and it took only a few hours to fly from Ilyara's borders to the mountains that were a three-or four-day camel ride away. The glasswings rode the wind, rising toward the mountaintops effortlessly, and his first glimpse of the worrisome gap came as a flash of moonlit granite beneath them. From above, it looked barely a hand's-breadth wide, and not much longer, although it visibly twisted sharply at one point, a jagged break between massive, dangerous peaks.

Then they shot over the gap itself, and found an army.

RASIM HADN'T UNDERSTOOD how mountain passes worked, not really. He'd imagined they were just lower points between many peaks that went all the way back down to what he thought of as ground level. He'd been thinking of the *pass* as the narrow, twisty canyon that he'd meant to block off.

But beyond that narrow twisty canyon lay a valley only a little lower than the peaks around it. It stretched north for miles toward another set of peaks that also had a canyon-like gap in them, and then beyond that, another valley, a little lower but still basically *high*, stretched out. *That* was what a mountain pass really was, a series of peaks and valleys that connected safely enough to cross, not just one little gap in an endless reach of mountains that went all the way up and all the way down again. Valleys stretched west, too, rougher and higher than the one at the gap, but still almost passable. To the east, peaks rose again quickly, blocking the way, so the valley they flew over was the last chance to cross into the Ilyaran desert.

And the Moranese army filled a great deal of the valley floor leading to the actual tiny gap that Rasim had imagined *was* the pass.

Their camp was laid out in circles, growing smaller around a central circle that had soldiers bristling around it, visible even late at night under the fading moonlight. The ground in the middle looked barren, almost writhing with night colors, and Rasim had no idea why they were facing in rather than outward. Kisia, pressed against his back, whispered his name in dismay, and Rasim nodded helplessly. He waved, catching Desimi's eye. In silent agreement, they shot back over the mountains to the Ilyaran side before somebody glanced up and saw three journeymen flying overhead.

It was not easy to talk to someone on another glass-wing, not with the wind witchery that stormed around them. On the other hand, Rasim didn't trust himself to weave a separate thread of skymastery so they could talk. He was afraid any loss of concentration might mean the glasswing would lose interest and he and Kisia would fall out of the air. So he shouted, because between the wind and the distance, the Moranese prob-ably wouldn't hear him anyway. "We have to stop them!"

"We can't," Kisia yelled. "They're sure to have enslaved witches with them!"

"So you two should go back to Ilyara and warn them, and I'll stay to try to stop this!"

Desimi gave a big laugh that was almost lost to the sound of wind. "I don't think so, Sunburn!"

"But there's no point in closing it and then not staying to defend it if there are witches who can undo our work!" His glasswing hovered with wingbeats so fast Rasim couldn't see them except when it shifted angles, which all of the wings seemed to be able to do independently.

Kisia shrugged against his back, shouting, "So we'll stay. You can't be allowed to be the only one who acts on terrible ideas!"

"Everyone might be safer if I didn't, either!"

Kisia's snort carried through the whipping winds. "Maybe, but we'd be a *lot* safer if stupid Guildmaster Pydasho hadn't decided to try to take over the world, so I don't think there's much point in you kicking yourself!"

"No one is going to be looking up for us!" Desimi yelled. "We can probably drop right into the middle of their camp! There's something *weird* there, did you notice?"

"They probably have all their witches in there and don't trust them! *Oh*." Rasim twisted toward Kisia. "You and Sesin could both purge heartbreak in Moran. Do you think you can do the same with mindkiller?"

"Probably, but wh—oh." Kisia's face brightened. "Oh! You think if we get close enough I can maybe purge their enslaved witches so they don't have to follow orders anymore. Would it work?"

A wild smile ran across Rasim's face. "Maybe that's why they're all facing the middle of camp, instead of keeping an eye out for enemies approaching from outside. Maybe they're trying to control their witches. If that's what's happening, trying to free them is worth it, right? Desimi, can you—?"

"I can't purge anything!" the bigger journeyman called. "But I can try to close off the gap so they don't have anywhere to run except home again!"

Rasim nodded, and the journeymen split up. Desimi's glasswing skimmed downward toward the narrow canyon, while Rasim guided his back over the mountain again to bring Kisia toward the center of the Moranese camp. She whispered, "There are so many of them," against his back, and he nodded unhappily. He couldn't even easily count the number of campfires, much less guess at how many people each of the tents held. Some were large, barrack-like, while others were smaller but far greater in number. They *all* seemed to have their entrances pointing inward, toward the middle of the camp, which made no sense.

"The witches must have gotten really dangerous," Kisia breathed. "I wonder if the mindkiller isn't working as well anymore."

"I don't know, but something's going on. It looks quiet in the very middle, though, down there on that hill. If I bring us down really close we can jump to the ground without the glasswing's wings waking anybody up, I hope."

"Maybe we should jump from higher," Kisia said dubiously.

"Not unless you know how to heal a broken leg in a few seconds, or run on one."

Kisia made a disgruntled noise that obviously meant no, and a few minutes later they leaped from the glasswing onto a twisting mass of stone.

THEY BOTH FROZE as the ground moved under them, long slow uncomfortable shifts that scraped stone against stone. Rasim lost his balance and fell into a slowly-closing crevasse, although Kisia's hand shot after him and hauled him up again. They lay on their bellies, gasping with confusion and fear, as the stone continued to grind beneath them, until Kisia, in a strangled whisper, said, "It's a snake. A stone snake. Like in the Northlands. Get down. Get off it, I mean.

Somebody's going to see us!" She gave him a push, and they both went over the far side of the snake in a rush, landing with a thump.

The huge beast behind them continued to move, but they held still, hoping they hadn't been noticed. Now that he was on the ground, his heart beating wildly and his stomach churning with nerves, leaping into the middle of an enemy camp seemed like one of the dumber things Rasim had ever done. And, as Kisia had said, he'd once jumped off a mountain onto a dragon.

Somehow no one had noticed them. Rasim had no idea how that was possible, given that even from above, it was clear there were sentries awake and focused on the middle of the camp. His gut went to ice as a murmur sounded somewhere nearby, tension rising in voices. Kisia elbowed him, and he dared a glance around the slowly moving coils.

The snake's face was barely a dozen steps away. Rasim's belly clenched so hard he thought he might need a necessary. For a few seconds he couldn't move at all, hypnotized by fear and awe. The snake's massive stone coils scraped over themselves as the huge creature shifted uncomfortably, as if sleeping on top of the soil went against its very nature. It was orange in the campfire light, but Rasim had no idea if that was its natural color, or reflection from the fires. Its spine was at least half again Rasim's own height, and its scales were smoother than the rough boulder-like skin of the Northern snake, but not sleek. Its eyes flickered open to gaze directly as Rasim, almost as if it knew he was there.

It looked miserable.

Kisia elbowed him again, and he flinched, looking where she wanted him to, this time. He immediately wished he hadn't.

Enslaved Ilyaran witches sat in a loose circle around the stone snake, shuddering with effort. Rasim couldn't feel any power flowing from them, but he wouldn't, not if they were stone witches, struggling to contain the terrible beast. They, too, looked miserable, in a very similar way to the snake itself. Their eyes were half open, but rolled back, glazed, as if they were almost completely unconscious.

Dread sluiced through Rasim as he tried first to imagine how much of the will-sapping mindkiller drug they must be on, to be only semi-conscious yet still working witchery. Then a worse thought struck him: that they had been given *delzjha,* the Shenryalan drug that could push a witch to burn through her power until it killed her, and she would be happy about it. He had used it once in a moment of great need, and it had been so extraordinary that he'd asked the *Wafiya*'s first mate, Hassin, to dump what remained over the ship's rail, so he wouldn't be tempted to use it again. Even now he could remember the thrill of uninhibited power coursing through him, and hoped he'd never be near the stuff again.

Whether it was *delzjha,* mindkiller, or something else, the enslaved witches were all too clearly using everything they had to keep the huge snake subdued.

Its eyes closed again, membranes nictitating across the stony pupil as it lost its battle with awareness. Kisia carefully slid her hand into Rasim's, holding it so hard his bones ached. A shiver started in Rasim's bones and rose all the way to his skin, lifting the hairs on his arms as he put his mouth by her ear and breathed, "We have to free it."

"We what?" Kisia managed not to raise her voice, but she somehow puffed up like an upset cat. "We *what?*"

"It's miserable," Rasim whispered. "And anything they want it for can't be good for Ilyara. We have to free it. If you can purge even just a few of the witches out there of whatever drug they're on, I bet they'll lose control and it'll run."

Kisia, quietly but very prissily, said, "Snakes don't run. They slither." Less prissily, she added, "How did they *catch* it? Where did it come from? You're the only person I ever met who made giant terrifying magical animals appear out of nowhere!"

"I didn't make the one in the North appear!" Rasim hissed indignantly. "It was already there! Remember? The mountain garrison's walls were witched so it couldn't get out. Telun and Milu were the ones who woke it up!"

Kisia opened her mouth and shut it again, blinking at him, then blinked again. "Did you really not set the *Wafiya*'s ropes on fire?"

Exasperation flooded Rasim. "No! I don't think so! What does that have to do with anything?"

She, in a superior tone, said, "Shh," and shrugged

thoughtfully. "I don't know. I just thought all the extra witchery was you. I forgot the Northern snake was awake before we got there. So other people *can* wake these things up." She tilted her chin up, considering the vast, restless creature they hid beside, while Rasim gaped at her with indignation.

After a few seconds, though, the answer clicked in his mind. "Cindu."

Kisia echoed the name like a question, then exhaled it a little harder as she understood. "Cindu. You think he woke a snake from under the city when he attacked Moran with stone witchery?"

Rasim crouched like he needed to be smaller to hide from the idea, but he nodded. The enslaved stone witch, once freed, had torn Moran's river walls down, and then shaken the city to the ground with a massive outpouring of power. It could easily have wakened a stone snake. "There were probably enough witches in Moran to subdue it, but…Kisia, if this thing came up from below Moran, the city must be even more badly destroyed than we thought, and…"

"And we already thought it must be really bad." Kisia crouched, too, the two of them small and insignificant next to the stone snake's enormous bulk. It was cool, like deep earth, and the scales that Rasim leaned against were glass-smooth in places, and rough as shark skin in others. "Do you…do you think it's the right kind of rock to dive into the mountain here, if we free it?"

"I don't know. And I don't know if we'd be lucky enough for it to just want to run away, or if it would want to get back at the Moranese for capturing it."

Kisia was silent a moment before speaking in an extremely pragmatic tone. "Well, if it smashes them all, that's one less problem for Ilyara to deal with."

"Except we're right here to smash too!"

She shrugged. "You'd keep us safe."

Rasim smiled weakly. "Have you ever thought maybe you have too much faith in me?"

A little to his surprise, she met his eyes, hers large and dark and intense in the shadows, and her voice was very soft as she said, "No."

For some reason, Rasim's jaw, and then his whole face, slowly got hot. A nervous twang ran down the whole middle of his body, sending sparks all over his skin, and he ducked his head, wondering why it was suddenly so hard to breathe. "That's, um. That's nice of you. Maybe not very smart. But nice."

Kisia laughed very quietly and leaned in to brush her lips over Rasim's hot cheek, which got even hotter. "I'm flattered. Now excuse me, because I'm not very smart, I'm going to try to make a bunch of stone witches all really sick at the same time. Why don't you try to convince this gigantic terrifying snake that it really just wants to dive into the heart of the mountain, just in case I succeed?"

Rasim, speechless, nodded, and pressed his flaming face against the snake's cool side, trying to ignore Kisia's gentle gathering of sea mastery in favor of somehow convincing an elemental beast to flee rather than fight when the moment came.

It was hard, when someone was right next to him,

working a magic he could feel. He hadn't really paid attention to how she and the healer's apprentice, Sesin, had purged witches during the chaos in Moran, but he was certain that Kisia's approach now was much, much more delicate than that had been. For one thing, this wasn't quite as much of an emergency, but more importantly, it would be best if no one else noticed what she was doing. Neither of them knew if there were any sea witches around to feel her working, or whether they *could* feel it if they were near, but she obviously thought being cautious was better than being fast, this time.

But it was a lot easier to admire her careful craftsmanship than it was to be sure his own inert stonemastery attempts were getting anywhere. Rasim put his palm against the snake's side, trying to concentrate on how it shifted and grumbled like a rock slide waiting to happen, and wondered if it could hear him, if he thought at it loudly enough. Maybe he didn't need to use magic. Maybe he could just *think* it away.

A little grin curled the corner of his mouth. Thinking something away would definitely be magic. On the other hand, he couldn't try shaping the stone beneath the snake, because they already knew that made a barrier to where the strange creatures could go, so thinking at it didn't seem any less likely to work than stonemastery in general. It just needed to forget that this army had held it captive, and sink into the mountain top, returning to sleep, or returning home.

Returning home, returning to something like peace, sounded so good that heated tears stung his eyes. If sentiment could convince the snake to leave them alone, then Rasim would succeed effortlessly.

He was almost certain it was going to work, until Kisia made somebody barf so loudly it woke up the whole camp.

CHAPTER THIRTEEN

The first few seconds of retching were so appalling that Kisia and Rasim both just froze, not even sure what was happening. Rasim had never heard anything like it. The poor witch whose system Kisia had purged sounded as though her vomiting started at her toes, with the intention of ejecting them through her mouth. There were other much less dramatic sounds of sickness all around, but there only needed to be one making noise, if it sounded like *that*.

Then Kisia, her voice thin and high with controlled hysteria, said, "She must have been a camel in a previous life," and Rasim's near-tears from a moment earlier became an overwrought sob of contained laughter. Above the sounds of their panicked humor, people began to shout as the sluggish stone snake surged above them, shaking off its stupor. Arrows filled the air at an astonishing rate, plinking uselessly against the snake's granite scales, but causing considerable threat to the sick witches on the ground.

Rasim couldn't feel stone witchery, but skymastery's light, easy dance was easy to grasp. He seized the wind, casting arrows away, and someone's angry voice rose, warning about magic. "I don't suppose you can just make everybody throw up?"

Kisia shot him a wild glance that suggested she might be able to, but aloud, she said, "I don't know if I could walk afterward, though."

Rasim grimaced. "Never mind, then. But we have to stop their witches—" As he spoke, the air witchery he worked suddenly fought him as someone else attacked. Rasim hissed, "We're Ilyaran and trying to help," into the wind at the other caster. The magic trying to grab his faltered, and Rasim felt a brief new struggle as the distant witch looked for a way to do as the mindkiller and his master told him he must without hindering Rasim's efforts.

The stone snake smashed belly-down across two tents at once, and Rasim thought maybe it wouldn't matter who helped who. They were all going to get squished. Desperate, sure it wouldn't work, he cried, "Run! Run away!" to the snake. Instead the creature's huge lashing tail slammed into him, and for a few seconds he knew nothing but the rush of wind around him as he flew through the air.

He landed hard in *something*, he didn't want to know what, and, dazed, lay there unable to think anything except 'flying on a glasswing is more fun.' Somebody shrieked his name, and he wondered about that for a moment before realizing it had to be Kisia. No one else knew who he was. He thought he'd better get up so she wouldn't worry, but his entire body ached and his head hurt from whatever he'd hit it on.

Cloth suddenly folded down around him, billowing like falling sails, and Rasim belatedly realized he'd hit a tent. That had probably saved him breaking anything, but his head hurt tremendously and getting up struck him as exceptionally difficult. Harder than the earliest shift on the *Wafiya*, which always meant waking hours before the sun rose.

Then a sword slipped under his chin, tilting it up, and all of his other problems seemed very small and insignificant.

The solider on the other end of the sword had a hard-set mouth and large, frightened eyes. He flinched every time the snake slammed down, but he moved the sword a fraction of an inch and indicated Rasim should get up, or get skewered. Rasim gave the tiniest nod he could, not wanting to cut his own throat, but it was enough: the soldier moved back half a step so Rasim could actually move.

Rasim whispered, "Sorry," and even sort of meant it as he seized sky witchery again and slammed the hardest wind he could conjure into the soldier's chest. The man, totally unprepared, simply fell over backward. Rasim made a desperate scramble for stone witchery at the same time he scrambled to his feet. Getting up worked; pinning the soldier down with rock didn't. Still, Rasim leaped over him and ran, which was better than having a sword at his throat.

He'd only been out of the fight for a few seconds, but an appalling amount of destruction had been wrought in that time. The snake whipped around like it was dying, and a hundred feet of snake was a lot of thrashing. Arrows, spears, and even swords bounced off it, although it didn't seem to notice at all.

The stone witches that Kisia had purged were mostly on their feet, trembling with the effort of trying to control the massive monster. Rasim didn't think they were doing it because they'd been commanded, or because they wanted to stay where they were. They just couldn't get away until the snake was subdued.

Subdued. That's what they'd done to the Northern snake. With ice water, which they didn't have now, but they did have a *lot* more stonemasters than they'd had then. They could try something else. Rasim yelled, "Shape it a channel! Something it can fall into!" to absolutely no avail. He could barely even hear himself in the cacophony. He started to conjure air witchery to amplify his voice, thought better of it, and looked for somewhere to hide, first.

On one hand, a lot of fires had gone out, so it was much darker, which could make hiding easier. On the other, people were running everywhere now, and all the quiet spaces between the tents were long gone. Rasim sighed, glanced around for Kisia, then gathered air witchery to bellow, "Work together and shape a channel into the stone! You can cover the snake with it once it's in, and it should rest!"

He spoke Ilyaran, because he didn't know nearly enough Moranese to say all that, and he saw a number of witches look sharply in his direction. Within a few heartbeats, they'd begun to coordinate, and the mountain reshaped itself under the awesome power of Ilyaran witches working in concert. They didn't just shape a channel for the vast snake to settle in: a huge hole opened in the valley floor, and as one of its coils slithered in, the snake overbalanced. It bit at the ground, trying to drag itself back out, but the stone it tried to grab betrayed it under the witchery being worked: a tremendous chunk of granite simply detached from the mountain and went with the snake as it fell.

"Leave it some unworked stone!" Rasim cried. "Give it somewhere to go, somewhere deep and safe!"

More witches looked his way, and for a moment he was glad that their masters probably thought they were still under the influence of mindkiller. The drug made witches and their magic respond to authority, sometimes regardless of who the authority *was*. Rasim's certainty, in this case, made him authoritative enough. He added, "I've got a free seamaster journeyman with me, too. If you've been throwing up, you probably don't have much mindkiller left in your body. Don't eat or drink anything the army gives you," in a murmur that he let the wind carry to the witches he could see.

It turned out Kisia had been right. Telling enslaved witches they suddenly had their freedom, and hoping they'd stay to help, wasn't a good idea. At least half a dozen of the working witches bolted toward the edges of the camp. One, either more powerful or a lot smarter, opened the stone beneath her feet and disappeared into the mountain. Rasim had seen a Shenryalan earth sorcerer do that, but never an Ilyaran stone witch.

Almost as soon as she sank into the valley floor, the snake's attempts to escape grew more frantic. Rasim swore and ran across the smashed-up center of the camp, hoping he could make a difference by getting his hands on the huge magical beast. Assuming he could avoid getting squished by it in the process, at least.

He was nearly there when Kisia tackled him, knocking him sideways in the heartbeat before an arrow flew through the space he'd been in. She yelled, "You are going to get yourself killed!" right in his face.

He yelled, "I was trying to help!" back. Beneath their yelling, a shuddering rumble shook the mountaintop, and Kisia rolled off him so they could both sit up and see what was going on.

Stone rose, higher and higher, to envelop the raging snake in a dome. Soldiers screamed and scattered, or stood frozen in horror as the world broke apart around them, maybe for the second time. Rasim couldn't imagine what it would be like to watch your home rise and surge and shatter, and then to have the land you stood on, thousands of miles away, do the same again. For a heart-twisting moment, he understood the impulse to invade and destroy Ilyara that the Moranese people must have shared. Witchery had devastated their world once already, and was now doing it again.

Then movement at the upper edge of the dome's curve caught his eye, and a shock ran through him as he realized the stone witch who had submerged was now up there, reshaping the mountain around the tiring snake. The bubble she'd built pressed down, down, down again, until the ground was as flat as it had once been, and the snake was buried somewhere in the depths of the valley. She remained on a rise that hadn't been there before, though, looking slowly around the encampment. Rasim's stomach seized. "If she decides to kill everybody, I can't stop her."

Kisia went ashy. "Talk to her. You have to try."

Rasim nodded, trying to scrape air witchery together as the stone witch on the mound continued her to examine the valley, only stopping when her gaze finally landed on Rasim. Someone loosed an arrow at her, but stone leapt upward so casually it looked alive, and stopped the arrow's fall with shattering grace. Nobody else tried, as she walked on a ramp of stone that appeared beneath her feet, bringing her all the way to Kisia and Rasim.

Like almost all the slaves he'd seen in Moran, the woman was thin, although her face still held a certain natural roundness. Stonemaster Lusa had been round like that, but hers had been a kind shape. This stone-master's roundness could cut, somehow, like all the soft edges had been honed to a blade. She pulled her lips back from her teeth, wetting them with her tongue like they tasted of poison, and spoke careful words in a language obviously now long-unfamiliar to her.

"Tell them," she said in Ilyaran. "Tell them that if they come for me, or any of us who leave now, that I will break the spine of the earth and send deepest fires of Coluth's molten heart to melt their city, to boil their waters, to scorch their lands, and to burn out the very name of Ilyara from the memory of time itself."

Rasim's jaw dropped. "You want me to tell *Ilyara* that? Not the Moranese?"

"Moran enslaved me," she said, still speaking carefully. "Ilyara, though. Ilyara didn't come for me. If she still lives, tell Guildmaster Gailuan that Kiraluna hopes she spends the end of her days suffering in the grinding depths." Her lip curled, and she stalked away. Most of the stone witches who hadn't already run followed in her wake. A handful of soldiers stepped forward uncertainly, clearly thinking they should stop the escapees.

Spikes of glass-sharp stone rose from the broken mountain top so fast Rasim barely saw it happen. They shot up to within a hair's breadth of the soldiers' chests and throats, knocking their weapons aside. Kiraluna spoke in Moranese, her tone itself a flat warning. She gestured, and smaller spikes rose in a dangerous circle around her, then faded back into the ground as she stared uncompromisingly at the Moranese soldiers.

Kisia breathed, "What's she saying?"

Rasim shrugged. "I'm pretty sure it's something like she could kill everybody here in a heartbeat if she felt like it and this is their one chance to not die horribly."

As he spoke, the soldiers fell back several steps, and the spikes collapsed back into the ground. Kiraluna and the other stone witches walked on without another challenge, heading not toward the narrow mountain gap, but west, where the valley stretched long and rough but more or less low through innumerable mountain peaks. It curved north after a while, or the mountains rose to block it off again, and he could hear the thundering, shaking sound of avalanches in the far distance in that direction. Still, a dozen stone witches probably wouldn't have much problem working their way through mountainous territory if they felt like it.

It belatedly struck him that the sun had risen some-time recently. He'd been able to see Kiraluna on the curve of the dome she captured the snake under, so since then, at least. Their plan to sneak out of the Moranese camp again before dawn had gone some-what wrong. He whispered, "Did you find any other witches to purge?"

Kisia lifted one shoulder and let it fall in the smallest of motions. "A few. One was a sea witch, so I showed him how. Hopefully he's gotten some of the others cleared." She glanced around them, and Rasim followed her gaze. Almost everyone was still watching the retreating witches.

A little too late, a thought occurred to Rasim, and as Kisia turned her attention back to him, he knew she'd thought it, too. "We should have gone *with* them, shouldn't we…"

"Oh, no," a woman's voice said softly from a few meters away. "Oh, no, I like how this has gone, instead. I didn't imagine I'd have the absolute joy of encoun-tering you again, Rasim, and yet look, here you are, delivering yourself straight into my arms."

Rasim closed his eyes and bared his teeth, trusting Kisia would understand the grimace for her, and gath-ered himself to face the woman who had approached. "Lady Amdria."

CHAPTER FOURTEEN

Amdria of Moran wasn't a tall woman, and her red-dyed, travel-stained trousers and tunic did nothing to add to what height she had. A vicious light of vengeance in her eyes gave her presence she otherwise might lack, though. Her dark hair was scraped back from her heart-shaped face, which had deeper lines around the eyes and mouth than she had last time Rasim had seen her. Cords stood out in her throat from the harshness of her smile. "What a *troublesome* little slave you are, Rasim al Ilialio."

"I just saved your entire camp from being crushed to death by a stone snake," Rasim replied as coolly as he could. "I wouldn't say I'm that much trouble."

Her smile tightened like a viper's. "We wouldn't have needed saving if you hadn't made my slaves sick!"

"You wouldn't have needed saving, ever, if you hadn't enslaved people in the first place." Rasim had meant to stay calm, but anger rose in his chest, bubbling and popping with eagerness to burst forth.

The last time he'd seen this woman, a friend of his had died. Agnet, the huge Northern fighter who had spent years in the Moranese arena, had been killed in the slave uprising after keeping Rasim alive for days, and the Shenryalan prince Bayar alive for months. Rasim wouldn't lose a minute of sleep if Amdria died the same way right now, with somebody's spear shoved through the back of her neck.

"Still so righteous," Amdria said in what sounded like real astonishment. "After destroying a city, killing thousands, starting wars, and yet you're still so sure of yourself, Ilyaran. Do you never doubt yourself, even with all the horror you leave behind you?"

Rasim's fists clenched of their own accord. He struggled to keep his voice even. "What Cindu did was horrific, and whether you believe it or not, I'm honestly sorry he wrecked your home. But I bet you don't know that Prince Lorens gave him the drug that made it possible for him to *do* that much damage, and you should."

Amdria's eyes widened very slightly, enough to tell Rasim she hadn't known. At his side, Kisia gave a near-silent hiss of triumph, like that should change everything, but Amdria's eyes narrowed again, anger scarring jagged lines into her face. "But you began the rebellion that led to Cindu's freedom—"

"Which never would have been possible if you didn't enslave people in the first place!" Rasim's shout sounded thin in the morning air, and he was sure it made him seem weaker, but he didn't care. "I don't care how you tell yourself the story, Amdria! What you do to people is wrong, and if you'd never done it, Cindu would never have had a reason to destroy your city!"

"Those ones walked away," Amdria snarled, managing to point after the retreating stone witches with her voice alone. "Why could Cindu not have done the same?"

"I don't know, and I'm sure you killed him before you could possibly find out! Ask the person who *owned* him!" Rasim shouted. "I bet they have an idea or two of what they did that was so awful that a whole city paying for it seemed fair!"

Amdria's lip curled and her gaze darted around the gathered soldiers, and those farther away, picking up the pieces of their camp after the snake's destructive rampage. A lot of people were watching, listening, but Rasim spoke almost no Moranese, so their entire conversation had been in Ilyaran. He bet very few of the people around them spoke *that*, so although everybody would know that neither he nor Amdria were happy, he doubted they'd understand what, exactly, they were arguing about.

Which was good for Amdria. She didn't need people questioning the line of command, or the way things were done in Moran. Rasim wished again that the guild had more language classes, instead of relying on pidgin speak at the docks, or Sunmasters being on hand to do the important translating.

His own words suddenly bounced back at him from the mountain walls, *didn't enslave people!* Even Amdria startled, like the world itself had taken up his cry.

Rasim smiled rather nastily. "See? Even the mountains agree."

The mountains shouted *seem fair! fair! fair!* back at them over the far-off sound of thundering avalanches, and Rasim's grin got even sharper. "Turn around, Amdria. Take your people home and rebuild your city. Don't try to take on Ilyara. You've already lost enough. There's no point in losing it all."

Amdria took a deep breath, setting the lines of her travel-stained clothes and examining Rasim for a long enough moment that he almost thought she might listen.

Then her own smile thinned to blade-sharp and she said two words in Moranese that he know all too well: "Kill them."

KISIA MADE A SOFT, terrible sound of fear that hurt Rasim's heart more than his own thrill of fright did. He whispered, "I'm sorry," and somehow she managed to pull a tremulous smile out of her terror.

"It's all right. We kind of knew we weren't going to make it this time. At least we're together."

That was as far as she got before a hail of arrows flew toward them. Rasim roared, shaping terror and anger into a wall of sky mastery. Wind blasted around them, a huge gust almost physical in its strength, and the arrows fell rattling to the ragged valley floor. Kisia, baring her teeth in a dreadful smile, grabbed his hand so tightly it hurt, and extended her other in concentration.

Another hail of arrows fell, and were knocked away by a fresh gust of wind. Rasim wished he could work stone witchery fast and certainly enough to raise a shield the way Kiraluna had done, but the wind would have to do as a third arc of arrows sailed toward them, and then a fourth.

Before the fifth, though, Amdria's pale golden skin tones greyed abruptly, shadows suddenly visible beneath her eyes as she clutched a hand over her heart. Her gasped, "Witch!" was barely audible through the howling windstorm Rasim kept up, but a glance at Kisia told him the Moranese leader was right. There was no remorse or regret in the set of Kisia's jaw, or in the black determination of her eyes. Rasim couldn't even find it in himself to believe it would be better *not* to take Amdria with them, if they were going to die. The more Moranese who died here, now, the fewer could ride on Ilyara later.

Amdria dragged in a breath that clearly pained her, clutching at someone nearby and trying to lift her voice to cry, "Stop. Stop!" The man at her side took up her call, ordering a cease-fire, and as the arrows stopped falling, so did Rasim's windstorm.

Kisia, though, clearly kept a grip around Amdria's heart. She loosened it just enough for the older woman's color to improve a little, but warned, "I can kill you before you kill us," with absolute confidence.

Amdria blanched, then forced a tight smile. "Murdering me wo—"

"I like to think of it as assassination." Kisia was all teeth and sharp edges, with no uncertainty in all of her being. "That's what you do to political opponents, right? Assassinate them, not murder. For the good of the people."

"It won't save your city," Amdria wheezed through short breaths. "Kill me or don't, but Ilyara will fall to the Moranese army, and you will be the first of our enemy to die."

"Probably." Kisia's smile was dangerous. "But you won't live to see it happen."

Amdria hissed, *"Witches!"* and this time it was an order, not a curse. Rasim felt sun witchery blossom behind him, and spun to face the attack. There were only a handful of sunmasters there, none of them young. Their united power rushed toward with such heat and speed that for a heartbeat, Rasim was caught in a fiery memory, little more than color and scent and fear, as if the entire world had become flame. The air, bruised orange and choked with smoke, was too hot to breathe when wind gusted through to clear it for a moment. The fire was everything, all-encompassing, inescapable.

But somehow there was water—terrifying, cold, trying to drag him down, but at least not burning as the rest of the world did.

And then there was nothing. Nothing, no trace of memory, no paralyzing terror, no story of what had happened next. There was only now, with a wildfire crackling around him, and a disdain bordering on anger rising in his chest.

Sun witchery, which had been so difficult to learn, filled him now. The interior flame that Sunmaster Endat had tried help him discover, and the Shenryalan spiritmaster Oyun had succeeded in guiding him to, came to life within Rasim as if it had been waiting for a true test before it fully merged with his spirit. Fire lived inside him, and the burning air around him was hardly more than an inconvenience. Most sunmasters needed a spark to work their witchery.

Rasim extinguished the inferno they'd spun, and crushed every other blaze near enough to reach, and it was *easy*. The witches he faced gaped, shocked and confused beyond comprehension. It took everything Rasim had to pull words from the power he commanded and to say, hoarsely, "Purge them, Kisia, if you can."

She made a humming sound of urgency beside him, keeping one hand extended toward Amdria and stretching the other toward the captive sun witches. For a blurry moment, Rasim didn't understand: they'd been holding hands, a few seconds ago. Oh, but he'd released her when he'd turned to the attacking sun witches. His mind felt full of fire, alive and licking and burning away thought.

A small part of Rasim thought maybe that was dangerous, but he didn't care very much. Everything was dangerous right now, and a lot of people wanted to kill him. If becoming fire would save them, he would give up his body and turn to flame, if he could. The thundering of the distant avalanches was in his ears now, fire roaring through his blood and pushing to overwhelm him.

Kisia barked, a small sharp triumphant noise, and almost as one, the enslaved sun witches lost control of their bodies, sicking up and more. The smell was quite awful.

Behind him, Amdria shrieked in confusion and anger. "Kill them! *Kill them!*"

"Do you *want* to die?" Kisia whirled toward the Moranese councilwoman, hands clawed in threat. Rasim lifted a palm, sending a wave of fire, almost as whole and rolling as water, upward to set falling arrows alight. As an afterthought, he ignited the ones that had been whipped away by his windstorm, too.

Someone braver, if not smarter, rushed toward the two journeymen with a sword. That was harder to knock aside with sky witchery, too large to easily heat with sun magic, and there wasn't enough water at this height to sweep the army away in a flood. Rasim wished again that he had any sense of stonemastery, or, barring that, a sword of his own.

But the weapons he had were made of magic, so he thrust a fistful of wind into the soldier's chest, knocking him back, and cast a ring of fire around himself and Kisia to keep them from attacking so easily. Someone threw a bucket of water over the fire, or tried: Kisia snatched the water out of the air and threw it back in the soldier's face. Rasim's head hurt with the weight of witchery being used, and the relentless rumble that felt like it shook the earth itself. He almost wished it was the stone witches they'd freed coming back. He couldn't cast stone shields fast enough to do them any good.

The sun witchery attacks had stopped, at least. Rasim could cast similar attacks himself, but didn't want to. He didn't want to kill people. He certainly didn't want to burn them to death. And maybe that was why they would die up there on the mountain top, a hundred miles from home.

He must have said that aloud, because Kisia cackled. "Maybe, but we're not going to go down easy." Soldiers were trying to step through the fire ring he'd cast, and dancing back fearfully. He could no longer see Amdria, had no idea whether she lived, and didn't want to ask. The world became one soldier at a time. He pushed them back with heat or wind, expanding the protective circle of fire around them, and knew that at some point, it wouldn't work anymore. Even Guildmaster Isidri had exhausted herself, working sea witchery. No one could keep it up forever. Not even with *delzjha*, the Shenryalan power-enhancing drug. If Rasim had that, he'd keep using witchery until he died. At least this way, even if he collapsed, he might have a chance at survival.

Well. He would have a chance at survival if he wasn't in the middle of an unfriendly army, fighting to extend his life by just one more minute, and another, and another.

There were so many Moranese, and no matter where he turned, someone else was pushing through the fire ring. They didn't even have to. Eventually he just wouldn't be able to keep it going anymore. But either they didn't know, or they didn't care. Or they were busy trying to deal with the witches Kisia had freed from the mindkiller. That heartened Rasim for a moment, as they fought back to back. But only for a moment, really. He didn't see a way this ended well for any of them, despite the huge thundering noise beyond their circle of fire, despite the shouts of fear and anger, despite the clash of fighting that seemed to take up all the sound and attention in the world.

Not until a small, sturdy horse gave a truly spectacular leap over the flames Rasim kept alive. The little animal landed nearly on top of the journeymen, who fell over each other as they surged back, trying not to be crushed. The shaggy little beast looked pretty enormous after all, from Rasim's vantage on the ground. It stomped and snorted, eyes rolling unhappily at being in a ring of fire, but it held still until Bayar of Shenryal, on its back, whipped his helmet off and grinned wildly down at his friends.

CHAPTER FIFTEEN

Kisia cried, "*Bayar?*" in astonishment, and somehow flung herself from the ground into the Shenryalan prince's arms. Rasim, still too stunned to move, gaped up at them as they hugged ferociously, raining kisses on each other's faces and shoulders. Then Bayar, still with a huge grin, leaned past Kisia to offer Rasim his hand.

"Unless you prefer the ground, 'sorcerer-child?'"

Rasim didn't even recognize the sound that burst from his chest at the question. It mixed laughter and a sob and a snort of derision all together until it was mostly a cough, but coughs didn't usually have so much emotion in them. He put his hand up and the Shenryalan prince—as small and sturdy as his horse, with a specially-build saddle to accommodate his unusually short limbs—hauled Rasim to his feet and into a hug as fierce as the one he and Kisia had shared. Still confused beyond belief, Rasim said, "Bayar?" in much the same way Kisia had, and the other boy grinned even more broadly.

"Rasim." His name was spoken with pure affection. "You've rescued me so many times. I thought I should return the favor."

"How?" Rasim's voice was hoarse. "I mean…how?"

Months of travel had done nothing at all to diminish the Shenryalan youth's smile, or the radiance of his beautiful face. Rasim had forgotten how astonishingly handsome the horse clans prince was, and Kisia looked thunderstruck all over again. He couldn't really blame her.

Bayar tilted his head at the ring of fire they stood in. "Perhaps you can soothe this for my horse's sake, and then I'll explain?"

Rasim, stupidly, said, "But the army," and Bayar's smile gentled.

"There's considerably less army than there was, my friend. You're safe now."

"But…" In some way, Rasim believed him: the fact that Bayar, who was meant to be hundreds of miles away, coming through a different pass entirely, was there at *all*, suggested that the Moranese army was no longer much of a problem. It still didn't make sense, and Rasim, who had been preparing to die just a few seconds ago, didn't feel like he was keeping up very well. But he let his sun witchery go, watching the tall flames fade into nothingness.

Their disappearance revealed an endless horde of Shenryalan riders thick on the ground, fighting the Moranese army. Or running over the Moranese army, really. It appeared that the Shenryalans had swept in from the west, smashed into the Moranese back line, and more or less trampled them into submission. Everywhere Rasim looked, cavalry threaded through the encampment, already in control. With so much of the camp focused inward, first on the stone snake and then on the magical battle at its core, the Moranese must have been totally unprepared.

Kisia, who seemed to be taking it in a lot faster than Rasim was, pounded Bayar's shoulder in glee. "How did you get here? What are you doing here? You were supposed to be three hundred leagues to the east!"

"You can't be here." Rasim fumbled for the map he had in his tunic, then gave up, still gaping around himself in disbelief. There was a gangly, long-legged Shenryalan dismounting a little distance away, and another, thicker one, bundled in the same heavy traveling furs and leathers that Bayar wore, struggling off his horse nearby. A little beyond them, a graceful rider in blue and white surveyed their conquest with satisfaction. Despite all that, Rasim said, "I've looked at the maps. There's no pass. You can't get here. You're not here. You can't be."

"And yet here we are," Bayar replied triumphantly. "We rode south from Shenryal, yes. We meant to take the sea pass, which would see us in Ilyara in two months from when we left. Another few weeks, from now. But as we reached the mountains, I thought, Rasim would do something magnificently stupid and dangerous instead of taking so long. What would he do? And so we rode across the mountains instead of around them, and here we are!"

"But that's impossible. There aren't any passes."

"There weren't any passes." Bayar lifted his hand, beckoning, and the gangly rider, having assisted the thicker one off his horse, strode over and without warning enveloped Kisia and Rasim into an enormous hug. The second, heavier rider joined the hug, squishing both of them breathless so Rasim couldn't even squeak a question.

Kisia squirmed an arm out and knocked the taller rider's hat back, then somehow managed to get enough air to shriek, "*Milu!*" with unbridled joy. "Milu, Telun, Telun is that you, Siliaria's fins, look at you two, you look Shenryalan!"

Milu, tall, slender, and an extraordinarily gifted stonemaster journeyman, flashed a brilliant grin into the tremendous embrace. From what Rasim could see, Kisia was right: although much darker and more tightly-curled of hair than the Shenryalans in general, Milu otherwise could be mistaken for one of the steppes people. He wore their brilliant, layered colors easily, and had ridden like a man born to it, rather than someone who had only learned a few months earlier.

Journeyman Telun, built like a wall and a little lighter brown in skin tones, made an even more pass-able Shenryalan than his partner did. "I look it," he said with a huge grin as they released the hug, "but I'm never going to be as good on an a horse as anyone in the tribes is, even the toddlers. You're alive!"

"Thanks to you," Rasim blurted. "What did you—did you do—did you do what I think Bayar—did you—?"

Telun beamed. "I've never seen you speechless before. Aye, yes, my Milu here casually rearranged a mountain range or two so we could get to you faster, and we weren't a minute too soon, were we?"

Rasim, half outraged, cried, "I would not have thought of that!" to Bayar, and felt his ears heat up as laughter rocked the people around him. "Well, I wouldn't have!"

"Probably not." Kisia knocked her shoulder into his happily. "Stonemastery is too hard for you. *You* would have called glasswings for everybody and they'd have ridden in as air cavalry."

"I—" Rasim wanted to protest, but it seemed fairly likely, now that she'd said it. Still, a little defensively, he mumbled, "I don't think I could hold that much air witchery at once."

Joy leaped in Telun's face. "Speaking of skymastery." He lifted his hands and gathered an eddy of air between them, spinning bits of dust and cruft through it so it could easily be seen.

Kisia and Rasim both bellowed, "Telun!" in astonishment, and Kisia jumped on him, hugging him with her arms and legs. He laughed and caught her without staggering or flinching as she gave his back a series of congratulatory thumps. "Look at you! A skymaster! And you're so old!"

"Hey!" Telun laughed. "I'm not that old!"

"You are for learning new witchery! And I should know!" Kisia let go and Telun, grinning, put her on the ground as she demanded, "Who taught you? Oyun? Is she with you? I bet she'd like to see Rasim again."

"The First Shaman does not travel with us," Bayar said with amused solemnity. "This is too great and dangerous a journey for one so old as she. But we do have sky sorcerers who have trained Telun, and spoken highly of his dedication to their craft."

"Rasim." A warm voice interrupted them as Bikat, Bayar's father, handsome in his blue and white robes, rode over from where he'd been watching the aftermath of the battle. "I'm pleased to see you've survived this long, sorcerer-child, and you, daughter of my wife's heart." He inclined his head to Kisia, then frowned, first gently, then with increasing concern as he glanced around. "Where is your third? Surely he has not fallen?"

"Desimi? No, he's fine," Rasim assured him. "He's over there closing off the gap so the Moranese army can't get out." He paused. "I guess we should go tell him to stop, huh?"

Genuine relief relaxed Bikat's shoulders. "Good. I feared for the future of Ilyara, for a moment there. I am glad my fears were unfounded. And that my son was right. I was afraid his plan to cross the top of the world was an act of madness brought on from being too long away from Shenryal." Bayar's father was as handsome as his son, his clothing indicating his status as King Horse, avatar of Shenryal's greatest god, and husband to their leader, Bayar's mother, the Great Mare. "We asked a great deal of your stone sorcerers, in making our way here. I hope there will be time for them to rest, soon."

"Mostly Milu," Telun said with an easy shrug. "I'm not a tenth the stonemaster he is."

Milu slid his arm around Telun's shoulder and pulled him into a rough embrace, mouth pressed against the shorter man's forehead. "And yet I would never have left Ilyara without you, so whether your talent matches mine or not, your heart far outstrips it."

"You always say that."

"It's always true." Milu sighed deeply, settling against Telun's side. "Although a nice long rest wouldn't go amiss, you understand."

"There's no more army," Rasim said faintly, as it hit him. "There aren't any more Moranese to attack us. We might get to have a rest. You saved us," he said to Bayar, almost blankly, and then, awkwardly because he didn't speak Shenryalan well, he repeated himself in Bayar's native tongue. "You saved Ilyara."

To his shock, a celebratory roar shook the air, feet and hooves thudding on the stony valley floor. Rasim finally realized he'd heard them coming, and mistaken it for far-off avalanches. A weak smile crawled across his face, then turned to sobs of relieved laughter as first Kisia, then Bayar, hauled him into jubilant hugs. Then Bikat hugged him, and he was dragged apart from Kisia, celebrating while being hugged by Shenryalan strangers. His bones felt wobbly, and his muscles even more useless than that, like relief was so strong he'd forgotten how to move properly. Someone handed him a flask, and he swallowed a huge sip of what he recognized too late as the fruity, orange alcoholic drink favored by Shenryalans. He coughed on its burning strength, wiped his eyes, laughed, and handed it back to the beaming rider who'd offered it to him in the first place.

Even a single sip of the alcohol made his thighs even more wobbly, but it also somehow fortified him, making taking another step and facing another day seems slightly more possible. Especially if that day wasn't going to be dogged by the fear of a Moranese army crushing Ilyara. Rasim staggered a little and searched for Kisia in the riotous celebration.

He found wreckage long before he found her. Whole swathes of the Moranese camp were visibly victim of the stone snake's wild flailing and frantic attacks. People were working between the crushed tents, searching for survivors and moving bodies where survivors couldn't be found. In other places, it was clear that the Shenryalan riders had come through at huge speed, tearing tents down, entangling soldiers wherever possible, and fighting where necessary. Rasim remembered, with an ache in his chest, that to kill another human being was one of the worst crimes in Bayar's tribe. They had been prepared to go to war to retrieve Bayar himself from Moranese hands; now they followed him into bloodshed and death to help Rasim, who had brought him home.

The horse tribes had undergone ritual and cleansing ahead of time to gain permission from their King Horse for such evil. Rasim's stomach hurt, wishing there had been another way, and yet he was terribly grateful that Bayar's people had come to save his own.

He realized, wandering through the camp, that the Shenryalans had spared as many lives as they could. There were a lot of prisoners, watched over by mounted riders. Most of them looked cold, tired, and not particularly happy, but also relieved to be alive. But the farther he wandered, the more he realized he was looking for someone in particular, and that she wouldn't be in the outskirts of the camp.

He turned back, focused now, and stopped at makeshift healing tents on his way, searching for Amdria of Moran. Rasim didn't think she would have run. Not with her whole army turned to the task of killing two journeymen. He didn't think she could imagine losing that fight, so there would be no reason for her *to* run.

Not until the Shenryalans swept down on her, and by then, it would be too late.

He found her in a healing tent, the first one that had been set up, barely a hundred feet from where he and Kisia had fought for their lives. She looked like she'd fought. There were defensive slashes on her arms where her shirt had been cut away, and splashes of blood that had nothing to do with the dark stain on fabric bound around her torso.

No one attended her. With a glance around the tent, Rasim understood why: she was dying, and there were others the Shenryalan healers might actually be able to help. He sat at her side, watching her labored breathing, watching sweat bead on her forehead and chills shake her body.

Her eyes opened abruptly and her hand rose, an elegant, dying dance. Rasim took it in his own, and for a few seconds she focused on him before peculiar humor traced over her face. "Troublesome slave."

"Lady Amdria." She didn't deserve the honorific. Rasim knew it. He said it anyway, and when her hand clenched around his, he didn't pull away.

"We lost," she said after a long time. "Fifteen years of planning. All lost today. Because of you. Troublesome slave."

"Yes."

"Are you happy?" Her eyes opened again, glittering bright. "I'm dying. Are you happy?"

"No."

"I've heard…" Amdria faltered, and for a while Rasim thought she wouldn't speak again. Then she gathered herself once more. "I've heard Ilyarans sing their dead to rest in the sea."

"The Seamasters do, yes."

"Will you sing for me, troublesome slave?"

Rasim studied her for several seconds, and then, very gently, said, "No."

Amdria laughed, a short startled sound, and her hand went lax in Rasim's. She wasn't dead yet: her chest rose and fell, but he didn't think she would speak again.

Instead, Bikat, the King Horse, spoke from the tent's doorway. "You don't need to be here, sorcerer-child."

"I think I do." Rasim's voice sounded thin to his own ears. "Not for her sake, maybe. But for mine."

"Then, if you will allow me, I'll join you." Bayar's father came to sit next to Rasim, and they stayed there in silence, watching Amdria until one breath drained away, and another never came.

When Rasim was certain she wouldn't breathe again, he stood, unsure of himself. Bikat put his hand on his shoulder, the gesture almost a question, but Rasim shook his head. "I'm all right. I feel…" He went silent, considering that. "Empty. I'm not sad. I'm not angry. I'm not glad, except for that it's over."

Bikat nodded, squeezing Rasim's shoulder. "Bayar and Kisia are near the fire."

"Thank you." Rasim, still feeling empty, left the tent to discover celebration and noise were still going on out there. Somehow it had all fallen away while he waited for Amdria to die, and now he wasn't quite sure what to make of it. He thought maybe relief could make its way through the emptiness, but celebration felt far away.

It took a little while to find *which* fire Bayar and Kisia were at. They sat close together, both wrapped in one of the brilliantly-woven, brightly colored Shenryalan blankets. Their heads were ducked toward each other's, intimate and comfortable. A funny little twist in Rasim's gut purged some of the emptiness and made him hesitate before interrupting them.

Eventually Kisia looked up, startled to see him even though he'd been standing nearby for several minutes. Her gaze was filled with all kinds of complicated emotion, which was exactly how Rasim felt as the emptiness in his gut faded. She managed a lopsided smile. "Hi, Rasi. Bayar was just telling me how I'm his sister now, according to Shenryalan law. Because of how Irlin made me her heart daughter, and gave me her clan's tattoo." She gestured clumsily at her shoulder, and her smile, determinedly bright, remained crooked.

Rasim, remembering how they'd stood apart from everyone else to say goodbye in Shenryal, and how Kisia had only let herself look back once after leaving Bayar, felt a terrible surge of pity and relief rush through him all at once. "I'm sorry. Or I'm…congratulations? You already had a lot of brothers."

Bayar gave a low laugh that sounded like Kisia's smile looked. "And I had no sisters, so I've come out better in this bargain than my…friend…has. What did you want, Rasim?"

Rasim's heart ached for the two of them even if he didn't fully grasp why. He couldn't think of an easy way to say it, so he just said, "Amdria's dead," and waited.

"I didn't do it!" Kisia said defensively.

Bayar's eyes widened in mild horror. "I hope not."

"Well, I almost did earlier. Kind of. I was trying not to because I thought Rasim wouldn't like it, even though they were all trying to kill us. I was just… squishing her a little. Internally."

Bayar leaned away from her slightly so he could look horrified, more or less at her ear, because he was too close to really see her properly. "Squishing?"

"Kisia's got a natural talent for healing," Rasim said

proudly, then made a face. "But if you can heal, you can…not-heal, too."

The Shenryalan youth's eyes widened. "I'm glad she's on our side."

"So are all of us. No, it wasn't you, Kees. She got stabbed in the fight and just died in one of the healers' tents. I was with her."

"Why?"

"I don't know. It seemed right."

"Of course it did," Kisia said, sounding so much like Desimi that even she heard it, and added, "*Sunburn*," for good effect.

Rasim's eyes widened. "Desimi. We should go tell him it's all over." Rasim considered the two of them there, and with another lurch of his heart, said, "*I* should go tell him it's all over?"

"We should," Bayar said firmly. He rose and offered Kisia a hand, his smile a little sad. She stood, too, looking down at him helplessly, and Rasim realized they were almost exactly the same height while sitting, even though she was much taller than he when they were on their feet. Bayar murmured something in Shenryalan, and Kisia almost laughed. Then he lifted her hand and kissed the knuckles, which made Rasim wish he'd had the presence of mind to turn away before that happened, and they hugged before Bayar released the Ilyaran girl's fingers. "You said Desimi was closing off the gap? He has found stone witchery in himself, as well as earth sorcery?"

Rasim grimaced. "Yes, and he's going to kill us for

not coming to get him right away, and for him having to do all that work when we didn't need it anymore."

Bayar smiled. "Then perhaps we should ask Milu and Telun to join us, so that he at least doesn't have to undo it all again, too."

CHAPTER SIXTEEN

Not only did the stone witches join them, but they wanted to know everything that had happened since they'd parted. Rasim put his palms up, said, "You get to tell it this time," to Kisia, and almost immediately wished he hadn't, because Kisia made him sound much more impressive and heroic than Rasim thought he deserved.

It took an hour's unhurried walk to reach the gap, which, to Rasim's surprise, wasn't fully closed. It remained entirely open until the first switchback twist, and then narrowed so a very small person—Rasim's size, perhaps, or Kisia's—might squeeze through. Desimi, however, was nowhere to be seen.

Kisia said, "Oh," softly, and her voice somehow shone with pleased understanding. "He left us enough room to squeeze out."

Telun gave a belly laugh at the slender path and stuck his arm in up to the shoulder. "That's as far as *I* would have gotten. He must not have expected anybody but you to follow him."

"Well, we'll fix that." Milu stood in the still-open part of the switchback, examining its jagged walls and sharp curves. "A lot of riders are going to have to come through here. It'd be much faster if I just…" He waved his hand, implying that reshaping a mountain range was a trivial effort.

Of course, he'd apparently been doing something very like that for some time, creating enough of a road for the cavalry to ride across the tops of mountains on. Rasim, speaking without thinking, said, "Do you think the Great Fire did something to us? Made an unusual number of really strong witches, maybe? Because, Milu, the magic you've been doing, that's…that's practically Coluth-level witchery. It's the work of the gods. And there's Desimi, and Daka from the Sunmasters' Guild, and…"

"You," Kisia put in, but Rasim made a face.

"I'm not sure I count. I met Siliaria."

"So did I!"

"And you can heal people!"

Kisia looked startled, as if the two things had never crossed her mind as being possibly connected. "Well, yes, but you're different. You're—"

"If you say 'Siliaria's chosen' I'm going to scream," Rasim warned.

Milu laughed. "I've never met any gods, but I'm afraid I was born ten years before the Great Fire, Rasim. I think Ilyara has always had extraordinary witches. We just don't usually work together."

Kisia, exasperated, muttered, "I was *not* going to say Siliaria's chosen, Rasim, I was going to say—" She broke off, eyeing Milu, and sighed. "Never mind. I'll tell you later."

"All right." Rasim gave her a brief smile, then blinked at Milu. "I forgot you were that much older than us. Right." His eyebrows drew down in a frown. "We really *should* work together more, though. The guilds are so isolated. From each other and even mostly from the city."

"Well, that's what the King's Guild is for," Kisia pointed out.

"True. All right, let's open the gap wider," Rasim said to Milu. "I've got to see Desimi's face. Besides, that way we can bring Bayar's cavalry home to Ilyara sooner, and celebrate our victory."

Kisia snorted as the stonemaster journeymen began widening the gap. "I'm not sure he'll miss having almost been killed by an army. Why did he even stay on that side?"

"Probably because he didn't know if you were going to succeed with purging their witches and didn't want to use enough skymastery to call a glasswing. It could have drawn attention."

Kisia looked skeptical. "Do you really think Desimi would have thought of all that?"

"Yes," Rasim said with more faith than certainty.

Kisia grinned like she knew it, then yelled happily as the stone ahead of them flowed open to reveal Desimi at the far end. She and Rasim both ran through, crashing into the bigger boy, who returned their hugs while gaping over their heads. "Is that Milu? And Telun? And *Bayar*? What did you *do* while I was out here, Rasim?"

"Ended the war, I think," Rasim said happily, muffled into Desimi's arm. "Bayar's people swept in and rescued us. A lot of the Moranese army got smashed. We'll tell you all about it on the way home."

"You ended the war while I was out here mucking with stone magic?" Desimi asked, outraged. "Why do you get to have all the fun?"

"But you were mucking with stonemastery!" Rasim crowed. "You did it, Desimi! You closed the gap!"

"And you gave us enough room to escape if we needed it," Kisia added, hugging the bigger boy again. "Thank you."

"*And* you didn't even get your arm stuck in the rock!" Rasim finished with a teasing grin.

Milu laughed out loud from the other end of the gap. "Did you? That's a rite of passage, Desimi. Every stonemaster apprentice I've ever known has done that at least once."

Rasim, stung, said, "I haven't," and Desimi's chagrin faded to smug pleasure.

"That's 'cause I'm better at it than you are."

"Well, that's probably true. Should we—do we—should we—" Rasim stumbled over his tongue and his thoughts, leaving Kisia to laugh at him.

"Should we go home? I think so. If you can make a glasswing flight safe," she added a bit more seriously. "You've been using witchery constantly for the past…" She glanced toward the sun, which was reaching toward the western horizon. "Pretty much the past day, Rasi. Maybe we should just sleep, and leave in the morning."

"It's too hot to fly during the day, even for just a few hours." Now that Kisia had suggested it, though, sleep sounded like one of the best ideas Rasim had ever heard. "Maybe until a few hours before dawn? Bayar, Telun, Milu, do you want to come with us?"

Bayar and Telun, in identical tones, said, "*Fly?*" and Milu said, "Absolutely not. I learned to ride a horse. That's enough for me."

Telun, smiling with both affection and disappointment, shrugged. "Then I won't either."

"Bayar?" Kisia asked hopefully.

The Shenryalan prince looked wistful. "I can think of nothing I would rather do than fly to Ilyara with you, but my father promised the Great Mare he would do all he could to keep me safe. I suspect Mother would not consider flying to Ilyara 'safe.'"

"Maybe," Desimi said slyly, "you shouldn't mention it. We could just leave early, and you could say you're sorry later."

"If I dare," Bayar said with a wry smile, "you'll know when I meet you in the small hours of the morning."

BAYAR *DID* MEET them in the small hours of the morning, just as the moons began to set behind the mountains. Unfortunately, so did his father, who chuckled at Kisia's expression of dismay. "A responsible leader consults with his council before making rash decisions," the King Horse told her. "Bayar chose well, in discussing your plans with me."

Rasim, remembering that leadership in Shenryal went from mothers to daughters, and had to be agreed upon by a council, wasn't sure Bayar's leadership abilities were actually all that important, in their culture. If he was to follow in his father's footsteps as the King Horse, it would be through marriage to the new Great Mare, because his mother had no daughters.

Except Irlin had adopted Kisia as her heart-daughter. Rasim's gaze jerked to her indignant face as she scowled at Bikat, and blurted, "Could Kisia be the Great Mare?"

It was late, and eerily quiet in the mountain valley. His question sounded very loud in the silence, and the handful of people who were awake nearby all glanced sharply at him, visibly surprised.

Even more to *his* surprise, Bayar's cheeks, always warmly red beneath his golden skin, glowed hot for a few seconds. Kisia stared at Rasim, then looked at Bikat, her jaw set with hope, confusion, and regret.

The King Horse, nearly as startled as his son, but less inclined to blush, let his eyebrows rise slowly as he met Kisia's eyes. "Technically, as Irlin's heart-daughter, yes. You would be eligible. But it would be a difficult thing to convince the elders and shamans of, sea-daughter. You are not of our people, and know little of our culture."

Kisia pulled together a strangely fragile smile. "So if I even wanted to try, I would need a strong King Horse at my side. A King Horse who knew everything, including how to rule." Rasim could see the cords in her neck standing out as she kept herself from looking at Bayar, although in the end, she did, with a brief, brittle smile. "I'm pretty sure the only person who qualifies is technically my brother now."

Her gaze returned to Bikat, whose handsome face was solemn and still in the moonlight until she said, "And I'm almost sure that was on purpose."

Admiration chased surprise across his expression, and settled on what Rasim could only regard as a profound respect. Bikat bowed slightly to Kisia, all his finery making it clear that he outranked her, yet obviously felt the tribute was her due. He spoke very quietly, really only to Kisia and perhaps Bayar, but there was hardly any other noise. Rasim held his breath so he wouldn't miss anything. "It was."

The King Horse sounded sorrowful as he met Kisia's eyes. "It was truly a gesture from the Great Mare's heart, Kisia. You paid a great personal cost to keep our son safe. Such sacrifice requires recognition, but more, Irlin desired it. The offer, the request, for you to become her heart-daughter was deeply meant, and that you accepted is an honor that she will carry with her for the rest of her life. She bears waves among her tattoos now, for her sea-daughter."

"But," Kisia said, her voice too loud and too sharp.

"But," Bikat echoed. "Bayar was long, *long* gone from our people, and our tribes are insular, uncomfortable with outsiders. That Oyun declared him uncorrupted by his time outside was a gift and a relief, one that most of us were glad to accept."

"But," Kisia said again, closing her eyes momentarily. Then she set her jaw and stared up at Bikat. "But he was…*friends*…with a girl from outside the tribes, and that girl almost died for him, and anyone who has ever heard a story in their lives knows how *that* kind of story goes, don't they? So making me her heart-daughter also meant making me…"

"Unable to choose me as a husband," Bayar finished quietly. "You could, perhaps, be the Great Mare, but I could never be your King Horse."

Kisia flinched like she'd been hit, and unhappiness flickered over Bikat's face. "I am sorry. For what that may be worth, Irlin and I are both sorry. It's clear you care for each other. But we have a nation to think of, the Great Mare and I."

Desimi, who'd crept up beside Rasim at some point, elbowed him. Rasim elbowed him back to shut him up. It worked, or at least Desimi had the sense to stay quiet, because anything he said would be loud in the silence, and draw attention to them. Rasim already felt guilty for seeing any of this at all. It wasn't his business, and it made his heart ache, and sent chills of relief through him all at the same time.

For a moment, something close to naked hatred spilled across Kisia's face, although she pulled her expression back under control and nodded stiffly before facing Bayar. "So you're not coming with us."

"I can't." The two words held a world of regret. Bayar extended his hands toward Kisia, a hopeless gesture, and she stepped toward him swiftly, catching his hands in hers. "I can't," he said again, this time in Shenryalan. "My people need me to be one of them."

He said something else, beyond Rasim's ability to understand, but Kisia gave a short, helpless little laugh that was full of tears, and everyone who was awake suddenly decided to turn away when Bayar pulled her into an embrace. Rasim felt his ears flaming as he stared fixedly at a mountain peak silhouetted by moonlight, and this time when Desimi elbowed him, he didn't poke him back.

A minute later Kisia stalked by both of them, saying, "Let's go," hoarsely. Desimi jolted into motion after her, but Rasim turned back toward Bikat and Bayar for a moment. They stood together, Bikat's hand on his son's shoulder, and he nodded at Rasim. "We'll see you in Ilyara in a few days, sorcerer-child. Good luck."

Rasim whispered, "Thank you," and ran after his friends.

Kisia said, "I don't want to talk about it," when he caught up, and so, although he and Desimi exchanged quick looks, they didn't. They went through the pass—wide enough now for a whole army to walk through easily—and Rasim shivered in the wind on the outer side of the mountain.

"At least it shouldn't be hard to call a glasswing, in this." Desimi cast another brief glance at Kisia, then at Rasim. "Maybe just one, this time? Even if it's not as fast, it'll be…"

"Warmer," Rasim said, although he thought Desimi might want to say 'comforting,' because Kisia looked miserable. She shrugged, Rasim nodded, and when Desimi began the working to draw a glasswing out of the wind, Rasim added his power to the magic. They were getting faster at it, like the glasswings were waiting now, instead of having to be lured from a great distance. Rasim wondered momentarily if the stone snake had been easier to awaken in Moran because of the one they'd encountered in the Northlands, but he forgot the thought as a glasswing settled in front of them. They crowded onto its fragile-looking carapace, Kisia wedged in the middle and Desimi at the back, because his longer arms meant he could hold on to two of them more easily than Rasim could.

He was pretty sure Kisia cried for part of the flight, but the wind whipped most of the sound away, and the back of his tunic dried quickly, so he didn't say anything, and hoped that was the right thing to do.

Sunrise was in their eyes, bouncing in brilliant golds and blues off the river as they flew straight over the city. Rasim got a glimpse of its fan-shaped sprawl, mimicking the delta it sat on, from above. There was much more *city* outside the city walls than Rasim had realized. Inside them, the widest streets circled the palace, but even the narrowest looked planned, slender shadows between the paler stone of the city's buildings.

Beyond the walls, Ilyara grew more organically, like a living thing with twists and bends and streets ending unexpectedly, but they were tidy and cared-for, just as the interior streets were. That, Rasim thought, was what 'Golden Ilyara' was really about: there were simply so many witches in the guilds that the city could be kept neat and safe almost effortlessly. So many other places had nothing like that at all.

Neither did they have the magnificent rising arches of the Seamasters' hall at the harbor. The pleated wooden buildings shaped like overturned, interlocking ship's keels looked even more like that from so far above. Rasim knew they were a luxury in stone-built Ilyara. Even so, until he saw the shining wooden hulls towering over everything around them, until he could compare them from above, he hadn't fully realized how unique they were. They were almost defiant of the way things worked in Ilyara, which made him grin. If he hadn't known they were far older than Isidri, he would have thought she'd insisted her guild live in wooden buildings just to let the Sunmasters know that Seamasters remembered when things were different in Ilyara. They tilted over the river, heading toward the ship-yards as hope rose in Rasim's chest. They could make things better, in Ilyara and everywhere. They'd already stopped a war. The rest should be easy.

He was still holding on to that thought when lightning spattered from the brilliant reflections on the river, and, like it had done to the *Wafiya*, shattered the glasswing beneath them.

CHAPTER SEVENTEEN

Kisia screamed in Rasim's ear. Then the three of them were all falling separately, the distance to the river below suddenly seeming very great indeed. Rasim scrambled for sky witchery, desperately trying to call another glasswing from amidst panic. The air rushing past him as he fell was fast and hard and frightening, and he couldn't grasp enough magic to shape any of it. Hitting the water from so high up could kill them.

Water sluiced upward, a huge rush that lowered the river's level up and down its length. They splashed into it from enough of a height to hurt, but not kill them, and for a few seconds Rasim was head over heels in the surging surf, scared, unsure which way was up, *wet*, but not dead. He burst back to the surface quickly, but the river, falling back into its banks, rolled him again. Water went up his nose and he swallowed enough to feel sick as it twisted him around before finally settling enough that he could flail his way out.

Kisia came up nearby, coughing and spluttering and wet, just like he was. She saw him and swam toward him through the choppy water with a few strong strokes, still wheezing as she asked, "What happened?"

"I don't know! Where's Desimi?"

"Right here." The big journeyman stood on the river bank, dry but with his fists clenched, as if he hadn't been sure of them surfacing. "I'm sorry. I tried to keep all of us safe and dry, but—"

Rasim worked a whisper of sea witchery, rising from the river to hug Desimi, wet and all. "That was you," he said hoarsely. "You brought the river up. Good thinking. Quick thinking. Thank you."

Kisia, shaking herself dry as she stepped out of the river, hugged Desimi too. "Thanks, but what *happened?*"

"I don't know," Rasim said again, baffled. "There was lightning? Like what hit the *Waf*—oh, no."

Another arc of lighting soared through the dawn air as he spoke, smashing into the Seamasters' hall. Panic twisted Rasim's heart as fire ignited where the strike had landed. Beside him, Desimi, with a roar of air witchery that reminded Rasim of Taishm's cry months ago, bellowed, *"Seamasters! Fire!"*

Kisia's hands were already extended as she struggled to lift the weight of water from the riverbed to the burgeoning flames. Rasim called witchery to help, but Desimi took it over with a growled, "Find out what's going on." For the second time, water sluiced upward with the power of Desimi's magic, soaking the Seamasters' guildhall.

Kisia gasped, "The wounded," in dismay.

Desimi bared his teeth at her. "They're better off wet than burned. Rasim, *go!*"

Rasim's didn't know if glasswings cared about each other, or if they were even aware of each other as they darted incorporeally through the air. *He* was aware of them, though, and one had just died helping them. His witchery was tinged with grief and apology, and he wouldn't have been surprised they refused to answer.

Instead, calling another was nearly effortless. It came, glorious with sunrise colors, its wings throwing prisms over Kisia and Desimi as they worked to protect the guildhall. Kisia yelled, "Go!" Rasim threw himself on the glasswing's back, urging it skyward.

There was too much light bouncing off the river. Sunrise had turned it to a blinding path of glittering gold, disguising anything on its surface. Rasim yelled, "Fog, I need *fog!*" and tried, for the first time, to conjure two magics at once. He didn't think he'd done it while fighting the Moranese army only yesterday. He'd been changing from one to another as fast as he could, then. Now, though, he needed to hold the glasswing in its form beneath him, *and* convince cool morning air to coalesce into water droplets that would break up the brilliant reflections on the river.

At least the river was warmer than the air, which helped. Rasim put one hand on the glasswing's back, like touching it could keep it with him, and curled his other toward the river, frantically encouraging the gentle clash of warm water and cool air that could cause fog. His head spun with the effort, and the glass-wing trembled beneath him, but after long moments, the relentless glare from the rising sun reflecting off the river began to lessen.

And on the river came a fleet of Northern ships, the fresh fog swirling around their low-slung keels.

Lightning shattered through the air again, but this time Rasim's glasswing was ready. It moved faster than he could imagine, twitching to the side in the air. He felt the hairs on his body lift as the lightning crackled by. The glasswing, to his astonishment, curled beneath him and shot innumerable glass bolts toward the boats. Rasim gave a hoarse cry of delight: he'd forgotten the fragile, beautiful creatures had offensive capabilities. Those slender glass bolts were poison-tipped, too, making death almost certain for anyone they hit.

He was only relieved when some of the nearly-invisible shards of glass hit home, ensuring a few of his enemy would fall. He cried out again, trying to gather more air witchery, although whether he meant to warn Ilyara or call more glasswings, he wasn't sure.

"*Rasim!*" An all-too familiar voice rang out, powered by nothing more than astonishment as Prince Lorens swarmed the mast of a Northern ship and waved wildly from its crow's nest, as if they were long-lost friends amazed to see each other again. "By the *gods*, you're persistent!"

Rasim's glasswing, more attuned to enemies than Rasim himself was, launched another flurry of poison glass darts. Lightning crackled again, this time in a net that disintegrated the darts long before they had any chance of reaching the Northern prince. The glasswing hissed, a sound Rasim hadn't known it could make. He hadn't known they could make any sound, in fact, much less one that indicated it understood that it had been thwarted. Rasim, feeling like he should back the gorgeous flying beast up, yelled, "Surrender, Lorens! You can't beat a whole city of Ilyarans!"

The Northern prince, still waving and actually grinning cheerfully, shouted, "I can when the Sunmasters are helping me!"

A warning tingle zipped down Rasim's spine and he leaned close to the glasswing, yelling, "Dive, dive!"

He didn't know whether the creature understood, but it did dive as a massive bolt of fiery *something* soared through the air where he'd been. The glasswing whipped around, moving so fast Rasim was nearly dislodged, and for a shocked moment they hung in the air, gaping at the world below them.

He'd known there were barricades around the Seamasters' Guild: Isidri and Asindo had told him about them, and had sent Rasim and the others back out through the shipyards and the river to avoid them.

What he hadn't known was those barricades hid catapults. Or had hidden the parts of them: in the growing light, he could see gaps where the buckets, the arms, the counterweights, had been removed from the larger barricade walls. Someone had practiced long and often to put the war machines together so quickly. They weren't huge, but they didn't have to be: Rasim twisted on the glasswing's back to see that the fiery blob that had shot past him had landed on the Seamasters' guildhall. It stuck, making it clear it was the same stuff that had been used during the Great Fire. To

Rasim's horror, in just a few seconds its deadly fire had begun eating through the guildhall's wooden walls.

They intended to destroy the Seamasters entirely.

The thought dropped into Rasim's mind and hung there, so obvious that he could now think of nothing else. They had tried before with the smaller Northern fleet almost a year ago, and Isidri's arrest. The guild had been disbanded, then, and only reconvened after Isidri, once freed, saved the city almost single-handedly. Having failed once, their enemies would burn it to the ground if they could, with all the guild members and hundreds of wounded Ilyarans locked within.

It didn't make any sense. Isidri had only told everyone that the Sunmasters hadn't always held sway in the palace until *after* the guild had been disbanded. She hadn't been any particular threat to them, before that. The Seamasters hadn't been a threat. There was no reason to try to destroy them that Rasim could think of.

Except Guildmaster Pydasho had said Laishn's heir, his son, had been so powerful with sea witchery that his talent was clear even in infancy. That they'd started the Great Fire to burn the child out, and if the rest of the city went with it, then the Sunmasters could pick up the pieces to start anew.

Everyone knew the baby boy had died in the fire, along with Queen Annaken and so many others.

Everyone knew that, but maybe Pydasho thought otherwise. Maybe he thought the only way to be *sure* was to wipe out the Seamasters entirely. Because surely if Siliaria was to have saved anyone during the Great

Fire, it would have been the royal heir whose connection to her was already so strong.

A rather dreadful idea seeped through Rasim's whole body, coiling in his gut and staying there, cold and awful. He shuddered, trying to push it away, and then another bolt of terrible sticky fire seared the air near him, and his glasswing was diving, speeding toward the barricades with a mind and a will of its own. Rasim yelled, "No, we have to tell them not to use water!" and tried to haul it another direction.

For a creature made of air, the glasswing was surprisingly difficult to guide. Rasim thought about the reins horses and camels wore, but had no idea how he'd fit a glasswing with them. His shimmering beast skidded to a halt in the sky above the first catapult and shot poison darts in great number, hitting very few of its targets, but causing men and women in Sun Guild colors to scatter. Rasim, without thinking, conjured fire in one hand, about to cast it into the barricade when Kisia screamed, "Rasi, no!"

He twisted toward her voice to find Desimi beside her, air witchery alive around him as he made her words carry: *They've got the sticky fire in there!*

For a moment he didn't know what she meant. Then sickness swept him. He *knew* that, he'd just seen one of their fireballs eating away at the guildhall, and he still had been ready to use sun witchery. For a heartbeat he wanted to blame the magic itself, because that was better than the possibility that he was, in fact, very very foolish.

In that heartbeat he nearly lost control of the glasswing, which dipped and faded as if it couldn't decide whether it wanted to return to the air itself, or fight. Rasim certainly didn't want to return to the fight, and it had only been going on for a few seconds. *He* would have destroyed the guildhall and half of Ilyara if he'd thrown that fistful of fire into the barricade, or attacked the catapults. The sticky fire would have exploded everywhere. He croaked a thanks toward Kisia, whose whole body relaxed for a heartbeat before she turned to say something to Desimi. The glasswing shot higher into the sky, taking Rasim away from the other journeymen. He gave a hopeful yell, trying to convince it to land in the guildhall yard, but it recoiled as if the injured there were a source of fear for it.

Instead it flickered higher, to where fire was taking hold of the hall's rooftops. They had burned once before, during the Great Fire. Rasim wondered for the first time if that had been on purpose, too. Now, though, he knew what they hadn't then: the sticky fire could be extinguished with sand.

There was a *lot* of sand around Ilyara.

He slid from the glasswing's back onto the roof of the guildhall and immediately wished he hadn't. There was a kind of peculiar security in riding the air-born beast. Being on his own two feet on the tremendous arc of the guildhall's roof fully lacked that security. On the other hand, he really needed to concentrate, and didn't think he could keep the glasswing tangible at the same time. From the roof, he gathered enough air witchery to yell, "Desimi! Get word through the city! Tell them a sandstorm is coming!"

Down in the surging crowd—the streets had gone mad in the minutes he'd been in the air—Rasim saw the big journeyman twist toward him, then wave a wild agreement. His voice boomed out, and some people scattered. Not enough, but some, and they would carry word. The fewer people out to be scoured by sand, the better, although Ilyara was huge. The delta it sat in was even bigger. But beyond them lay a desert as endless as the sea. Rasim didn't know if he could reach that far with his skymastery, or whether trying the slow sense-less power of stonemastery might do him more good, but the hall was burning beneath his feet and there was no more time to wonder.

He gathered the sand that had strayed into nearby Ilyaran streets as best he could, whipping it into the air with eddies and currents that felt as powerful as whirlpools in the ocean, to him, and dashed that sand against the guildhall's walls. It helped a little, but nowhere near enough. Cursing, Rasim reached farther with his sky witchery. Having *delzjha* would help him now. With the Shenryalan drug in his blood, he would be able to reach the desert easily, and save his guildhall. His home.

It would probably kill him, of course, so it was just as well he didn't have any, but for that heartbeat, he wished he did. For the next, Desimi's witchery came to life, supporting Rasim's, and working together they could reach much farther along the Ilialio, out toward the desert whose sands they needed so badly.

There were glasswings awakening to their witchery, all along the river. They felt the magic and were drawn to it, until the air seemed made of sand and glass. Rasim was afraid even he and Desimi working together couldn't reach deep enough in the desert to get as much sand as they needed, but there was a sudden odd rush, like someone on the far side of his witchery gave the sand a push toward him. With that rush, sand began to roil in the air, and spill down the river toward Ilyara at speed. Rasim, sweating and afraid in the growing flames, gave a hoarse triumphant shout, and pulled the witchery to him, hauling sand in to dump over the fire.

Someone stopped him.

For several long, astonished seconds, Rasim didn't even know how to respond, and in that time, a huge amount of his witchery came apart. Was *torn* apart. Desimi's support disappeared completely, and the sand he'd gathered in the twisting winds simply fell into the river as if he'd never bothered. He rallied, or tried to, grabbing at threads of air witchery, but they slid away as if he'd never commended that magic at all.

"That was a *very* good effort," Jhikara's voice said in his ear. "Genuinely stupendous. I don't know if I would have thought of it. Well done, Rasim."

"Then let me *finish*!"

"Well, no." The Skymaster guild's leader sounded amused. "No, I don't think I will. You might actually succeed, and your guild's survival will certainly mean the end of my tenure as Guildmaster. I'd rather not have that. So, no, I'm afraid not." Her voice disappeared, and so did any hope of suffocating the sticky fire with sand: Rasim could feel the pressure of her witchery keeping the winds out of his reach, ensuring he couldn't try that particular stunt again.

He gave an inarticulate yell that had no more strength behind it than any thirteen year old boy's voice did, and sank to the rooftop with his hands folded behind his head. He couldn't even call a glass-wing and get down, with the amount of power Jhikara was exerting to keep him isolated from skymastery. Rasim was surprised he could even breathe.

A memory edged at the corners of his mind as all around him, different kinds of witchery flexed and flowed. Sunmastery in the distance, where the barricades were, but mostly seamastery as the guild tried to protect their home despite Desimi still shouting about water not working on this kind of fire. His voice carried farther and more clearly than it had any right to. *He* still had access to his sky witchery, then. Rasim couldn't remember if Jhikara even knew the big journeyman could wield it. He took a shuddering breath, and the memory came clear. Jhikara, warning Guildmaster Pydasho that fire couldn't burn without air.

Probably even sticky fire couldn't burn without air. He could try a much smaller magic, one that might not even catch Jhikara's notice, and maybe save the guildhall that way. Head still down, like if he didn't move his witchery would be even less noticeable, Rasim reached toward the nearest raging ball of sticky fire, and pulled the air away.

It guttered, but even when that little patch of fire was out, Rasim felt as if a spark waited in it, ready to reignite. All it needed was an ember or maybe even just fresh air, and it would begin to burn again. Which meant it had to *all* be out before he could stop working this witchery, because if he left any of it even smoldering, he'd have to start all over. He wasn't sure if he could use that much skymastery without Jhikara noticing, but the sense of potential inside the sticky bombs made him certain anything less than total eradication of the fire would result in it roaring back to life. He stretched his little working farther, trying to smother the fire so fully that even letting his magic go wouldn't allow it to burn again.

Another slow thought dropped through his mind, and left him feeling stupid. He was a *sun witch* now, too. That was why he could even *feel* the potential lurking in the sticky mess. He didn't want to think too hard about the fact that he was definitely using both sun and sky witchery at the same time, for fear he might lose control of them both, but if he was a *sun witch*, he could just *put the fires out.*

The Sunmasters, as a guild, hadn't been able to stop the Great Fire, although Rasim now knew their guildmaster had been working against them. That Pydasho had *started* the fire. But even so, the fire's stickiness, the explosive clinging aspect that refused to go out with water, those were *hard*, even for sun witches. Or they had been thirteen years ago, with no guildmaster or king to guide them.

Rasim didn't have a guildmaster or a king, just a horrible idea at the back of his mind that he hoped wasn't true, and a bone-deep need to do something impossible. He rose, knowing it made him a target, but somehow unable to work all the witchery he needed to while cowering in a ball on the rooftop.

He didn't have to pull *much* air away, even though there were patches of sticky fire all over the guildhall roof now. The flames licking higher would go out with nothing below to feed them. All he needed to do was what he did to bring air with him underwater, only... opposite. In the sea, he pushed the water away to give breathable air room; now he had to push air itself away. It had to be possible.

Air was so *heavy*. Rasim had learned that fighting in the Moranese arena, but he'd forgotten until now, because he'd mostly been trying to stir it up since then, not create pockets where it wasn't. It wanted to push back down into the empty spaces he made, and sweat began rolling off him even though he stood perfectly still.

But it worked, slowly. The second part was harder: reaching into the pitchy goo, searching for those sparks that wanted to reignite. They weren't really fire, though. He couldn't *do* anything with them, or even find them. Potential, it turned out, was impossible to grasp. He could smother flames everywhere else, and did. The fire died quickly where it burned naturally, even with his concentration split between two kinds of witchery. But he didn't know how to stop the sticky stuff from flaring up again. He was terrified that even if managed to quench it all, it would come back to life as soon as he stopped the desperate outpouring of witchery.

The guildhall lurched under his feet. Rasim staggered, panic clawing his belly. He didn't want to fall, and he didn't want to know what awful thing was happening that could make the whole guildhall move. A horrid, obvious idea leaped to mind, and he looked toward the desert, suddenly sure he would see another stone snake rising from the sands. *That* would cause the earth to shake all over the city.

In the distance there were clouds of sand, like the storm he'd tried to conjure earlier had awoken even after Jhikara stopped his witchery. Closer, darker dust boiled up, like something had collapsed. Maybe the city walls, although they'd only been breached in one place, if that was true. He couldn't see what had broken through, though. If it was a stone snake, the whole city could fall.

A second booming thud rattled him so hard he had to sit, or risk sliding right off the roof. Wind gusted around him, throwing dust in swirls and making his perch even more precarious. A third crashing boom shook the guildhall.

Rasim, stomach and hands clenched, climbed to his feet again, searching for the source of the quakes.

A vast golden dragon rose into the air above the palace.

CHAPTER EIGHTEEN

S hadows shifted, deepening and brightening as the dragon's huge wings beat the air. It rose higher, then higher still, a massive beast colored like the sun itself, all fire and brightness. People screamed as debris fell from the thing's shoulders and back, as its terrible tail lashed and knocked buildings over. It hadn't risen from the palace, Rasim realized: it had come from beneath the Sunmasters' guildhall, like it had been resting there for untold centuries.

Now it shook itself like it was casting off sleep. Everything beneath its wingspan had been destroyed, and that was just an accident of awakening. It landed in the streets and flung its wings open, so fast and powerful that buildings broke with their impact, and threw its head back with a roar so loud that nothing else in all the world could possibly be heard. It took a few pacing steps, but the streets were too small for its dreadful size. It looked cramped and furious, until with a few terrible beats of the massive wings, it rose into the air again. Its long neck snapped around, fiery eyes searching the city. Rasim, with an icy chill, felt certain it was looking for him.

And he would have to let it find him, too, because in the handful of seconds it had been awake, it had already caused appalling destruction to the city. He couldn't let it do anything worse, not if he could stop it. Heart in his throat, body trembling with fear, he glanced around for a way off the still-burning guildhall roof, then realized that probably all he had to do was call sun witchery to get its attention.

It took a moment to nerve himself up, and in that moment, the biggest glasswing Rasim had ever seen coalesced above the dragon and smashed down with fighting pincers and poison darts.

RASIM GAVE A HOARSE, short scream, so rough it hurt his throat, but barely heard it under the thrumming of the vast glasswing's fast-beating wings. The wind from their effort swept the city, sending Rasim to his belly on the guildhall roof. Then he was sliding, fingers clawing to find a grip that didn't exist. Maybe he would just slide all the way down the side of the curved building, but maybe not. He fumbled for sky and sea witchery both, hoping desperately he could catch himself, but even if Jhikara hadn't limited his reach for skymastery, there just wasn't far enough to fall. Far enough to hurt or kill him, yes, but not far enough to save himself, even with a surge of river water.

Sky witchery *did* respond, startlingly powerful, given he hadn't expected anything at all. Even as he picked up speed, sliding down the roof's arch, a brief panicked bolt of laughter curdled his gut. Probably Jhikara was too busy trying to deal with a glasswing the size of the *Wafiya* to keep his witchery in check.

He hit the bottom of the roof's most pronounced curve, and was in free fall, still arching away from the building's side. Despair smashed through him as he threw sky witchery wide.

A glasswing appeared beneath him, catching the brunt of his fall. It also rolled with the weight of him, dropping him again, but at least he only had a few meters to fall now, instead of dozens. He hit the ground so hard he couldn't breathe. No one running for cover stopped to help him up.

He dragged a breath back into his body, grateful that at least no one had stepped on him.

Someone stepped on him, driving the air back out of him as soon as he'd thought it. Rasim rolled to the side, whimpering and gasping as he searched for some kind of protection until he could climb to his feet. A huge shadow roiled overhead, followed by a glimpse of glittering glasswing and a blast of golden dragon fire as the tremendous beasts fought over Ilyaran skies. Screams rose, barely audible beneath the sounds of fighting, and so many *people* ran in every direction. Rasim wheezed, then, able to breathe again, sat up, trying to understand what was going on.

Some of the desperate runners were trying to get the injured out of the guildhall's yard. Others were simply trying to escape, and others still were clearly there to fight: Rasim saw bolts of fire being answered by living water as the guilds warred with each other for the first time in remembered history.

Kisia was there suddenly, grabbing Rasim into a hug and gasping relief against his ear. "I thought you were dead. You fell so far."

"What's going on?" Rasim buried his face in Kisia's shoulder for a few seconds, wanting to assure himself of her safety as much as his own, but the question slipped out anyway. "How long was I on the roof?"

"Long enough for Lorens's ships to get to the harbor," Kisia whispered. "Isidri and Asindo are there now, with half the guild. Desimi's with them. They're holding it for now, Rasim, but there's a *dragon*."

She didn't just mean the dragon; Rasim understood that. She meant the lightning-wielding Northern witches, and the glasswing, and the sticky fire still burning the guildhall, even though he could feel the weight of sea witchery drowning the more ordinary fire that grew from those central sticky points. She meant, what were they going to do about all of it. Rasim had no idea, and said, "I think the dragon and the glasswing might be my fault," unhappily.

Kisia gave a wild little cackle. "I think we're beyond fault, Ras. Besides, Jhikara's out there fighting with guildmaster-level skymastery, and…well, they all are. All of them," she repeated emphatically. "But I don't think it matters. I don't think stopping all the magic is going to make a *dragon* disappear."

"It might make the glasswing disappear, though.

They only come when they're called."

Kisia thrust a finger upward, not that they could see the air battle right now. "Did that thing *look* like something that comes when somebody calls?"

Rasim shook his head. The enormous glasswing, like the dragon, looked elemental, impossible, and entirely...*on purpose*, if that was the right way to think of it. It looked as if its presence was its own idea, not something coaxed out by magic users. There was another rumble of the earth, a shake that went on and on and on, and from the ground, Rasim couldn't tell what was causing it. He hoped to all the gods and goddesses that it wasn't another dragon.

It stopped as quickly as it had started, but screams suddenly rolled toward them again, warning of disaster. The embroiled titans smashed into the ground nearby, shaking it with their weight and strength. Stone turned to dust, swirling madly through the air as the glasswing's many wings beat as it frantically tried to gain altitude again. Rasim caught a glimpse of the dragon's long neck lashing as it turned itself over, regaining its feet. It spat flame upward, but the glasswing was well out of reach by then, darting across the sky so fast that Rasim didn't know how the dragon had caught it in the first place.

An image of the dragon pouncing like a huge cat playing with a bug flashed through his mind and came out as a broken laugh. "I don't know how to stop it."

The dragon surged upward again as he spoke, wings spreading and visible over the guildhall walls as it launched itself toward the sky again.

And fell, thunderously, with a peculiarly familiar lurch, like someone had grabbed it by the leg and kept it from rising. It roared with anger, then, wings and neck flailing, with pain. A cheer rose as the great beast struggled, and Rasim suddenly realized why the lurch seemed familiar. "A stonemaster caught it! That's what it looks like when people try to walk when their feet have been caught in stone! Oh, clever, that was clever!"

A fresh deep buzzing of wings sounded as the glasswing darted down, then spun one tight, triumphant-looking circle before positioning itself above the trapped dragon and letting loose a barrage of poison darts. Glass glittered, dangerous and beautiful, and the dragon's scream was nearly drowned out by the glasswing's hugely pleased hiss. Rasim, horrified, said, "They're killing each other."

"At least something can," Kisia said grimly.

Lighting flew across the sky in the wake of her words, slamming into the glasswing. A wing shattered, falling in shards of glass that had the people below screaming as they ran for shelter. The glasswing screamed too, spinning more erratically toward the source of the attack. Poison shards shot overhead like starfall. Kisia grabbed Rasim's hand and bolted for the shipyards, which was the closest route to the harbor.

They dodged terrified sea witches and the helpless injured as they ran, becoming part of the surging chaos within the guildhall grounds. It had to be worse in the streets, Rasim thought: at least there *were* walls to protect them here, and the battling titans hadn't smashed into them. Another arc of lightning smashed toward the glasswing. Rasim looked back to see it dart to the side, narrowly avoiding being hit, and abruptly dug his heels in, stopping their headlong rush. "Metal, we need metal, big metal, Kisia! A lightning rod!"

"What?" She jerked to a stop, wobbling for balance. "What? Why? We—to draw it." She actually closed her eyes a moment, teeth bared with frustration and thought. "Because what else can stop lightning besides a lightning rod. Water can't, fire can't, air can't. Stone, maybe, but you can't work it fast enough."

"Desimi might be able to," Rasim said desperately. "Where is he?"

"I told you, he's with Isidri at the harbor. It's bad down there, Rasim." Kisia's eyes opened wide. "I don't know how many lightning witches they have—don't they work metal, Rasim? Isn't that one of the magics they had? Metal working?" She grabbed his tunic, almost shaking him. "You're part Northern. Rasim, can you find *metal witchery* in you?"

"I doubt it!"

"Desimi found earth sorcery when he needed it! You have to do this *right now*!"

"Well I'm going to need metal to even try!"

Kisia swore and spun, searching their surroundings, then swore even more violently. "Everything in Ilyara is made of stone!"

"I *know* that!"

Above them, another arc of lightning met, and shattered, an oncoming hail of poison darts. Liquid glass fell in a deadly rain, sending even the last holdouts running for cover amidst screams. Rasim sent a blast of sky witchery upward, trying to make a dome that would redirect the falling glass, or at least slow it enough for people to get to safety. It worked within the confines of the Seamasters' grounds, but everything beyond what he could see remained in danger. Rasim, like Kisia, swore. "We have to get out of here. We can't fix anything from inside the guildhall."

"You want to go *out*? Where the dragons and the glasswings and the fires and the—" Kisia hauled him toward the outer doors even as she rattled off the reasons to not do that. "What about the King's Guard? They have swords. We could raid their armory."

"Do you know where it is?"

She gave him a frantic glare over her shoulder. "In the barracks? I don't know! Do you have a better idea?" They burst on to the street and both immediately ducked as a catapult flung another fiery burden toward the Seamasters' hall.

Rasim, suddenly incensed, bellowed, "That! Is! *Enough!*" with enough air witchery that for a few seconds, everything around him actually went still. For a moment he was reminded of fighting in the Moranese arena. The audience there had never experienced the true power of a wind storm. Until Rasim had made it happen, they hadn't known that the air itself could drive straw through wood or even stone.

If it could do that, Rasim thought, it could tear wood apart, too, and he was *very* angry when he thought it. He splayed his fingers and seized bits of fallen glass in the wind, then threw them with violent speed into the catapults' arms.

Wood burst everywhere, splinters flying and the terrible, hideous sticky fire raining down from the catapult bowls. Screams rose even before the dreadful stuff hit anyone, and pure rage made Rasim throw protective domes above the catapult operators. Kisia shrieked, "Are you crazy?"

"*No*," Rasim yelled furiously. "I'm just *better than they are!*" He didn't exactly mean it the way it sounded, but he didn't know how to phrase it better, either, except, "Killing people doesn't solve anything!"

Kisia, slightly hysterical, said, "Given what's going on, I think you might be wrong, but let's run away instead of arguing about it," which seemed like a good idea. They bolted through the passageway Rasim had made with his witchery, and their attackers, either astonished or grateful that they weren't burning alive, chose not to follow.

That, and as soon as Rasim released the witchery, the pitch base of the sticky fire hit the ground around them, and they were suddenly very busy making sure no trace of flame came anywhere near them to ignite it. Kisia, casting a wild glance back, grunted an admission that maybe murdering them all hadn't been necessary.

Half a street onward they found rubble and destruction. A handful of buildings were completely smashed, with dozens more damaged. The injured were everywhere, and even those who weren't hurt were dust-covered, sweaty, exhausted, and terrified. Rescue efforts were ongoing, those who could trying to dig people out from under fallen buildings and tend to those who were hurt. Stonemasters were among the rescuers, shoring up broken houses and reshaping the fallen stone to allow people access to those who had been trapped. Rasim slowed, stomach clenched with fear and dismay. "We should help."

Kisia swung around and grabbed him by the shoulders. "Rasim. *Rasim*. Look at me. At me, not the mess." When he dragged his gaze to hers, it was to find fierceness in her dark eyes, and a resolute set to her jaw. "This is only going to get worse, Rasi. Even if they stopped the dragon, there are witches loosing lightning at the city. There's a fleet in our harbor. There are Sunmasters trying to set Ilyara on fire. The only way this doesn't get worse is if we stop it at the root. Remember when you told me I couldn't heal everyone?" She let go of his shoulders, gesturing angrily at the wreckage around them. "This is like that. We have to stop the big stuff so we can fix the littler things."

Rasim swayed, shivering from the insides of his bones all the way out. "You're right. I know you're right. I just...got caught up."

A wry smile pulled the corner of Kisia's mouth. Rasim's sudden impulse to kiss that smiling corner was so sharp and strong his ears went hot and he almost didn't hear her answer.

"I know. I get caught up, too. But I have this friend," she said through the blood rushing in his ears. "He reminds me of what we're trying to do when I lose sight of it, and I do the same thing for him. So we can come back to help here later," she said gently. "Right now, we have to find a way to stop this war, Rasim."

"I thought we'd already done that."

Kisia pointed toward the mountains. "We stopped *that* war. We forgot about the other one on its way. And—Siliaria's *blood!*" She ducked as another arc of lightning, and then another and another, winding together into a thick, dangerous braid, shot across the sky above them. Threads of sizzling electricity slammed into the ground as the Northern witches struck out against the glasswing, which screamed its defiance above the city in a sound like the howling wind. Rasim and Kisia, like everyone else, ran for cover, although as they ducked into a broken building Rasim realized he could make shelter, if he concentrated.

A bolt of lightning smashed into the ground a few meters away, and he decided maybe concentration was going to be in short supply. Still, he tried, eyes closed tight as he put a hand on the half-wrecked stone wall, encouraging it to take a shape that would protect people. Every time lightning fell, he flinched, and for a rueful moment imagined a stone shelter full of hiccupy shapes, like his magic would jump and reform the stone slightly with each startle he took.

Nearby a terrible blast of lightning made the whole earth shake, and a sudden roar of triumph filled the air. Kisia fumbled for Rasim's hand, but he had already opened his eyes, searching for what he expected to see: the golden dragon, freed from its stone prison by the crashing lightning, leaped into the sky. Even at the distance the huge beast was clearly injured, its hide pierced by the glasswing's poison darts and gold-sheened blood running down its sides, but *injured* and *out of the fight* were clearly different things when it came to dragons.

For a few seconds, Rasim could do nothing other than gape upward. The skies were the soft hazy blue of morning, with the day's heat not yet burning the haze away. Lightning shattered through the clear blue, striking unpredictably, although the target was the enormous glasswing, which glittered so brilliantly in the morning sunlight that when it turned just right, Rasim was blinded by light smashing off its prisms. It cast rainbows across the lightning, impossibly beautiful for the heartbeats they lasted, and through it all the dragon flew, spouting fire that had no more chance of stopping lightning than a summer breeze did.

The lightning fell like rain, though, crashing into the city everywhere. Rasim staggered out from under their shelter, looking toward the harbor. He couldn't actually see it from there, but he could see the strands of lightning flying from Northern ships, rising into the sky and colliding together or scattering across the sky. Aloud, but barely able to hear himself in the noise of war and magic, he said, "There aren't enough of them to make this much lightning."

Kisia was at his side, almost yelling in his ear to be heard. "There's not enough of you to pull an inlet up into a mountain cave or create a windstorm, but you did it anyway. Maybe they have one really powerful lightning witch."

"Maybe, but no, look." Rasim gestured, trying to point out the relatively few strands of lightning that banded together and became more and more and more as they spread over the city. Hairs rose up on his arms, his nape, everywhere, partly because of the electricity charging the air, but also because a worrying thought was rolling over him. "There's more witchery happening than there are witches."

"There are thousands of witches in Ilyara," Kisia pointed out. "And I bet almost all of them are using their magic right now."

The hairs on Rasim's arms stood up, sending a shiver all the way through him as he spun toward Kisia. "That's right. That's it. That's exactly it. Kees, how often do we all use our witchery at the same time?"

She laughed, sharp and worried. "Never? That's ridiculous. There are too many witches to coordinate across all the guilds. Even when a guild has to do some kind of big magic, the king focuses it."

"Right! Never! We never do this! There's too much magic!" He reeled back toward the harbor, nearly breaking into a run, but lightning slammed to the stone in front of them again, rapid bolts that looked for all the world like an animal stalking toward him. "Kisia," he said in a thin voice, "Kisia, run."

"*Where?*" She grabbed his hand and ran anyway, pulling him with her as glass and fire and lightning fell all around them. Rasim dared one look back over his shoulder and stumbled, taking Kisia down with him. They both crab-scrambled, trying to get up, trying to keep moving, as the lightning, swift and deadly and sizzling, came onward, step by step, until a vast and snarling thunder wolf emerged from the magic.

CHAPTER NINETEEN

Fresh screams erupted everywhere as more thunder wolves stalked out of the lightning. Like the dragons, the glasswings, and all the other creatures born in magic, they were enormous. Their eyes burned a deadly blue, and white fur crackled like uncountable strands of lightning moving together as one.

"They have teeth," Kisia whimpered. "It's not fair, why does something like that need *teeth*?"

They had claws, too, claws that sounded like lightning strikes as they touched the ground, and they had growls like thunder. Rasim croaked, "Get inside," and then lifted his voice, forcing himself to project. "Get inside if you can! I don't know what else will stop them!" He didn't know if stone would either, but it had to be better than standing gaping in the streets.

Someone said, "And if the dragon falls again?"

The dragon might not fall, but Rasim's stomach did. He'd forgotten the one danger in the direct face of another. "The cellars!" Kisia called. "Go below the city. Hide there. They're solid. They'll hold."

Whether they would or not, no one had any better ideas. Most people rushed away, although a handful of men and women in Stonemaster tunics came out of the distant rubble, muttering to each other. There was someone else with them, someone Rasim caught a brief glimpse of, then lost in the surging dust, but for a heartbeat he'd been sure he was looking at a Shen-ryalan. Almost as soon as he thought it, an older woman, with greying hair falling loose around her shoulders, said, "Get to shelter, children," and Rasim forgot what he'd half-imagined. The woman went on, her tone grim but firm. "We lost the dragon, but we can hold the line against these wolves for a little while."

"*Stone*," Rasim gasped, feeling foolish. "You can ground them."

Kisia, still crab-walking away from the pacing wolves, muttered, "Well, we knew that, you're just not good enough at stonemastery to make it work," which seemed both entirely fair and completely unfair all at the same time.

The Stonemaster gave them both a brief, hard smile. "We can ground them, at least for a while. I just hope everyone's thinking the same thing." Then her eyebrows flickered down as she examined Rasim. "You're not one of ours. What does she mean, you're not good at stonemastery?"

Rasim blurted, "King's Guild," hoping that would be enough, and the woman's dark eyes cleared briefly.

One of the others barked a warning as the thunder wolves gathered, moving together like a pack, now. Lightning snapped between them, making them seem like one incredibly large beast, although they each moved a little differently. Sick dread rose in Rasim's throat, but the Stonemasters stepped in front of them, unbelievably calm in the face of living lightning. There *was* a Shenryalan sorcerer. A Shenryalan sorcerer fighting alongside the Ilyaran stone witches. Rasim stared in bewilderment, then yelped as the thunder wolves' pack leader surged forward, not quite as fast as lightning itself.

It slammed into a wall that simply hadn't been there before. All its crackling presence spread across the stone, broken into sparks and fading away.

If lightning could sound surprised, the rest of the pack did. They didn't howl the way real wolves did, but the crackles and snaps of their electric voices popped with confusion. A second wolf threw itself against the Stonemasters' wall before the whole pack began yipping and snarling amongst each other, like lightning holding a conversation with itself. "Go," the woman said again, and this time Rasim and Kisia staggered to their feet and ran.

The wolves were everywhere, appearing as lightning careened across the sky. For a moment, Rasim tried to imagine what it would be like to be a creature born of magic. Like the glasswings, the thunder wolves felt *real*, not like something that had been created by the witches wielding lightning, but things that had always lived inside it, and were rarely seen in their physical forms. It was as if the massive lightning storm, or the twisting windstorms, were a doorway the strange beasts could walk through.

Dragons were different. So were the stone snakes, and maybe even the sea serpents that the Ilyaran fleet encountered from time to time. None of them had come through a magic-made doorway, or at least, Rasim didn't think so. The dragons and stone snakes seemed to be more *present* in the world, and the serpents simply swam the seas as their domain.

But they were drawn to magic. All of them, whether they were always part of the world, or remained hidden until huge amounts of witchery were used. So they might all fade away if everyone in Ilyara stopped using magic immediately. That seemed so unlikely Rasim gave a high-pitched giggle as they ran. Kisia glared at him and he gasped an apology as they ducked around corners, searching for a pathway that wasn't filled with lightning, wolves, or both.

At some point, Rasim thought, the Northern witches would stop trying to kill the glasswing, and go back to throwing bolts directly into buildings. It didn't matter that stone didn't conduct electricity well. The sheer concussive force was destructive enough.

And the wolves were figuring that out. The first few had simply thrown themselves against the Stonemasters' wall, but now Rasim caught glimpses of them pressing together, electricity bouncing through them until the pack leader spat bolts of lightning that seemed to come from all of them. Stone shattered under the vicious strikes, no matter how many Stonemasters stood against them. Rasim still couldn't feel the weight of their magic, but he could see the concentration and focus they displayed, trying to protect their city and its people. Choking dust swirled as the wolves paced forward, explosive with lightning.

A few of the beasts seemed to realize that they didn't have to attack to pass, either. They leaped the barriers that the Stonemasters raised, energy crackling off them in dangerous flashes. The best anyone could do then was protect themselves, either by running, or pouring magic into the streets and shaping roofed shelters that the tremendous thunder wolves walked over. Then earth rose up in a muffling wall and simply flopped over a wolf, like Kiraluna had done with the stone snake's dome, but less elegantly, and with more dirt. Rasim said, "Desimi?" hoarsely, but if it was the other journeyman witchmaster, he couldn't see him.

Another wolf was absorbed by an earthen blanket, and Rasim almost imagined relief in the creature's eyes as it disappeared. He wasn't sure the vast lighting beasts had any particular desire to hurt anyone. Storms didn't, generally. They just *were*. Rasim was fairly confident that, like storms, the thunder wolves—and the glasswings, and perhaps even the dragons—just *were*. It was just that usually, storms didn't actually grow feet and walk through streets like pack animals, or flock across the sky like vast insect swarms.

He still couldn't see Desimi, who was the only person he knew who could possibly be working earth witchery in Ilyara just then. His mind flickered to the Shenryalan sorcerer he'd seen, and almost rejected it.

He'd seen him, but it wasn't *possible*. Shenryalans didn't come to Ilyara to trade, and there was no way they could have gotten to the city from the mountains already. But someone was working earth magic.

It didn't matter, not then. "We have to get somewhere high. Somewhere we can see what's going on."

"Too bad you fell off the guildhall roof, then!"

"I didn't mean to!"

"The palace," Kisia said. "It's the highest point in the city, at least, what's still standing in it. And besides, Pydasho might be there and I'm going to pulverize his heart if I see him. That should take the fight out of the Sunmasters."

"Or they'll decide he's a martyr and never stop fighting," Rasim snapped. The streets surged beneath their feet as they ran, impossible amounts of stonewitchery being worked in an attempt to protect Ilyara's citizens. The stone witches had to do it, but Rasim was certain their tremendous workings would cause problems of their own. There was nothing he could do, though. He could barely keep his feet from one step to the next, the idea of Kisia murdering Pydasho was taking up the rest of his concentration. More to the point, trying to think of how to *stop* her took all his concentration.

The dragon's wings cast a shadow over the city, and a huge gust of wind knocked Rasim off his feet. He scrambled up again, bracing himself against another gust from the beast's huge wings, but there wasn't another one, and he thought that maybe, inside all the noise of the fighting and running and electricity and everything else, that he *didn't* hear another beat of the massive wings. He blurted, "Up!" and ran for an intact building, shouting an apology to the people already inside as he bolted for the roof.

A moment later he burst onto it, three stories high, flat, covered with poles and clothes that protected an early spring rooftop harvest from the sun, and also blocking his view of the city. He yelled, "Sorry!" again as he knocked the canopies down, and after a moment had cleared enough of the roof to see everywhere.

The dragon had come to rest on another building halfway across the city, its wings drooping and its head lowered as its huge sides heaved for air. The glasswing screamed furiously at it from another quarter of the city, where it darted through the sky at great speed, trying to dodge bolts from the thunder wolves prowling the streets. Other, smaller glasswings had joined it, turning the sky to a rainbow of glory where the sun refracted through their slender, translucent wings and bodies.

It was all stupidly beautiful, Rasim thought. Deadly, but absolutely gorgeous. The dragon's huge golden sheen reflecting sunlight more softly than the glasswings did, and their quick bodies danced through the air like something choreographed. Spikes of blue-white lightning shot past the glasswings, sometimes hitting one and burst it into glittering shards that fell to the ground like snow in the desert. Sun witchery sent red and orange flares through the other colors, all over the city, as the running battle for Ilyara rolled through its streets. The dragon spread its wings wide, casting another shadow over nearby buildings, but didn't try to launch itself into the air again. Smoke from innumerable fires swirled in the eddies its wings created, both lovely and dangerous. Rasim couldn't see the harbor from where he was, but he could see lightning spattering in that direction, and hoped his guild mates were all right.

Kisia, wheezing breathlessly, caught up with him on the roof and hit his shoulder several times. "If you're going to run away, tell me first!"

"I did!"

"I was watching my feet so I didn't fall over and when I looked back you were gone!" She straightened, wiping sweat out of her eyes, and misery ran across her face. "Ilyara's going to fall if we can't stop this soon. Not even to the Northerners. Just to all this magic."

"It's going to get worse," Rasim whispered with unhappy certainty. "The Stonemasters."

After a beat of confusion, Kisia groaned. "If there are stone snakes in Ilyara, they'll wake them up, won't they? But we can't tell them to stop, either. We have to stop *all* of it. Rasim, what are we going to do?"

He pressed his hands to his temples, eyes closed as he spoke slowly, his thoughts not running away with his tongue, for once. "You said something earlier. Something about the king. The king channeling the guilds when we have to do a big magic."

"Right, and Ilyara burned in the Great Fire because Laishn wasn't *here* to channel the Sunma—" Kisia broke off and made a sound like she'd bitten into a rotting fish. "Well, that's part of why Ilyara burned," she concluded grimly. "Overlooking Pydasho's treachery."

"What if we need him? Or somebody else in the royal family? There's…there's Faisha, and Alaisha. And Taishm. That's at least three people who can guide witchery, right?" His eyes popped open and he seized Kisia's shoulders. "All right. All right, what we need to do is find them. Taishm will be hardest, unless he's come out of hiding, I wouldn't stay hidden while my city was burning, I'd go to the palace—"

"We need you," Kisia said clearly. "*You* can guide the magics, Rasim. *You* can control all of them. Because *you*—"

Rasim lifted a hand, not wanting to hear how that sentence finished. He was almost certain it touched too closely on a thought he was trying very hard not to let himself think. "Even if I can, I can't do all of them. We need—oh, Desimi! Telun, oh, Siliaria's *teeth*, Telun is in the mountains with Bayar still—*Taishm!*" He gathered skymastery and bellowed the king's name, then, almost in the same breath, yelled, "Skymasters! Hear me, and make me heard! *Taishm*," he roared again, dizzy with effort. "Taishm, we need your help! Where are you?"

Witchery carried the cry much farther than it would go on its own, but not far enough. Not into the depths and crooks of Ilyaran cellars, or even to half the city. The king himself had been able to use sky magic to deliver a message from the palace all the way to the harbor. Skymastery was easier than stone witchery, but Rasim didn't think his talents stretched that far.

A few sky witches did take up his call, amplifying

it, carrying it through the city. In other places, though, Rasim could feel the magic falter, or even be shut down entirely as witches loyal to Jhikara decided he was an enemy. Suddenly angry, Rasim yelled, "You're on the losing side, Jhikara!" into the wind, and heard her laughter come back to him a few seconds later.

"Perhaps, but look what's out there, Rasim." If he could see her, Rasim knew the Guildmaster's eyes would be shining. "Look at those glass creatures. Look at what lives in the wind. Ilyara's rigid guilds and rules deny us so much. Look what we could be, instead. We could be *gods*."

Rasim, who had actually met a god, snorted. "You're wrong, Jhikara. You don't even know how wrong you are. Help me find Taishm, and you might come out of this alive."

Her laughter danced around him again. "What a threat, Journeyman. You certainly won't kill me, although your fierce friend might try. I wonder which would give out first, my heart, or her breath." Then the Guildmaster's voice was gone, and Rasim's shout no longer echoed through the city.

Kisia put her hand on Rasim's arm. "I'll find Taishm. You get down to the harbor and talk to Desimi."

"You're going out into that alone?" Rasim gestured at the roiling city in dismay.

"So are you," Kisia pointed out. "I'll be careful. I promise. You be careful too. And Rasim?" When his eyebrows lifted curiously, she said, "If you run into Jhikara, kick her ass."

Surprise made him laugh, albeit nervously. "If you run into Pydasho, *run*."

A sharp smile curved her mouth. "He's a fire witch, and I'm a water witch called sister by the goddess of the sea herself. I'll take my chances."

Rasim said, "Kisia," in alarm, but she was gone already, dashing back down through the building they'd stormed. He took a few stumbling steps after her, then sighed and turned back to look at the city for a moment. The dragon still had its wings spread, but it watched the skies warily, as if expecting an attack at any moment. Luckily—if that was the right word—for it, the glass wings were too entangled with the power snapping off the thunder wolves to bother with the dragon anymore. Rasim was half certain he could see the streets breaking apart as something huge moved beneath them, too, and had a sick moment of remembering they'd told people to hide in the cellars to avoid the lightning.

The vast magical beasts' fight had nothing to do with the human one, Rasim was almost certain of that. The creatures thundering through the streets and skies were elemental, and unaccustomed to even encountering one another. They seemed to be natural enemies, but Rasim thought if he was an impossibly huge monster, if he saw a *different* impossibly huge monster, the obvious response would be either to attack it, or run away. And in a situation like this one, with magic boiling everywhere in the city—magic that attracted the beasts in the first place—attacking each other seemed more likely. Maybe they fed on it. Maybe they didn't want to share. Maybe they were just excited to be in the world, and were making the most of their moment. It would have been rather wonderful, if wasn't wrecking block after block of Ilyara.

But they were, and they had to be stopped, so Rasim took a deep breath, and ran for the harbor.

CHAPTER TWENTY

The docks were in chaos.

Rasim didn't know what he'd expected. He didn't have any sense of how long he'd been trying to get through the city before turning back. For a moment he couldn't even remember *why* he'd been trying to get through the city instead of helping on the docks. Then a bolt of lightning that wasn't yet a thunder wolf sizzled by, and he remembered they'd been going to look for metal, to make a lightning rod with.

That still seemed like a good idea. Too bad he'd forgotten it while running from thunder wolves and ducking poison darts and trying to stay alive. Maybe Kisia would think of it on her way to find the king.

Which seemed like an impossible task, but Rasim put that aside. Everything was impossible right now, not least the fight going on in the harbor. It took long moments for him to even begin to understand what was happening, and when he did, it was bad enough that he wished he didn't.

Water witchery was *not* a good magic to fight lightning sorcery with. In the wake of the *Wafiya*'s death, Hassin had pulled lightning witches into the sea and drowned them, but they had clearly learned since then. Rasim couldn't see the Northern witches, but every time water rose to sneak its way on board a Northern ship, lightning shot out, connected with the water, and lit up the harbor's whole surface.

And the thing was, docks were *wet*. They didn't have to be soaking to conduct the lightning: damp was enough to be dangerous. There were witches on their hands and knees, clearly pouring everything they had into keeping the docks dry, but there were many other people stirring up storms in the harbor, and water kept splashing dangerously onto the docks.

The water nearest the Northern ships was slushy with ice, too: another witchery the North had and Ilyara didn't. Isidri could work with ice, but no one else in the guild could, and it was dangerous for the old Guildmaster. The slush was obviously making it harder for Ilyaran witchery to slip past Northern attention. They needed another approach. Something the Northerners wouldn't see coming, and which would force them from the safety of their ships into the city itself.

Rasim cast a frustrated glance toward the harbor's far shore, and the stretches of Ilyara that spread on the river's other side. The Stonemasters' guildhall was over there, as well as the Skymasters. He wanted them to be doing something clever, but the truth was that the witches on that side of the river were just as busy trying to fend off thunder wolves and poison darts falling from the sky as the ones on this side were.

Worse, as he watched, towers of dust rose and billowed as buildings collapsed, and he caught a glimpse of something huge and fast slithering across a rise over there. He imagined he could hear the sandy rasp of the giant snake's dune-colored scales through the Ilyaran streets, and for a moment Rasim sagged. He'd hoped, somehow, that the vast amounts of stone witchery wouldn't waken a stone snake here, and because he hadn't seen one on this side of the river, he'd let himself believe they were safe. But of course it would have awakened closer to the Stonemasters' Guild, where their power was concentrated. Another building crumbled, and Rasim shivered. Even with Ilyaran witchery, rebuilding the city would be the project of a lifetime.

Assuming anyone survived to rebuild.

Desimi and Isidri were shoulder to shoulder on the docks, standing on a jut of stone that hadn't been there before. The ancient guildmaster looked small beside her young companion, but her hair flew wildly in its braid, electricity all but seeming to lift it. Rasim could feel the power she poured into the harbor, keeping the Northern witches from freezing it. Desimi threw bolt after bolt of water at the Northern ships with one hand, and with the other, protected Isidri with stone shelters that were shattered by lightning as fast as he shaped them.

Not nearly enough of his water blasts broke through the lightning web to ram the ships, but some of them did. A glimmer of an idea finally awakened in Rasim's mind. There were so many other sea witches spread along the quays, fighting together but essentially with individual attacks. They were *good* at working together: sea witches had to, to survive storms and the unpredictable seas. But they'd never been taught to fight as one. They'd never had any reason to.

No guild in Ilyara had been taught to fight as one. That was what the monarch was for, to gather the huge power of a guild into one skilled working of magic.

Rasim's feet were moving, slipping him through small spaces between his fellow guildmembers as if acting on their own while his mind ran ahead of him, trying to put all the pieces together. He raised witchery more than once, supporting the magics around him, but he kept moving forward, until he'd reached the jetty that Desimi had shaped out over the harbor. Very distantly he heard Asindo's voice calling to him, in warning or alarm, but he walked forward to join Isidri and Desimi.

Desimi grunted, "Sunburn," without really even looking at him. "About time you showed up."

A surprised laugh cracked from Rasim's chest, and Desimi managed a quick thin grin at him. Up close, the big journeyman's strain was clear: he was sweating and ashy from effort, the power pouring from him simply immense.

Isidri, at his side, looked worse up close, too. The network of lines in her ancient face were deeper than Rasim had ever seen them, but her jaw was set with a determination as great as Desimi's. Even with Rasim there, they worked in tandem, with Desimi's power shoring the old guildmaster's up. He might not be able to work with ice himself, but as long as Isidri guided the power, he could help her.

Which was exactly what Rasim needed of him. Hope flared in his chest and he stepped a little closer, until the three of them were a warm little knot of witches on the seawall. "Desi, in a minute I'm going to take over supporting Isidri."

"Really," Desimi said through his teeth. "And what am I going to do?"

Rasim took a deep breath. "You're going to channel the rest of the guild's witchery, and smash through the Northern lightning to sink their ships."

Desimi shot him a disbelieving look. "And how am I going to do that?"

"I don't know exactly, but it's important, so you're going to figure it out." Rasim turned his head away from the two beside him and gathered sky witchery one more time. "*Seamasters*. On my mark, focus your witchery on Desimi! Let him guide it!"

A slightly baffled shout of agreement ran along the docks, and Rasim took that as good enough. He and Desimi had traded magic back and forth often enough now that taking on the weight of witchery that supported Isidri's was an almost comfortable ritual. Rasim breathed laughter. "Easier when I'm not just out of slave chains."

Desimi staggered a step anyway as he was left to work with stone witchery alone. A thick stone wall rose from the jetty, protecting the three of them as the big journeyman turned to Rasim with panic in his eyes. "You should do this. You're the smart one. You're Siliaria's favorite."

"Don't be silly, boy." Isidri sounded almost cheerful. "You've been using sea witchery like it was as natural as breathing since the moment you were brought into this world. Rasim's a bright boy with a lot of potential, but you were born to this."

"But I can't feel other people's witchery like Rasim does. How do I know it's there?" Desimi's voice was tight with worry and fear.

"Stop using yours," Isidri said gently. Rasim had no idea how she could talk to him so calmly while maintaining the tremendous power she was using. "Let it all go. All of it, Desi. Just for a moment, to feel what's going on around you with other witches. Rasim learned this early, it seems, perhaps because his power was never strong. Most others never learn it at all. But you can do it, boy. Just let the witchery go."

"I don't think I know how." Desi closed his eyes, shivering, and kept one hand on the stone wall he'd built. Isidri thumped his wrist.

"Let that go too, lad. Empty yourself."

Instead, he cracked one eye open. "That makes it sound like you want me to pee."

Isidri cackled. "If necessary, yes. Just not on me."

Rasim said, "Oh!" in sudden understanding. "Like Endat was trying to get us to do for sun witchery, Des. Oyun finally got me to do it, in Shenryal."

Desimi cracked the other eye open to glare at him. "Oyun roasted you in a tent over an open fire until you barfed. We don't have time for that." Ever so slightly less grumpily, he added, "But I know what you mean. I remember what Endat wanted us to do. A couple times I almost thought I had it, but it slipped away."

Rasim bit his tongue on suggesting that one of those times was when the *Wafiya*'s ropes had gone up in flames. Desimi closed his eyes again, exhaling slowly. His shoulders dropped a little, tension leaving his body, which Rasim thought was incredible, given the noise and chaos around them. He barely dared look away from the harbor as he poured witchery into the water for Isidri to shape, but he couldn't help glance at Desimi again when the bigger boy breathed, "Oh," in understanding. "Oh, I get it. The weight you talked about. I *did* know about that. It's just it wasn't—" He broke off with a sort of laugh, and Isidri, sweaty and trembling, cackled again.

"It just wasn't very much compared to your own, eh, is that it, lad? You just rolled on over it, because your power was stronger? I went on the same journey. Call it to you, Desimi. All that witchery? You can guide it."

The old woman's confidence tore at Rasim's chest. He had always wanted someone to believe in him that much. Isidri was so *certain*. He wondered if she would have been as sure of his abilities, if he'd tried to be the guide for this particular working.

Desimi's hands opened, fingers twitching in a familiar pattern: twisting one direction, then another, weaving below, twisting again, crossing over and under. The gestures were mesmerizing, quick, and so absolutely certain that it took Rasim a few seconds to recognize them: Desimi was making a rope. Every sea witch in the guild knew how to do that, but he doubted anybody but Isidri could do it with magic.

Anybody *else,* at least. Rasim couldn't see the power, but he could feel it, braiding together into something far, far stronger than any individual witch, even Isidri, could manage on their own. The witchery wasn't yet active in those strands: the seamasters were still throwing everything they had at the Northerners. But the 'rope' Desimi wove gathered the shape of each witch's individual power, until the big journeyman gave a rough nod and said, "I've got it. I think I've got it," to Rasim. "Tell them to do—whatever they're supposed to do."

"Seamasters!" Rasim lifted his voice again, using sky witchery to carry it. "Seamasters, now!"

The guildmembers had focused their witchery together hundreds of times in their lives. Rasim wasn't entirely sure what he was even asking of them, just then, except utter trust. And to his staggering relief, he got it: there was a shift in the power being used, as instead of guiding it individually, they handed off its *intent* to Desimi. There was no terrible deluge as hundreds of sea witches offered magic to a single user, only the desire, the knowledge, and the power to create a tremendous working.

Desimi shouted, a rough raw sound of shock as he took on the magic of a guild. Isidri fell back a step, moving out of his way as he spun toward the fleet of

Northern ships in the harbor, and shaped witchery like nothing Rasim had ever seen.

He had worked incredible sea witchery himself, commanding the sea beneath the frozen Northern harbors and breaking up the ice with it. He had, in desperation, worked significant skymastery, too, and at least defended himself well with sun witchery.

It simply didn't compare to the magic of a guild focused through a single wielder. He could feel, through the power he too offered Desimi, how the big journeyman's talent grasped and drew on what he was offered and made it more than any one person could ever imagine. His *own* witchery alone had managed to slam through some of the lightning barrier slammed into the Northern ships; now Desimi had not just his natural strength, but that of the guild. He gathered not one, but dozens of balls of water as if it was effortless, and with a ferocious thrust, sent them across the harbor's slushy surface at impossible speeds.

More than Rasim expected bashed into the Northern ships, finding breaks in the lightning web to careen through. The first ones hit high as Desimi got used to lobbing water like he was the catapult that threw it, and the next ones rushed lower, closer to the surface of the water.

Not all of them broke through: in many places, lightning struck in shattering bolts. Water exploded into steam, hissing and splashing dangerously. Desimi stopped the spatter almost thoughtlessly, an easy, effortless flick of magic while he concentrated the bulk of the guild's power on the attack. Rasim knew that lightning dissipated across the surface of water, but he had never imagined what would happen if lightning hit a fast-moving *ball* of water.

It didn't have time to dissolve, not entirely. Not at the speed at which Desimi threw them, dozens after dozens. Lightning leaped from one ball to another, dancing across the surface of water that wasn't connected to the harbor at all, unable to fully discharge for a critical heartbeat of time.

When those lightning-ridden water bombs hit the Northern ships, fire and panic erupted on them. Rasim knew instantly that at least one lightning witch had been lost: the web of electricity lost some of its strength, thinning in places. A roar went up among the seamasters, and if anyone had held back before, they no longer did. Rasim had experienced the terrible, joyful power of the *delzjha* drug; this was almost like that, except surrounded by the comforting knowledge that this was the *guild* at full strength, sharing power for a common purpose. It lacked *delzjha*'s dreadful glory of heroism, the burning certainty that the user was the only one who could possibly command such power, and was so much better for it.

The harbor waters steamed where icy slush hit the leading edge of lightning-laced water bombs. Out of the entire guild who were present, only Isidri hadn't joined Desimi's weaving, her attention still completely focused on pushing back the ice. Her power surged as the bombs began to hit, gaining territory while the ice witches on board the ships faltered. Water roiled again, huge churning bubbles more like the base of a waterfall than the generally-still harbor. Isidri made no effort to quiet those waters, but sent those bubbles sloshing through the slush, spilling into the punctured hulls of Northern ships. One of the ships gasped, and sank with more speed than Rasim expected. Northern sailors fled from it into the icy waters, and onto the nearby ships.

He hadn't seen Lorens except for that brief moment very early in the morning, and didn't catch a glimpse of his blonde head fleeing the remaining ships. Rasim hoped he'd been on the one that sank. The harbor water burped a huge splashy surge, like it was satisfied with the meal it had made of the Northern ship. Rasim wasn't the only one who saw it that way: a laugh, low and tense, ran through the gathered guild.

That laugh turned to shrieks as a sea serpent, alive with chunks of ice and snapping electricity, twisted up from the water, coiled around a ship, and crushed it into pieces as it dragged it beneath the surface of the water. A second coil rose and snared another ship so fast no one had even caught their breath yet, but piercing cries of terror split the air in the aftermath.

Within seconds, the beast threw itself out of the water again, huge and glittering with ice so deep a blue it matched the lightning sparking from its scales. No one, not even Desimi, could move as the thing rose and rose into the air, vast and terrible with witchery. It *looked* like the serpent Rasim had killed, if that creature could have taken the ice and the lightning and become one with it. It moved with sinuous, sea-born grace, unbothered that ice chunks fell from it as it swung around, and comfortable with the ability to drop its terrible jaw and spit lightning at a ship below.

The mast caught fire, sails igniting as Northern sailors threw themselves overboard, trying to escape the serpent. Given the electricity that poured off the beast, Rasim wasn't sure that was wise, but he didn't know what else they could do, either. The serpent fell across two ships, its body shuddering a moment before a massive blast of lightning exploded from every surface of its skin.

Almost as one, the seamasters on the quays ducked, screaming, trying to avoid the concussive force of electricity rolling across the harbor, and their united power began to unravel.

"*Hold!*" Desimi's voice rose hugely, a vast bellow encouraging the seamasters to stay with him. "*Hold!*"

Rasim felt their power wobble again, then strengthen as they put their trust in the young journeyman. He had no idea how to fight a lightning serpent, but Desimi, it appeared, did. He flung himself upward into a rising spigot, one hand extended to call a steel blade from the harbor where a Northerner had lost it.

Isidri murmured, "I don't think so, lad," and a wall of water came up to smash Desimi back down onto the docks as she leaped into the fray herself.

CHAPTER TWENTY-ONE

Like Desimi, the ancient Guildmaster swept a weapon up from the tumultuous harbor. Hers was a piece of wreckage, a length of wood shattered into sharpness from the lightning strikes. That was probably smarter than a metal blade. Rasim had been afraid the lightning crackling around the ice serpent would leap into the sword and then into Desimi.

Isidri rose on the waves like Siliaria herself, utterly in her element as the great beast thrashed and threw itself around the harbor. Desimi, soaking wet, scrambled to his feet with a cry matched by half the guild. The rest, like Rasim, were mute with horror as Isidri flung herself from one side to the other, faster than the serpent could attack. After a few astonished seconds, Rasim suspected she was anticipating the monster's movements through the water itself, as if it warned her of how the great creature's muscles twitched, and thus which way it would move.

Even as she dodged, she cast bolts of weaponized

water that cracked the serpent's icy scales, and at least once, turning its electric charge against itself: lightning bolted through her watery attack as it hit the serpent, which lit up blue all over. Ice shattered in chunks from its rimed sides. At the same time, Rasim realized that the whipping whirlpool that lifted Isidri wasn't carrying lightning to *her* because it wasn't just one rising spigot of water. Time and again, with impossible speed and craft, Isidri dropped one working and spun up a new one, stepping from one to another just a little faster than the serpent could attack.

Rasim had watched Captain Nasira walk across the surface of the sea as she left the drowning *Wafiya* behind. It had cost her. It was *nothing* compared to the extraordinary witchery Isidri worked now. Every step brought her closer to the lashing serpent, her confidence unshakable as she moved across the water.

For a heartbeat, Rasim wondered why they'd never seen a sea serpent like this one before. Theirs were scaled like giant fish, not crusted with lightning and ice. But then, they wouldn't be, not in Ilyara. This was a thing drawn to ice and lightning and water magic all at once, and Ilyara was a hot desert delta, not the kind of place ice ever formed naturally. Rasim tried to remember whether anything like the ice serpent had been painted in the heroic Northern murals, and realized that if his story was painted there, this might well be the kind of serpent they envisioned.

Desimi, helpless with fear, gave another hoarse shout, dislodging Rasim's racing thoughts. Isidri ducked under a barrage of lightning so terrifying that the whole guild cried out, and Desimi whipped witchery together again. Just his own, this time: Rasim didn't feel any of the strange draw and focus that said the big journeyman was concentrating the power of a guild in one working. But then, everyone's magic was scattered, at best. Most of the witches on shore had let go of their witchery, too stunned to act as they watched their guildmaster dance with a sea monster.

"Desi, no!" Rasim gathered witchery of his own to blunt Desimi's, although his heart sickened with it. Desimi's brute strength slammed against his own resolution, the bigger boy searching frantically for a way around the way Rasim kept the waters at the quay's edge from responding. Rasim knew if he reached a little farther, Desimi would be able to work his witchery, because he was afraid if he blocked much more than the closest waters from answering magic's call, he would doom Isidri. But Desimi was too scared and angry to think that clearly. He bore down with witchery so strongly that Rasim staggered, and when that didn't work, surged toward Rasim, prepared to use his physical power.

Then Asindo was there, a heavy hand on Desimi's shoulder. The new Guildmaster's tone was as solemn and sick as Rasim's heart. "Let Isidri face this one, lad. She knows what she's doing."

Desimi's magic cut away so abruptly that Rasim nearly fell. The other boy made the sound that Rasim wanted to, a helpless, desperate sob. "But I could help!"

Rasim shook his head miserably. "I don't think you

could, Desi. Look how fast she's moving. Feel how fast. None of us could keep up. We'll only be in her way."

"But—" Once again, the hoarse helpless cry was the sound Rasim felt in his chest, in his stomach, all the way through him. By sheer luck, he had survived an ordinary sea serpent's attack. Quick and talented as Isidri was, a single mis-step would be her doom. Sick with anticipation, Rasim turned to watch the battle with clenched hands and rigid jaws.

Isidri simply didn't mis-step. Had it been less frightening, Rasim would have watched her fight with undiminished awe. She moved gracefully, swiftly, hounding the serpent with water blasts that slowly began to permanently dislodge icy scales. Rasim couldn't tell if they were actually melting, or simply breaking away. Beneath the ice scales, the beast was glacier blue, a deeper and more beautiful shade than the serpent he'd fought, although he remembered with a shock that as they'd dived, his serpent had begun to glow blue. Maybe that glow had been the same power that now let this beast contain lightning. Its glacier-colored skin looked thin, delicate, in a way its icy scales didn't, but electricity still slithered across it in smooth crackling bolts.

The old Guildmaster was slowing, though. No one could keep up the level of witchery she was working forever, or even for very long. Still, every step through her whirlpools saw her advance on the serpent, and magic poured from her as if it was limitless. Rasim held his breath and clutched Desimi's arm as they, and every other member of the guild, watched helplessly to see which of the combatants would triumph.

A roar rose on the quays as the old Guildmaster, with a nimble leap, crossed the distance from her whirlpools to the serpent's neck, and jabbed her piece of broken stick into its neck for purchase. The serpent shrieked, a familiar sound to anyone who had encountered the creatures on the sea. It sounded like the ships' whistles, but deeper, more resonant, sharper, all at once. It lifted hairs on Rasim's nape, and sent a cold shiver through him as he remembered the last time he'd heard that scream. The fleet had lost so many ships that day, and it had set Rasim on a path he'd never expected to take.

But then it shrieked again, this time seeming agitated. Lightning sparked against its skin, but didn't fly in deadly bolts the way it had before. Rasim nearly laughed, although his heart was too much in his throat for a sound to emerge. "It can't use lightning on her without zotting itself. Not as long as she's on it."

And Isidri looked like she could ride the serpent's spine forever. A wild grin split her wrinkled face as she crept forward, using the flotsam staff to stabilize herself. Another flash of memory shuddered through Rasim. He'd used his belt knife that way, deep beneath the sea. The serpent hadn't even noticed as he plunged the little blade into its side, dragging himself up toward its head. Not until he'd thrust the knife into its eye, and swirled.

Isidri's braid whipped in the wind of their battle as she inched forward, one gleeful old woman on the ride of her life. The serpent twisted and snapped, but she'd stepped onto it too close to its head for it to bite her. When it crashed beneath the harbor's surface, the guildmembers screamed, but Isidri's laughter could be heard rising through the waves. Rasim thought the fighting must have stopped across the whole city while Ilyara awaited the outcome of this single encounter.

She was going to win. Certainty flashed over Rasim. Old or not, Isidri crackled with power, and the serpent's most dangerous weapon was turning back on itself now. It had hardly any ice left at all, and its glowing blue skin looked incredibly vulnerable without the chunky scales. Without the lightning to command, the ice was its main defense against tooth and claw, and Isidri had a claw.

The serpent, screaming in anger now that it had failed to dislodge her under the water, reared high into the sky with such speed that it briefly pressed Isidri against its spine, all but flattening her. She hung on to her jagged spear of wood with both hands as the serpent whipped back and forth. With each jerk one way or another the watching guild shrieked and gasped and bit their hands, trying not to distract Isidri from her efforts. When she wouldn't come loose, the serpent whistled again, an ear-cracking sound that surely had to silence and still the entire city. It rose higher yet, blasting another whistle at the apex of its stretch as it towered over the ships' masts, the city, over everything in the whole wide world except the old guildmaster.

Isidri came to her feet as it screamed, lithe and sure-footed as an apprentice, and ran the last few steps up its spine to its skull. There, she lifted the jagged spear, and with absolute glee, cried Siliaria's name into the silence as the serpent's whistle ended. Power exploded from her, visible waves of magic as she drove the sharpened weapon down, cracking the beast's bony skull with impossible strength.

The serpent died, but Isidri al Ilialio died with it.

CHAPTER TWENTY-TWO

The serpent fell in slow collapsing waves, coiling down into the harbor waters with tremendous splashes. Isidri, so much smaller, seemed to fall much faster, to the sound of a terrible cry from the guild she had led for so long. Hundreds of hands stretched outward, as if in catching her, they could undo what had happened.

They couldn't: Rasim knew it. He had seen, as they all had seen, the incredible pulse of power that had erupted from the Guildmaster as she had wielded the power of a god for one single heartbeat. The serpent was disintegrating under that power now, as if the shock of it had been so great that it didn't remember to come apart immediately. But dreadful chunks of flesh and blood fell with great splashes that soaked even the Seamasters, who together acted with one purpose alone: to save Isidri from falling awkwardly into the depths. Every sea witch on the quays sent tendrils of gentle water to catch their fallen Guildmaster, so she was brought to shore on the strength of their love.

She looked so small, in death. Fragile, ancient, an empty shell that had housed a great spirit, now fled. Rasim couldn't think for grief as the guild brought Isidri to Asindo's arms, and for the first time, saw their new Guildmaster bow his head in tears.

Desimi shook Rasim's clutching hands off his arm and threw a fist so fast Rasim never could have stopped it, even if he hadn't been blinded by tears himself. He staggered with the hit, stars flying in his already blurred vision, and ducked the second punch mostly through old instinct as Desimi shrieked, "*I could have saved her!* I could have—I could have—"

His blows lost strength, and so did his knees, until he dropped to them at Rasim's side. Rasim knelt, too, pulling the other boy into a shaking hug as Desimi flailed and choked with sobs.

"Rasim." Asindo's voice was heartrendingly soft. "A touch of skymastery, if you can?"

Through tears, Rasim nodded, struggling to weave a little witchery so Asindo's low, broken words would carry. "None of us could have saved her," the Guildmaster said. "Siliaria knows Isidri always did do exactly what she wanted to."

Somehow, impossibly, even in the grip of the newest and rawest grief, a chuckle broke through the gathered guild. "Today she wanted to protect her guild as only she could do. Today," Asindo said, his voice strengthening, "*we* will do for Ilyara what Isidri has done for us. We will grieve, Seamasters, but first, *first* we will win this gods-cursed battle that has been brought to us, and we will show the world why war does not come to Ilyara!"

A cheer rose, ragged at first but gaining power as it changed from simple noise to a brief, heartfelt chant. "For Isidri! Is-i-dri! *Is-i-dri! IS-I-DRI!*"

Beneath the call to arms, Asindo, with weary regret, said, "Too much has already been asked of you, Desimi, Rasim, but I'm afraid I have to ask for more yet."

The boys, still curled around each other in shared grief, looked up at the stout Guildmaster, his braid wet over his shoulder. Isidri, in his arms, was dry, the only witch on the docks who hadn't been soaked in the battle. Her white braid fell long and gentle toward the ground. Rasim, trembling, rose and tucked her braid across her chest, tidying the old woman a little. She looked more than peaceful, he thought. She looked satisfied.

"Anything." Desimi's voice was a raw broken sound. "Anything you need us to do, Guildmaster. Anything."

"We have to stop these beasts." Asindo held Isidri's weight as if it was nothing, and also the greatest burden he'd ever carried. "I don't know how, but I do know they seem to respond to witchery, and you two are my only—" He broke off, searching for a word.

"Witchmasters," Kisia said in a small thin voice. She stumbled onto the quay, her eyes dark and huge with unshed tears. To Rasim's shock, Taishm followed her, his gaze bleak with loss. Kisia made a listless gesture, her face drawn and older than her years. "I found the king, but I wasn't fast enough. I'm sorry. I'm so sorry."

Like the boys, she dropped to her knees, shaking with sobs. Rasim dropped again too, pulling her into a hug that she resisted at first. "She believed in me. She chose me. She let me do what nobody had ever done before. What are we going to do without her?"

"Finish what she started," Rasim said hoarsely into her hair, before looking up at Asindo. The Guildmaster still stood unmoving, as if to move would begin a life he wasn't yet prepared to face. Rasim's throat and chest clenched, but he forced himself to speak. "You're right, Guildmaster. They're drawn to the magic."

It took a moment to go on. His chest hurt so much. "There aren't any more lightning attacks happening. I think we might have killed all their lightning witches. Maybe the ice witches, too, because…" Because ice wasn't reforming on the harbor, but everyone could see that. "I don't think the lightning witches being dead will make the thunder wolves disappear, but maybe there won't be any more. If they hit stone unexpectedly they dissipate, so the Stonemasters should be able to deal with them."

"The Stonemasters," Taishm said in a raw voice, "are under siege from a great horned sand snake, though."

Rasim's smile felt awful. "One thing at a time, your majesty." He thought, briefly, about mentioning the Shenryalan he'd seen, and the earth witchery that had been worked, but decided not to. He still didn't entirely believe he'd seen it. He was just losing his mind a little, because of all the chaos.

Taishm cracked a hard laugh, but nodded, then spoke, his words running ahead of Rasim's thoughts.

"Dispel the thunder wolves, then rally the Stonemasters to destroy the snake? And the Skymasters to tame the winds, and the Sunmasters that dragon, but Rasim, two of those guilds have betrayed Ilyara."

"You can guide the Skymasters." Rasim usually enjoyed being quick. Now he only felt tired in every bone of his body. "Desimi can manage the Stonemasters."

Desimi's head came up, bewildered. "No, I can't!"

"You can." Rasim waved his hand toward the mourning sea witches as evidence that his witchmastery meant Desimi *could* guild a guild.

"And the Sunmasters?" Taishm watched Rasim with a thoughtful frown that cleared a little, then returned forcefully as Rasim spread his hands.

"It's going to have to be me."

"You think you have it in you?" Grim concern filled Taishm's voice.

Rasim shrugged helplessly. "I'm going to have to. Oyun said I had a natural talent for sun witchery, and I can use all the other Ilyaran magics. That's what the King's Guild was for, right? To see if we could? Well, I can, so I should probably be able to guide a guild, too."

"You're thirteen."

"So is Desimi!"

A brief twist crossed Taishm's mouth. "True. Well, I have little choice anyway. The only other possibilities are my cousins, and while Alaisha's heart is in the right place, her gifts for witchery are even weaker than mine, and Faisha...." He sighed. All Rasim knew about Taishm's second cousin was that she'd spent years hoping to marry him out of an affection for power, rather than for the good of Ilyara, or even for the good of Taishm. "No one knows where she is anyway."

The king hesitated before letting it go and bowing briefly to Asindo. "Guildmaster, if I may second your journeymen to me, I think this effort is best run from the palace rather than the docks."

"Bring them back to me alive." Asindo spoke in a tone most people, never mind kings, wouldn't tolerate. Taishm only nodded, beckoning to the journeymen and making no objection when Kisia joined the boys. The four of them stood together as Asindo, finally forced to move, took the first heavy step away from the quays, bearing Isidri in his arms.

Most of the guild followed, falling into two lines behind the Guildmaster, ragged at first and then gradually, perhaps intentionally, also falling into step with one another, so a near-silent march of witches escorted Isidri back to the guildhall for the final time. The only sounds to break their silence were sobs, muffled or choked except where grief couldn't be held back, and echoing across the quiet harbor.

For what felt like the first time in forever, Rasim remembered to look for Northern ships to see what was left of their fleet. A number of the long boats had come out unscathed, although not, apparently, any of those that had carried their witches. Rasim didn't know if that was luck on the serpent's part, or if Isidri had drawn them into the huge beast's path to ensure their destruction.

At least one of the ships had broken ranks and was

moving away, back toward the river mouth. Others were swarmed with extra sailors, angry and frightened. Rasim didn't think any of them had made it to this side of the harbor; it was possible there were some soldiers now on the other shore. He couldn't imagine that would go well for them.

Desimi, voice almost perfectly even, said, "Can I sink them?"

Taishm made a harsh noise in his throat. "Nearly every part of me wants to say yes, but a thread of wisdom tells me no. They don't seem to be much danger to us now, and should probably be considered prisoners of war, or perhaps even let go to tell the world why Ilyara has gone unconquered for so long. Either way, I would just as soon let Janna of the North-lands decide how to deal with her rebellious crews than do it myself."

"What about Lorens?" Rasim almost didn't recognize his own voice, but he was all too afraid he recognized the viciousness in Taishm's smile as he said, "Lorens is another matter entirely."

"We have to find him first," Kisia said. "After that it's anybody's game."

Rasim felt a stab of angry agreement pierce him. He didn't think he liked the idea of vengeance, mostly. Prince Lorens might be a special case.

The last of the gathered sea witches had passed them, by then. The guildhall, which had been barri-caded for weeks, now stood open to allow people to enter. Another pang shot through Rasim's chest, and he wasn't surprised to feel Taishm's hand on his shoulder. "I'm sorry, Rasim. I need you now."

He nodded stiffly. "Guildmaster said mourning later. I just…" Jaw set resolutely, he looked up at the king. "How are we going to get to the palace with you in tow? Last I knew, Pydasho wanted to kill you."

A smile that had nothing to do with anger or grief touched Taishm's lips. "As it turns out, I *am* still the king, and as such, command a certain loyalty." He lifted a hand, fingers swirling in a signal, and an army melted out of the shadows.

LED by the fierce Commander Yalonta, the King's Guard had been gathering, waiting patiently for Taishm's signal. Rasim's heart clenched in borderline panic when they began to appear: he thought he would have noticed them, especially since the last time he'd met her, Yalonta had been arresting him.

She was smaller than Rasim expected for a guard, and for an Ilyaran, surprisingly light of hair. Not as bright-haired as the Northerners, but deep gold, a lot like Rasim's was, now that it was bleached. She was strong-faced, not exactly pretty, but interesting to look at. Dozens of guards in the king's livery were with her, although a few of them were in ill-fitted uniforms, and Rasim swore they looked more Shen-ryalan than Ilyaran. When he mouthed 'how?' at Yalonta, she gave him a toothy smile. "I saw your friend here striking out on her own, and thought if anyone in this besieged city knew where Taishm was, it would be you three."

The smile faded into regret, though, as she said, "And when the battle was met at the harbor, I knew that no matter where else she meant to take him, she would come back to her guild first. So we came, and we waited. I'm sorry for your loss, Journeymen."

"And you knew?" Rasim asked the king. "You signaled for them."

"I saw Yalonta as we were coming to the docks, and bid her stay. Too much had already happened. Now, though, we must go quickly. Too much is still happening." Taishm glanced upward, where glasswings still turned the light to rainbows as they soared through the sky, and where the injured dragon dodged their attacks. Lightning still rolled through the streets with the pacing of thunder wolves, and Rasim couldn't imagine the disaster being wrought on the other shore by the great stone snake.

"I was using witchery after witchery in the mountains," he said to no one in particular as the guard formed up around them. "Why didn't the dragons and glasswings come then?"

"Because it was only you," Kisia replied. They were already moving by then, Yalonta's presence at the head of an armed brigade enough to clear the streets of what people there were. "Oyun said that dragon in Shenryal came to you because you were all out of balance. You're balanced now, and just your witchery alone wasn't enough to rouse a whole mess of monsters. Which is just as well. We had a hard enough time with one."

Taishm exhaled explosively. "Yes. I understand if I have a kingdom at the end of all this, it's in large part thanks to you, Rasim. I didn't think they would come through the high pass."

"You can pay me back by ignoring me for the rest of my life," Rasim muttered. "I just want to help rebuild the guild and sail and not do anything exciting or political again, ever."

"Well, that's not going to happen," Kisia said. "You're going to be in the palace."

"I thought we were friends. Why would you say something that mean?"

Kisia gave a quick sharp laugh, but her answer was drowned by a crackle of lightning as a thunder wolf bolted from a broken-down alley. Rasim didn't know how the guard stood their ground: he shrieked and flung his arms up, too exhausted and overwhelmed to do anything else.

Taishm, though, flicked his fingers and a stone wall erupted from the ground. The thunder wolf crashed into it and dissipated, licks of lightning making after-images in Rasim's eyes. Desimi, gaping, said, "How did you do that so fast?" and peculiarly, the rest of the rush through the city amounted to a lesson in stone witch-ery. Desimi still wasn't anything like as fast as the king by the time they approached the city center, but he visibly improved in that little while. He even offered Taishm a brief, crooked grin. "Maybe I can teach you earth witchery, after all of this."

"That," Taishm said with evident sincerity, "would be *fascinating*. I wonder if I can learn, at my age."

"I propose we deal with the problems we have in front of us first," Yalonta said through her teeth. "I'm glad the boy's mastery is coming along so fast, as I understand the job he has in front of him, but let us not forget we have a coup on our hands, Majesty. This is not the time for playing with new magics."

"I did say afterward!" Desimi said indignantly.

"You did," Yalonta admitted. "It was Taishm's enthusiasm I was trying to curb."

"Oh. All right."

"Our plan," the commander said to Taishm. "Did we have one, or were we just going to storm the palace with forty guards and three journeymen?"

"I thought we would take a side entrance," Taishm admitted. "One of my old childhood passageways."

Enthusiasm lit Yalonta's eyes. "I always *have* wanted to know where those were, and where they led."

"I'll give this one up to you," the king said as he diverted their little army down a street that didn't obviously lead to the palace. "You're aware of the Convergence room?"

"I've heard of it," Yalonta said dubiously. "It exists?"

"We study there, when we're children. It helps us to learn the different witcheries. It's also easiest to guide a whole guild's magic from inside it. As far as I know, no one has ever tried having three witches guiding three different guilds' magic before, but these are unprecedented times." They slipped down an alleyway, this one rough with rubble before Taishm cleared it with another effortless gesture.

Desimi, indignant again, said, "There's a place that

makes doing multiple magics easier?" as Rasim, equally indignant but keeping it to himself, wondered why the journeymen in the King's Guild hadn't been given access to this room, if they were supposed to learn several kinds of witchery.

A moment later it occurred to him that nearly half the members of the new King's Guild had gotten on a ship and sailed away about five minutes after Taishm had formed it, and was glad he'd kept his mouth shut for once.

Then they were underground, finding their way to one of Taishm's secret passages, and everyone felt as though they should be quiet. That didn't really make sense, Rasim decided. They probably should have been quiet on the streets, not under them. Still, he didn't want to talk either, and was glad when the passageway led to a narrow set of spiraling stairs, then opened onto an extraordinary room.

It was round and domed, with slender columns of stone supporting open-air windows in its upper third. Rasim instantly knew it, although he'd only ever seen it from the outside: it was the highest part of the palace, visible all over the city. He had never given it a second thought. From the outside, it was airy, beautiful, a symbol of the city. From inside, it was that and more.

All four Ilyaran witcheries were represented in it, each given a quarter of the dome, with pathways between them, separating them from each other. Rasim was fairly certain each quarter faced its guildhall, with their distant placements around the city. The Seamasters' quarter was done in moonstone and water, with etchings of Siliaria and the sea worked into the stone. Each of the others had their own stones, their own gods, their own element, although Rasim, glancing at the fiery Sunmasters' quarter, didn't know how the soft fire opal didn't crack under the heat of the embers kept burning there.

Rasim took a short, shaking breath, and then a deeper one, eyes closed as he stepped into the room. It *resonated*, somehow, calming him despite the fact that the city was being destroyed around them. The burbling spring of the water witches' quarter was such a relief that he wanted to sit down in it, but the other quarters had their appeal, too. Even the Stonemasters' quarter, he realized: for the first time ever, he had a sense of the stone, patient, waiting, quiet, like it was aware of him. Aware, but not particularly *interested*: the other quarters pulled at him more strongly.

Even Kisia breathed, "Oh," in soft astonishment. "This feels…centered. I almost think even I could guide a guild from here."

"No." Taishm spoke almost as softly. "Not without drawing on the other guilds' witcheries. For balance, as your friend in Shenryal said. This place was built to make that possible. Or easier," he said with a brief glance at Desimi. "I suppose it must always have been possible, or no one would have thought to build a room to make it easier. Rasim, Desimi, come with me. We need to be in the center of the room."

Prince Lorens's voice was silky, smooth, and entirely unexpected. "Do forgive me, Taishm, but I would not take another step, if I were you."

CHAPTER TWENTY-THREE

Too late, Rasim realized there were four doors to the round room. The one they'd come through was the Stonemasters' door. That suddenly made sense; it was the one from beneath the ground itself. Lorens had entered through the Seamasters' door, which made Rasim's chest fill with irrational rage. It didn't really matter, but the Northern prince didn't *deserve* to be associated with the Seamasters in any way, not even such a small one as walking through a door.

He looked unruffled and calm, even bright and beautiful, as always. He hadn't been in the Ilyaran sun long enough for his pale skin to burn, and his astonishingly yellow hair was pulled back. It made his blue eyes seem larger and showed their constant amusement off to his best advantage. He looked, Rasim thought, like the kind of man who *should* be a leader: handsome, trustworthy, confident, well-presented. Especially for someone who had fled a sinking ship. Or maybe he hadn't: maybe he'd abandoned his fleet earlier so he could work his way to the palace and his allies.

Those allies were entering the room now, too, Pydasho through the Sunmasters' door, and Jhikara through the Skymasters'. A gust of wind slammed the Stonemasters' door on most of Taishm's guard: only the king, the journeymen, and Yalonta had made it through the door before it closed. The commander of the guard strode forward, intent on putting herself between her king and his enemies, but Taishm raised his hand, murmuring, "Stay, Yalonta. I can't afford to lose you today."

"Taishm—"

"It's an order, Commander."

Yalonta snarled but fell back, fury etched in her features. Taishm nodded, clearly grateful, although most of his attention was on the three who'd entered the room. They were all so different, Rasim thought, that they could have looked a little silly as allies. Instead they seemed dangerous, Pydasho's broad form and fanatical eyes like a barely-contained wildfire, and Jhikara's slender height and wild smile glittering with excitement. Between them, Lorens, who had no magic, still wore the sword he always carried on his hip. Compared to the two brown-skinned Guildmasters, his pale Northern complexion made him look almost like a thing made of steel, ready to cut.

If Taishm thought any of them looked like trouble, he didn't reveal it in his voice. "I thought we were friends, Lorens. But I thought that about Roscord, too. I had no idea I was so bad at choosing friends."

A brief expression of regret flashed across Lorens's face, but with the way he shrugged, Rasim couldn't tell which was real, the regret or the acceptance. "It was never really about you, Taishm. I was relieved when Annaken married your cousin, because it meant one more person who wasn't between me and the throne, but *gods*, my mother plans to live forever and my sister is so…" He curled his fingers inward with frustration. "*Your* throne passes to the next available family member. Ours goes through the women's line. It would have been my mother, then Annaken as regent for Inga, and then Inga and her daughters, and only me if the rest of them were dead. It's difficult, being seventeen years old and knowing that you'll never amount to more than a useful liaison, perhaps someone to marry off when a treaty needs to be made."

The blue in his eyes went flat, as cold and deadly as a deep sea or the blade of a sword. "So when I came to Annaken's wedding and Pydasho approached me to discuss the question of succession in Ilyara and the North, I was already more than ready to listen."

"So that's all it is," Taishm said quietly. "Power."

Lorens's eyes flashed again. "Power is *all* there ever is, and you would know that if you hadn't had it handed to you because of us!"

Their conversation had been so civilized that Rasim wasn't at all prepared when Pydasho threw a roaring fireball that expanded hugely in size as Jhikara's witchery sped it forward. Taishm, though, had apparently been waiting for it: he lifted a hand and closed it like he was catching a toy, once more effortlessly mastering a magic he wasn't believed to be good at. Pydasho's witchery winked out, but a second blast followed at speed, and then another and another, until the room was nearly a swirling inferno.

Rasim, remembering again what Jhikara had said about fire and air, reached for sky witchery, and found it blocked. The dancing touch of Jhikara's magic taunted him, and the Skymaster herself gave him a wicked grin that flattened into nothing when Taishm, unbothered by her efforts, snatched the wind away and the inferno died.

Desimi breathed, "We're *not* witchmasters," in awe. "We're just apprentices."

Sudden shadow fell over the room, seconds before a thundering crash shook it. Rasim flinched, looking up to see if the domed roof had cracked, and was doubly surprised that it hadn't when it became clear the golden dragon had smashed into it. The huge beast scrabbled for purchase, then launched itself off the roof again, a host of glittering glasswings in pursuit. Rasim, helplessly, said, "We have to stop them."

"But Taishm's our sky witch!" Kisia hissed. "This wasn't supposed to happen all at once! I didn't know Lorens would be here!"

Something between laughter and desperation twisted a sound from Rasim's chest. "See, that's what happens, things just keep piling up and happening all at once! Desimi, can you, with the wind?"

"But—" Desimi gestured at the king and the two Guildmasters, who were locked in a battle that didn't look like much from the outside, save for the brief bursts of witchery that flared to life and died again. Neither Jhikara nor Pydasho were gaining any ground, but neither was Taishm.

"No *but*," Kisia whispered. "You're going to have to. Taishm's busy. And maybe if you can rally the Skymasters, we can use that against Jhikara somehow."

Desimi bared his teeth at her, but also shrugged, because apparently he didn't have a better plan any more than Rasim himself did. "Just go really slowly," he suggested in a whisper. "So they don't notice us moving to the quarters."

"Either that or go really fast," Kisia said brightly, then gave them both a grin almost as wild as Jhikara's when they gaped at her. "Look, it's not me doing it, so I get to have bad ideas about what you should do!"

Rasim and Desimi exchanged glances, and, as a glasswing actually spun through one of the open windows above their heads, decided fast was better. They bolted left and right, skidding toward the sun and sky quarters. Rasim felt a burst of heat above him, and heard shouts from all three of the magical combatants as Taishm protected him from Pydasho's attack.

"Go, lads!" The king strode into the center of the room, resolute and drawing fire as the boys placed themselves in their quarters.

Witchery had been done here for a long, long time. Rasim knew it immediately, as if ancient power had actually marked the stone of the Sunmasters' quarter. It drew him in, offering him the confidence to work with a tremendous magic, although he also sensed something almost like expectation. The history of this place, although not often used for this particular purpose, *expected* that the sun-wielding witches of Ilyara would be offering their power to be shared. It wasn't meant to be dragged out of them, which Rasim was afraid he might have to do.

The relief carving of Riorda, shaped in the rich oranges, deep reds, and honey yellows of fire opal, looked down at him from the quarter's wall. She'd been portrayed with a gentle benevolence, a gift of fire in one hand, and all the things that fire made possible at her feet: cooking, the warmth of a home, light to see on a dark night, even the renewal of life after a wildfire. Those were the aspects she emphasized, when she gave Ilyaran witches the power of her domain.

Its other uses—destruction, warfare, death—were represented in much less detail, as if it was important to acknowledge them, but suggesting they were not the things the goddess wanted her gifts used for. Rasim, unsure of himself, said, "Your guild has been led astray, Goddess. I'd like to fix it, but I might need some help. They're not going to want me to guide their magic."

He sat down cross-legged, as close to the embers as he dared, and stretched his hands over them, feeling the heat and encouraging flame to lick upward. It did, but not painfully: each lick felt like a strand of power. Rasim took them slowly and began to braid them in the same way Desimi had done with the Seamasters' magic: making a rope.

Some of it came easily, almost curiously, as if the witches whose power he requested were fascinated by the idea of someone asking for it. Other strands were more neutral, like their wielders didn't know or didn't care that their magics were being gathered for a greater working. But many, many, *many* of them resisted, and Rasim, abruptly confident that any working with reluctant magic would be disaster, allowed himself to remain aware of those ones, but didn't try to do anything with them.

He could feel Pydasho's witchery specifically: it was so close, and so angry, and so very strong. Taishm's power kept Pydasho's lashes of sun magic from hitting Rasim, and he was certain the king protected Desimi in the same way. He had no idea how long Taishm could keep it up, and even less idea how long it would take to coax a guild into taming a dragon.

Up until that moment, Rasim hadn't realized that was his plan. It made a sort of sense, though: the dragon, drawn by fire magic, at least symbolized the renegade guild's rebelliousness He drew breath to suggest that Desimi do something similar, then decided he had plenty to deal with without doing Desimi's thinking for him. The other boy had already shaped an entire guild's magic into one working. He was ahead of Rasim in that regard.

A clash of metal turned his spine to ice. He twisted just long enough to see Lorens closing with Taishm, a flurry of blades in the middle of the focal room's floor. Horror seized Rasim by the throat and he turned back to his efforts, wondering how Taishm could possibly maintain two magical defenses and a physical one.

He should probably assume that the king couldn't, and get busy with his own part of this. It was harder, with swords smashing together and the sounds of grunting and fighting behind him, but a brief, soothing memory came to him: the calm quiet of fire in the darkness, as Oyun had shown him how to reach.

A thread of amusement wrenched through him, too, as he also remembered throwing up and voiding until his eyes watered, which hadn't exactly been calm. But finally finding the flame had been, and it was still there, waiting for him to return. Its gentle crackling helped drown out the fight, and it felt natural to bind the witchery he'd been offered to that internal flame.

It came to life with an enthusiasm and power he hadn't expected, creating a pull of its own. The least resistant of the sun witches were drawn to it, as if the bright magic overcame their reluctance. With each new working that joined Rasim's, someone else became intrigued, until the rope he had woven felt substantial and strong. There were still many sun witches who refused to join him, their convictions stronger than the pull of magic, but Rasim didn't think he needed them all. He only needed enough.

And he had enough, now. Enough to cast a web, or a net. A net, of course: he was a Seamaster at heart, and for all the politicking and fighting they'd been involved in the past year, the Seamasters were mostly fishermen, helping feed the tremendous city of Ilyara. Rasim knew how to weave a rope, and he knew how to weave a net from those ropes. That he was doing so with magic instead of fibers seemed almost inconsequential.

Pydasho's witchery crashed down on his when he tried to cast the net. Rasim cried out, shocked, and heard Taishm's grunting curse behind him. The Guild-master cackled, advancing toward Rasim, but suddenly, awfully, Kisia was there, her voice thin and defiant. "Not while I'm here."

She had water to use, Rasim realized. Like all the other quarters, the staggeringly beautiful moonstone carving of Siliaria was fronted by her element: a spring burbled through the pool at her feet. Kisia already had a working in hand, one element against another. Pydasho, incredulous and imperious, said, "You're an *apprentice.* Isidri's experiment. Her *pet.*"

He didn't know, Rasim thought. Pydasho didn't know yet that Isidri was dead, and he didn't know that invoking her name in that moment might be the worst thing he could possibly do in a room with three heart-broken sea witches. Kisia's voice went cold and certain and strangely adult. "Siliaria called me sister, witch. I invite you to try me."

Pydasho's witchery faltered as he gaped at the jour-neyman prepared to face a master in battle. In that moment, Rasim cast his rope—the net was gone, too hard to re-weave so fast—and as fire met water in a raging billow of steam, he lassoed a dragon.

THE LASSO DID NOT—THANK Siliaria—pull the dragon into the focus room, like a physical piece of rope might have. Instead, a connection opened between Rasim and the tremendous, injured beast, as if they were both creatures made of fire, which would always merge with itself if it could. They were one, and one of them was dying. The glasswing poison seeping deep in the dragon's blood would kill it soon. The wounds were hot spots, even in the midst of flame. Rasim was drawn to them, and found there was a part of himself that was still separate, after all. That part, impulsively, sent a lick of sun witchery into the nearest wound.

Power poured from him in a deadly rush, sucking magic into the injury. Hope flared inside him, a flame itself. He could heal the dragon, if he had enough time. He had no idea how much time had passed since he'd sat down at the Sunmasters' quarter in the focus room. It could have been seconds. It might have been hours. But if only he had a little more of it, he could heal the giant golden beast of its injuries, and *something*, at least, would be salvaged from all of this horror. He found another poison piercing in the dragon's hide, and sent sun witchery into it again. That same almost-sickening sensation of magic rushing out of him happened again, and a sharp certainty, clear as a voice in his head, rang through him.

This would take the sun witchery from him, burn it clean out of him as the cost of a healing beyond human comprehension.

"Take it all." He didn't know if he spoke aloud. He thought maybe he hadn't, any more than the voice in his head was exactly a voice. It was something speaking to him, though, and it was something listening.

"All I ever wanted to be was a sea witch, anyway. I don't need the air or fire or stone. Just the sea. Siliaria's gift to me." There were tears on his face, scalding away as if his skin had become fire too. "That's all I ever wanted. I'll give that up too, if I have to. Because it's not fair. It's not fair to let the dragon die because we're clumsy and dangerous and didn't know what we were doing. The glasswings and the thunder wolves can go back home into the wind and the lightning, they're less —they're less *physical*. They don't live in the world the same way we do, or the dragon does. It isn't fair to punish them for our mistakes. Take it all," he said again. "Let the dragon live."

The fire didn't go out: that would be too simple. Instead it flowed from him, burning brighter and brighter, using the strength of half a guild to shore up his offer. The dragon's gold-tinged blood felt like fire itself, drinking up the power it was offered, and one by one, the terrible dead spots, the murky places where glasswing poison roiled beneath the golden skin, burned away into healthy hide. Every patch of poison drew sun magic from the guild, and *out* of Rasim, draining the witchery from him. It felt like a bad cut, like blood being siphoned away, each pulse leaving him a little weaker.

Fire couldn't burn without air. The dancing power of sky witchery chased the sunmastery, feeding it as it poured through the dragon's huge body. For a moment, that draining strength touched on his sea witchery, but shied away again: water was fire's antithesis, and the dragon's healing wanted no part of it.

The beast was already stronger, wings beating more powerfully and its voice rising in relief above the city. There didn't seem to be any deadly glasswings to poison it again, which meant—a bolt of triumph rushed through Rasim, pulling a wild smile across his face. It meant Desimi had succeeded. All he had to do was finish healing the dragon, and then the city would no longer be under siege from monsters.

As if boosted by his sudden determination, there was a final rush of magic, all the power pouring into the dragon's wounds. Air and fire flickered in Rasim, and died. He fell back into his body as the dragon screamed with relief and gouted flame above Ilyara. Then, as the last of the guild magic he'd channeled loosened and fell apart, the dragon leaped higher into the sky, and with strong, desperate wingbeats, flew into the desert.

Its scream forced a lull in the focus room's fight, or at least in the physical battle between king and prince. Witchery still lashed, blurring the walls into invisibility with its speed, but Rasim, weak and shivering, pushed to his feet to watch Lorens fall back a step.

"You can't win like this," the Northern prince said in breathless astonishment as he panted from effort. "I have *Guildmasters* on my side. A decade-long *plan*. You have a weak king and a handful of children!"

Desimi gave a rough laugh as he came to flank Taishm opposite of where Rasim now stood. "You have a funny idea of weak."

"And I'm not a witchmaster, but I am a water witch." Kisia, jaw set with resolution, came to put her hand in Rasim's, and then took Desimi's. Her fingers were cold and her eyes were bright with fear and anger. "The way I see it, that makes us one whole King's Guild against a couple of masters and a prince without a kingdom. You should probably give up now."

Rasim, a little too honest for his own good, barely caught himself before blurting that he'd just given up all his sun witchery. Taishm still had all the magics, so Kisia wasn't *wrong*. She just wasn't right the way she thought she was. Pydasho and Jhikara both physically leaned in to their magics, determination now laced with panic as the possibility of losing everything loomed large. The whole room spun with power, air and fire doing battle with stone and water until he could barely see anything beyond the magic. He didn't even know who was working which witcheries on their side: he and Kisia wielded water, but whether it was Desimi or Taishm mastering fire, air, or stone, he couldn't tell. Not anymore. There was a hollowness inside him where the sun and sky witcheries had been, an almost-familiar sensation of having been drained beyond use. The *delzjha* had done that to his sea witchery. Rasim assumed the stone witchery was gone, too. He never had been able to sense it anyway. What he did feel was a weariness in his bones, and a hope it would all be over soon.

He was still hoping that when Yalonta, whose job had nothing to do with magic and everything to do with soldiering, slipped up behind the Northern prince and thrust a knife into his back.

CHAPTER TWENTY-FOUR

A shocked cry broke across the focus room as Lorens fell. Even the Guildmasters lost control of their power for a moment. Taishm made a snapping motion with one hand, as if physically cutting off their access to witchery. From the sudden enraged struggle on Pydasho's face, and the baffled, borderline amusement on Jhikara's, like she couldn't believe this was happening, Rasim thought that was exactly what the king had done.

Yalonta wiped her blade clean and knelt, placing it at Taishm's feet. "Forgive me, my king. He was the only one I could strike at."

"Ah." The small sound caught in Taishm's throat. "Under the circumstances, Commander, I believe even the Northlands will understand. You will receive no censure from me. Please stand. Open the door, and bid your guards to settle the restlessness in the city. We have had more than enough of war in Ilyara."

"Your majesty." Yalonta put her fist over her heart, then rose and strode away to do as she'd been told.

Taishm watched, regal and uncompromising, until a flash of irritation rushed over his face and he cursed. "That was so well done, I hate having to call anyone back. Yalonta?"

The commander turned in the doorway, her eyebrows elevated, and Taishm, annoyed, said, "Please have someone fetch heartbreak, too. I only figured out how to block a witch from their magic in the past few days, and I can't hold it forever. I need the wretched heartbreak, and didn't think of it until just now."

A little smile crawled across the corner of Yalonta's mouth. She was apparently entirely unbothered by just having killed a man, which Rasim supposed was a good trait, in a soldier. "I would have anyway, Taishm. Just give me a minute."

"Thank you." The king no longer sounded irritable, although his brief pleasure faded as he returned his attention to the two helpless Guildmasters and the dead prince between them. "This is not how I would have chosen for things to end."

"You wouldn't have chosen for any of it to start," Kisia said. "None of us wanted this to happen. Well, *they* did, but things haven't gone well for them, and really, I think that's much better than them winning."

Taishm, by degrees, turned his gaze toward her. "You're a ruthless child, aren't you, Kisia al Ilialio?"

"People keep telling me that. Pretty soon I'll start thinking I am, and then you'll all wish you hadn't."

The king examined her a moment, mouth pursed.

"You're a nice, kind, delightful, gentle young woman, aren't you, Kisia al Ilialio?"

Kisia burst out laughing, and suddenly, while nothing was really all right, things were much better than they'd been. Taishm drew all three journeymen into a hug. "You've done well, children. Exceptionally well. Thank you. I thank you, and Ilyara thanks you."

He also released them with a sigh, and, casting a glance at the Guildmasters, said, "I need to address the city, but I can't call up any other witchery while I hold these two down. Desimi, Rasim, could one of you conjure a little air witchery for me?"

Rasim, his stomach gone to knots, said, "I can't."

Taishm gave him a sympathetic nod. "You've done enough, lad. More than anyone could ever have asked of you. As have you, Desimi. If I need to wait until Yalonta returns with the heartbreak, another five minutes probably won't really matter."

"No, I can do it. But I think you need more than a little, if you're going to talk to the whole city." Desimi closed his eyes, and although this time he wasn't weaving the power of a guild, his hands still fell into the comforting motions of rope-making, until he was evidently content with his working. Rasim still couldn't feel it, and swallowed an unexpected lurch. He hadn't known he would miss the sensation of other people working magic.

Taishm murmured, "Thank you," and then with a full voice, warned Ilyarans—citizens, Sunmasters, and Skymasters alike—that the rebel Guildmasters had been arrested. Their coup was over, and anyone still fighting would be treated harshly by the city guard. Obviously conscious of the strain he was putting on a journeyman, he only spoke for a minute or two, and nodded his thanks again when he'd finished.

Desimi, with a relieved huff, shook his hands like he was releasing all the magic, and wrapped his fingers around the necklace Taishm had given him almost a year ago. "You're welcome. Can we—can we go home now? To the guildhall? It's just...everyone's going to be..." He obviously couldn't quite bring himself to say *mourning Isidri.* Rasim didn't want to say it aloud either.

Yalonta entered briskly, carrying vials and escorted by two positively enormous guards. She waggled one of the vials in front of Jhikara's face. "You can just go ahead and drink this, or they can pin you down, pinch your nose, and pour it down your throat. Your call."

Jhikara, lip curled, chose to drink it; Pydasho did not, and Rasim thought the two guards were rather glad of the chance to force the stuff into him. Like every other witchery drug Rasim had ever seen, heart-break worked fast. Within almost no time at all, Taishm relaxed as the two Guildmasters lost the ability to reach their witchery. Then, with a sigh, the king said, "Yes, of course, children. You can go home. If Guildmaster Asindo would let me attend Isidri's funeral, I would be grateful beyond words."

"You're the king," Kisia said. "He can't stop you."

Humor flickered over Taishm's face again. "You still don't like that, do you? The idea that I have the unearned power to rule, or place myself where I'm not necessarily welcome?"

Kisia looked around the room and a little grudgingly, muttered, "Maybe not *completely* unearned."

Taishm chuckled. "Well, thank you for that. And yes, I could come, and no one would stop me, but I'm not of your guild, Kisia. I don't actually have the right to be there, and I do have enough respect for your ways that I wouldn't want to be where I wasn't wanted."

Rasim said, "Thank you," before Kisia made it any worse. "We'll tell Asindo you'd like to come. It...I don't know when. Soon. We don't...linger."

"If you'll allow me, I'll send a guard with you to report back when it's decided," Taishm offered gently.

"Yeah. Yes. That would be good. Please." Rasim nodded jerkily, and Taishm gestured for Yalonta to find someone to send with them. They left the palace a little while later, knowing that the king might have sent them home in a carriage if the streets weren't destroyed. It was a long walk, all three journeymen quiet, although the city itself was anything but. Everywhere Rasim looked there was destruction and its aftermath, the injured and the dead and those left behind. Tears leaked down his cheeks as they walked, and Kisia put her hand in his. It helped a little.

Sunset came on as they reached the guildhall. Rasim stood at its closed gates, swaying so much he had to put a hand on the tall arched wood to steady himself. "It only started this morning. At sunrise."

Desimi spoke for the first time since they'd left the palace. "That's why you don't pick fights with witches."

"I guess so. That and the...the monsters." Rasim, still swaying, looked upward, trying to shape thoughts.

Ideas came halfway to him, then slipped away, his mind too tired to hold on to anything. "At least it's over now. Come on, help me with the doors."

Together, the three of them pushed the heavy doors open, and found whip-thin Captain Nasira, accompanied by Lady Donnin of the Islands, just on its other side. Nasira turned, something glinting in her eyes as she saw the journeymen, and her voice was both as sharp as ever, and desperately gentle. "There they are. Siliaria's fins, Journeymen, I didn't expect you to have all the fun without us!"

RASIM WHISPERED, "NASIRA?" hoarsely, and then in utter confusion, "Lady *Donnin?*" as the Islands leader, once a pirate, turned with smiling tears in her eyes.

"Rasim." She stepped forward to hug him, but Nasira got there first, pulling all three journeymen into a powerful embrace.

"How?" Rasim couldn't put more of a question together, but Nasira, chuckling roughly, understood.

"The Island nations were closer to where the *Wafiya* sank than anywhere else, and you had allies there. I convinced your Lady Donnin to sail us south—"

"By which she means she stormed in, demanded my ships, and put her witches to work on all of them so we made the journey in half the time my sailors would have," Donnin interrupted with wry amusement. Her silver-blonde hair was tied back in a complicated knot that looked like something a Seamaster would weave, and her fine-cut features were still so beautiful that Rasim thought she could stop a city by walking through it. She also seemed happier than she had the last time Rasim had seen her, and the way she looked at Nasira suggested the captain had something to do with it. "Your captain is a force of nature, Rasim."

"I know." Rasim tried not to make the words a sob, but it was a near thing.

Nasira shot an equally dry glance at the Islands lady. "We hoped we would sweep in to save the day, if it needed saving, but we came in late this afternoon to find the Northern fleet in pieces, along with half of Ilyara." Sorrow shadowed the hard lines of her face. "We heard about what Isidri did. Part of me wishes I'd been here to see it."

"No one who was will ever forget."

The captain nodded, then tilted her head toward the guildhall. "Let's bring you to Asindo. He'll be glad to see you're alive. As am I, Journeymen. All of you."

"Us too," Desimi said roughly. "I mean, you. Alive. You too. You know what I mean!"

"I do." A smile actually touched Nasira's lips as she nudged them into motion, although seconds later another choke of relief seized Rasim when the *Wafiya*'s first mate, Hassin, pulled him into a hug. His smile turned to bewildered tears as he caught a glimpse of Sunmaster Endat's round head.

"How can I be this happy and sad at the same time?"

He didn't expect anyone to hear him, much less answer, but to his surprise, Nasira's arm went around his shoulders. "That's the way of grief, lad. Not a soul among us is ready for life to keep going when someone we love dies, but we can't stop it, and we can't stop living in it. Isidri would understand." She snorted affectionately. "That old bat understood everything."

An awful snorting laugh of his own burst mostly from Rasim's nose, and Nasira grinned quickly at him. Then, bewilderingly, Milu was there, all elbows and knees, even in a hug. Rasim made a croaking sound of confusion and the Stonemaster journeymen set him back to grin hugely at him. "We watched you fly away and decided there was no way we were going to let you go back to Ilyara alone. Only when we got here there was a war going on, so we decided we'd better help with that."

Rasim, faintly, said, "We?"

Milu turned with an extravagant gesture, indicating not only Telun, who was to be expected if Milu was there, but an entire gathering of Shenryalans. One was unquestionably the earth witch Rasim thought he'd seen earlier in the day. Two others still wore the ill-fitting uniforms of Taishm's guard, and looked pleased with themselves.

"I did see... I thought I saw... *how?*" Rasim's head whirled so badly he tilted over sideways. Desimi grabbed him and set him on his feet again, but the big journeyman looked just as confused as Rasim felt.

Kisia, though, planted her hands on her hips and half glared, half grinned at the tall Stonemaster jour-neyman. "You thought 'what would Rasim do' again, didn't you? And you, no, wait, don't tell me!" She held up an imperious hand, gaze bouncing from the stone witches to the Shenryalan earth sorcerers, until her grin won out. "You woke that stone snake back up, didn't you. And you rode it to Ilyara."

Milu shouted with laughter, and then shouted in Shenryalan. All at once, the group of riders came to surround the journeymen, voices raised in excitement as they told their story in words Rasim mostly couldn't understand. Milu, talking through them, said, "That's what we did, yes, and it was the most exciting thing I've ever done. I'm only sorry we didn't get here sooner, and that there was so much destruction before we did."

"You did just fine," Rasim assured him dizzily, then gasped. "The hole in the city wall. That was you!"

Milu winced. "I misjudged how long it would take a snake that size to stop, and we...crashed, yes. But I'll fix it, I promise!"

Rasim said, "Thank you," helplessly, and then repeated himself in Shenryalan, to the obvious delight of the earth witches who had come to help Milu. A little vaguely, Rasim added, "I thought Shenryalans frowned on too much magic use."

"Apparently that rule only applies on the steppes." Milu grinned. "Out here in the rest of the world, well, the consequences are our problem to deal with."

Consequences, Rasim thought. Consequences like dragons, and glasswings. He nodded shakily, but, catching a glimpse of the Guildmaster, whispered, "I'd like to talk to Asindo, if you don't mind," and the Shenryalans let him go.

It took longer than he hoped to get to Asindo, and every step of the way told Rasim that Isidri's wasn't the only face missing. By the time he got to the Guildmaster's side, "Masira?"

"Tending to the hurt," Asindo replied swiftly. "Sesin is with her."

Relief exploded through Rasim's chest. He gave up trying to stand anymore, and didn't know if it was luck or someone's efforts that put a bench behind him when his knees gave out. "It's all so awful, Guildmaster. The city is so broken."

"Less than it might have been." Asindo sighed and sat beside him a moment, watching the grief-stricken revelries in the hall. "We needed the rest of our guild to come home, and everyone's heart is lifted for it, but there's so much loss. We'll sing the lost into the sea at sunrise, and again every day as long as we need to."

Rasim wiped tears from his eyes, to no avail. "Taishm wants to come sing for Isidri, if he's allowed."

The Guildmaster smiled. "Did he really think I'd say no?"

"I don't know," Rasim whispered. "I don't know anything anymore."

"You don't have to," Asindo said gently. "I'll send word to the king that he's welcome to join us. You should find your friends and sleep, Rasim. Dawn will come early."

"Everyone else is staying up, aren't they?"

Asindo looked thoughtfully over the hall. "Many will, yes. But none of them have had the—week?—that you have, Rasim. How long ago did the *Wafiya* sink?"

"I don't know," Rasim said again. "Maybe ten days ago. Captain Nasira would know."

"Ten days at most, then," Asindo said, still gentle. "The past ten days haven't been easy on anyone in Ilyara, but they've been harder on you than most. Rest. We won't let you sleep past the ships sailing."

Rasim tried one more time to find an objection, and instead, got up and went to bed.

CHAPTER TWENTY-FIVE

The morning came too early.

Rasim barely slept, but even if he had, he thought this particular dawn would have always come too early. If the sun didn't rise, then maybe somehow, impossibly, Guildmaster Isidri would still be with them. So when he woke after only a little sleep, long before daybreak, he just got up and went to the docks. There were hundreds of others already there, their restless, mourning feet having carried them to the harbor well before they needed to sail. The ships were readied in silence, and sailors filed onto them carrying bodies wrapped in clean white linen.

Isidri should have sailed to Siliaria's arms on the *Wafiya*, but it had died before her, as had the *Sinaz* and so many others. Asindo himself captained the *Bora*, the greatest of the ships the fleet had left, and all of the *Wafiya*'s crew sailed with him. Taishm was there, dressed in Seamaster colors out of respect, his face drawn and sad.

They hadn't even left the harbor's mouth before the sopranos began to sing, thin high voices stricken with grief. Their song, old as the guild itself, rose over Ilyara as the fleet made its way down a river still grey with morning twilight. The sky hadn't yet begun to color pink or gold, but the guild had been unable to wait.

They knew their river, though, and they knew their songs of mourning. They knew how long it would take to sail, and how long they had to sing in order to bring their dead home. It was a long time before the tenors joined in, filling some of the spaces broken by sobs as the sopranos sang. With their voices reaching toward it, the horizon blushed a sudden hot pink, and purple shot through the clouds. The altos came in as the ships reached the estuary, carrying the fleet out into the Ilyaran sea under a sky gone riotous with color. The sea itself was flat, as if it, too, mourned, but in doing so it reflected the deepening golds and reds of the early sky, until the baritones joined the song surrounded by the mirrored light of morning.

Witchery surged everywhere, the lightest and most delicate of magics, as gentle as the guild had been when they'd caught Isidri as she fell. One by one, the dead were given to Siliaria, as the basses finally brought their resonating voices to bear, and all but shook the surface of the sea.

There were so many. Rasim could barely draw breath, much less sing, but it would do the dead no good and no honor to break down now.. Still, there were so very *many* of their guild being offered to the goddess, and sung down into the depths of the water to find their rest in her arms. There were so many here and now, and so many others who had been lost over the past year, to serpents, to slavers, to age, and now to war. No one could sing long enough to fill the holes left by those losses.

There was a pause before Isidri's body was lifted from the *Bora*'s deck. Not a pause: a break. A silence, unlike any Rasim had ever heard in the mourning song, long enough that it was clear the ritual of it had ended.

Then someone began again, began anew, a single clear soprano voice. Rasim looked for it, and found Sesin, the healer's journeyman, in the *Bora*'s nest, eyes closed and tears streaming down her face as she sang.

One by one, range by range, they all began the song again, singing a fresh and singular goodbye to the Guildmaster who had served them so well for so very long. The sea, so quiet and still around the heartbroken fleet, finally began to stir, glassiness turning to gentle choppy waves that broke up the dawn reflections into fleeting things, glimpsed and then gone. Taishm, breaking from the song for a moment, chuckled tightly and murmured, "Stormbringer," as the waves grew in strength. "Remind me someday to tell you the story of your guildmaster, and my great-grandmother."

A few curious glances, including Rasim's, went his way, but only for a moment. Waves build around the ships as the baritones joined in the song again, and Rasim, in the breath of a phrase, whispered, "Sailors take warning," toward the red morning sky. Someone nodded, and the basses came in once more, deep and defiant of the growing storm. They would see Isidri laid to rest in Siliaria's arms, safely brought to the depths, where the goddess could embrace her as she deserved. A thrill of heartbreak and pride shivered through Rasim at that sensation of defiance, as if the guild would thwart the weather itself to do right by their guildmaster.

The sea churned again, hard enough to toss the ships, and resolution came into every voice and every strand of witchery being worked. Every witch in the guild worked as one to lift Isidri from the deck with threads of sea water, and to carry her gently over the rail to begin her descent into the sea. If it called monsters, so be it: this working would be shared no matter what.

Something happened inside the witchery, inside each and every delicate thread of magic. Something almost like Desimi's weaving of all their power together, but not quite. It felt more alive than that, Rasim thought. More primal, as if the sea itself had answered the Seamasters' song, and spread through their shared power to help them honor Isidri.

Desimi saw it first, and said, "Goddess's *ti—*" before strangling the curse in his throat as Siliaria herself rose from the sea to gather Isidri in her arms.

SHE WAS NOTHING, and everything, like Rasim remembered. A dolphin's tail and finned forearms, sleek dangerous points that were as much weapon as water-guiding. A woman's body, built of water that bubbled with power, and wild, wet hair that lashed around a face too remote to be human, but couldn't be seen as anything else. She was tremendous, inhuman in size, always changing, but this time she didn't carry her trident, or dive and disappear and reappear again. She simply rose up, and there was something in her ageless gaze that hadn't been there when Rasim first met her. Gentleness, maybe; maybe even youth. Kindness, and perhaps joy, if a goddess could feel such a thing. And sorrow: sorrow for this particular brief life's end, as if she had known and loved Isidri in life.

The guild had fallen silent, stricken with awe. Siliaria lifted her gaze, inhuman, depthless, ever-changing, and yet still so recognizable in grief, to look at them. Rasim swore she somehow, in that briefest of moments, looked at *each* of them, saw them all as individuals and as her chosen children.

He could have sworn, too, that there was a flicker of something in her eyes when they met his. Recognition, maybe, or acknowledgment stronger than what she shared with most of the others. He had forgotten how to breathe entirely, but didn't think it mattered. No one could breathe in the presence of the sea personified. It seemed as though the goddess's gaze landed on Kisia in the same way, a moment longer, a little heavier: something that said she knew them, and knew them well.

He might have imagined those stolen moments, though. He did *not* imagine that Siliaria swelled in size when she laid eyes on Desimi, her smile suddenly shark-sharp and full of teeth. Rasim didn't usually think of shark smiles as being delighted, but the goddess *grinned* at the powerful journeyman, and all of the fleet saw it.

Then she shrank back to the size she'd been—merely enormous, impossible, tremendous, rather than gargantuan—and flashed that silvery gaze around the guild again, this time expectantly.

For a heartbeat, Rasim had no idea what to do, but the answer came to him in sound, more than action. He began to sing again, taking the soprano line and starting their mourning song anew for the third time. This time, with the goddess waiting, the others joined in with each new line, until the basses rumbled, until the sea shook, until the world was nothing but air and sea and song.

Until, the Guildmaster's body cradled in her arms, Siliaria leaped high and dove deep, a spear of water to bring Isidri al Ilialio, beloved of the goddess, to her final rest.

CHAPTER TWENTY-SIX

A week of funerals passed. Bayar and his father
arrived with a small entourage; most of the
Shenryalan cavalry had chosen to go back home
instead of riding all the way in to Ilyara. They were
pleased to hear that Milu's plan and their earth witches
had helped to save the city, and reported that most of
the Moranese army had straggled home, no longer a
threat to anyone.

It was a week of Ilyara putting itself back together.
The Sunmasters not only needed a new leader, but to
rebuild their guildhall almost entirely after the dragon
rose from beneath it. Rasim heard that the Skymasters'
guild was doing a little better than that, at least, but
rumor had it both guilds were being shunned by most
of Ilyara's people. He hoped the city could find its way
to forgiveness, in time. For his own part, he didn't
think it mattered much. He wouldn't be studying with
the other guilds again.

Not even Desimi had been doing much with his

other magics. It felt as though the whole guild, maybe the whole city, just wanted to rest. The Stonemasters were at work, cleaning up and rebuilding. Seamasters helped when they needed dust and muck washed away, but otherwise…otherwise, Rasim thought, it was like everybody was a little afraid that using too much witchery would bring the monsters back. He was fairly sure it wouldn't, but he also didn't want to risk anything. Or worse, have to explain anything.

After four or five days, when the ships had returned from the morning's funeral sail, Kisia said, "Darrak," without any other explanation.

It took Rasim a minute to remember the tailor she'd healed during their first morning back in Ilyara. "You want to go see him?"

"I'd like to make sure he's all right." She managed the kind of fragile smile that seemed to be the best a lot of people could do these days. "I'd hate to have gone to all the trouble to help him just to find out a thunder wolf got him."

"Let's go," Desimi said. "We haven't been out of the guildhall in days." That wasn't exactly true, even if Rasim didn't count the sailing out to bury their dead every morning. They had gone to see Kisia's family, who had escaped the battle safely, although the buildings across the street from them had been smashed. The bakery had been running all day and all night since the war, handing out food to anyone who needed it. They, like everyone else, were exhausted, but there seemed to be a certain strength in pulling together. The bad times would end, if they helped each other out.

But it had been days, at least, since they'd been very far from the guildhall, so they went, the three of them picking their way quietly through a city that had grown back together in the time they'd been shut away. Rasim, watching a stone witch work to restore a shop, said, "We should offer help to Moran. It'll take them decades to recover, otherwise."

"You want to help the people who just tried to invade us?" Desimi asked incredulously.

Rasim sighed. "Part of me does. It's just so easy for us, Desi. In a few years, no one will know Ilyara nearly fell, but it'll be obvious in Moran for maybe the rest of our lives."

Kisia sniffed. "I don't know how long *you're* planning to live, but *I* intend to outlive Isidri. Even ordinary stonesmiths can rebuild a city in a hundred years."

"But it would be a lot faster if we helped." Rasim stopped arguing, though, if that was even what it was. He was starting to accept—well, not accept. He didn't think he would ever really accept that people didn't always believe help and kindness were the best thing to offer others. But he was starting to understand that not everyone felt that way.

"No way." Kisia's voice rose and she surged ahead of the boys a few steps. "That's Darrak, isn't it? In front of that shop? The one we got arrested in? *That's* his shop?"

"Woo." Desimi sounded impressed. "Didn't he say he'd make you some clothes in thanks? You'd better take him up on it. There was some nice stuff in there."

Rasim, fussing over details, muttered, "We were arrested in the cellars, not in his shop," but he knew what Kisia meant, and figured he deserved the glare she gave him before running off to greet the clothier. His face lit with joy, and he beckoned all three of the journeymen in to look over the cloth and clothes he had, and to offer them tea as he offered his sympathies on Isidri's death. Kisia was in high spirits when they left, and even Rasim felt better. They had saved someone, at least. They'd made a difference. He knew they'd made a lot of difference, but somehow seeing it in the shape of one single person helped.

At the end of a week, Taishm called them to the palace. He called everyone: Guildmasters, visiting dignitaries, even Captain Nasira. Yalonta herself escorted Rasim and his friends. Kisia politely asked the commander of the guard if she would like to put them in chains this time, too, and for a minute, Rasim really thought Yalonta would.

The throne room was full when the arrived, and fully formal. The journeymen wore their best tunics, and Desimi had his necklace, a mark of the King's regard, on the outside. Kisia had chosen not to wear a blouse under her tunic so the Shenryalan clan tattoo on her shoulder could easily be seen. Rasim felt a little underdressed, next to the two of them.

Bikat and Bayar wore their formal clothes, too, sky blues on Bikat and burnt oranges for Bayar, both lined with fur that had to be sweltering on an Ilyaran summer morning. Donnin's silver-green silk gown looked more suitable for the weather, but her pale face was already bright pink with the heat.

There were dozens, maybe hundreds, of people

Rasim didn't know, but Telun and Milu were there, which settled him a little. Sunmaster Endat, whom Rasim had barely seen since he returned with Nasira's crew, was now wearing Guildmaster robes. He nodded a grave greeting to the Seamaster journeymen, and Rasim, his heart hammering, nodded back. Endat had been friends with Lorens a long time. Rasim didn't know if elevating him to Guildmaster was good or bad.

Everyone else was indistinguishable in the swirling mass, which came to attention as Taishm arrived in the room. Without preamble, he beckoned Rasim, Kisia and Desimi forward, then, as if actually at a loss for words, said, "Well."

Rasim blurted, "I've been thinking," and the people who knew him laughed quietly. There were enough that the sound echoed through the throne room, making it seem more friendly for a moment.

Asindo, a few steps away and grinning, said, "We're not really laughing *at* you, lad."

"I know." They were, but he couldn't blame them. Him thinking was—well, not what had gotten them all into this in the first place, but certainly it was what had drawn attention to him, and kept it there for most of a year. "Still, I was thinking. About all of this, your majesty. About what happened in Ilyara, and why it happened. We know everywhere used to have quite a lot of witchery. A long time ago. Hundreds of years now, I think. And almost everyone has stories about monsters. Sea serpents, dragons, even the thunder wolves. I remember now."

He hesitated, glancing over his shoulder in search

of Northerners. Not enough time had passed since the battle for word to reach Queen Janna and Princess Inga, never mind for them to have come to Ilyara themselves. After a moment, Rasim shrugged and looked back at the king. "They had murals in the palace in Hongrunn. Mythological fights and heroic deeds. I didn't know what they were when I saw them back then, but there were lightning beasts in the paintings. Thunder wolves. So we have stories, is what I'm saying. Stories about ancient, magical monsters, even in places that don't have any witchery anymore."

Taishm's eyes were thoughtful. "Go on."

"I would have to ask someone *why* the North lost its magic. But I think it was because the creatures are drawn to it. The more you use at once, the more likely you are to call something. So it was dangerous. And probably a lot of witches died, until it just wasn't worth it anymore."

"But Ilyara," Taishm said, still thoughtful.

An odd burst of enthusiasm suddenly rushed through Rasim and he took a few steps forward, gesturing. "That's the question, isn't it? Why has Ilyara stayed so full of witchery for so long, when *everywhere* else has lost it? Your majesty, how old are the guilds?"

The king blinked. "As old as Ilyara. You know the stories, Rasim. Everyone does. 'Across the earth came Stonechild and Sky, fathers to all of the kings, by and by.'" He didn't quite sing the ancient lullaby. "The gods gave us four witcheries and told us to build four guilds around them. To take the orphans of the city into the guilds and teach them the magics. To ask those who left the guilds for other lives to forswear witchery."

"But we don't just ask them, do we? We insist. We give them heartbreak so they can't even use their magic anymore, and if they have children, we forbid them to teach them witchery." Rasim shook his head. "I don't think the gods told us to do all that. I think regular people who had seen what magic did were looking for a way to still use it without the side effect of…monsters."

Taishm leaned forward, fingers laced, gaze bright and interested, as if he and Rasim were the only two people in the room, and their conversation was between equals. Almost. Taishm did still sit on the throne, after all. "You think we've stayed strong because our witchery is so strictly regimented, is that it? Because we have no witchmasters, only masters of each particular witchery? Then what about my family, Rasim? The royal family has always been able to work all the magics, as far back as time remembers."

"But that's exactly it." Rasim stepped forward again, even more eagerly. "That's what I've been thinking about. The guilds not crossing over at all, that makes a kind of sense, doesn't it? Even if there are thousands of guildmembers, we hardly ever all work magic at the same time, and even less often all in the same place. But once in a while we do, and what do we do then? What are we supposed to do?"

Taishm sat back, fingers steepled as he examined Rasim. "Great workings are channeled through the king. Or queen. A single vision, guiding the witchery.

My cousin Laishn wasn't here during the Great Fire, so —" Pained recollection swept his face as he recalled the Sun guild's betrayals, but with a sigh, he went on. "Everything else aside, without the crowned monarch here, no one believed a magical working to end the fire could even be done."

"And that's the point," Rasim said. "I think using a witchmaster makes the witchery less…noticeable. To monsters, I mean. So that's the royal family's job."

"Because it's only one person working magic," Kisia said a little too loudly, like she'd just leaped to where Rasim was going. "I felt it when Desimi gathered the guild's witchery. *I* wasn't working any magic. I was just opening the channel to it, so he could draw on it. It felt weird," she added, then realized she'd drawn everyone's attention and shrugged. "That makes sense, Rasi."

He grinned crookedly at her. "I thought so. I've been thinking about it all week."

"Without talking about it?" Desimi snickered. "That must have been hard. Usually you say whatever you think as soon as you think it."

"Sometimes I say what I'm thinking before I even know I've thought it," Rasim said wryly. "I was trying really hard not to this time."

Another low laugh ran around the throne room as Taishm studied the three journeymen. "There are archives of Ilyara's early days. They haven't been studied in a long ti—"

He closed his eyes, briefly very human and ordinary before his eyebrows twitched up and his tone changed to chagrin. "No, of course they haven't been studied in a long time, because the Sunmasters are the royal record keepers. If this is true, and Pydasho was aware of any of it, he wouldn't have wanted these things to be remembered. Although perhaps if he'd explained any of it, I would have been less eager to try the King's Guild. He counseled against it."

"He counseled against it because he was trying to take over. Anything that shared power risked his!" Rasim, forgetting he was talking to a king, snapped the words, and from the corner of his eye saw both Bikat and Bayar bite their lips against grinning. "Uh. I mean. Your maj…" He gave up, partly because Taishm looked amused and mostly because he wasn't going to find his way out of that.

"Wait." Telun spoke, and sounded surprised at himself, but also dismayed. "Wait, does this mean I have to stop doing sky witchery? I was just starting to get good at it."

Three people spoke at once, including Rasim, whose, "Oyun said balance was as important as power," was lost under Taishm's, "That may be," and Milu's, "Or you could give up stonemastery, my love. It never suited you anyway."

"Oh." Delight splashed over Telun's face. "Oh, that's a good idea. Except…no, not if it means I have to go live with the Skymasters. You wouldn't be there. I'd rather be a poor stone witch than without you."

Milu ducked his head to murmur something in Telun's ear, and laughter spilled across the broad journeyman's face. He whispered something in return, and they leaned on each other, both looking satisfied.

Taishm, wryly, said, "I see I've complicated things far more than I meant to. Balance," he added, examining Rasim. "Are you balanced now, Journeyman?"

"It doesn't matter anymore." Rasim's hands went cold, shaking all of a sudden, as if he was about to confess to a terrible crime. "When I guided the Sun Guild's witchery, I decided to heal the dragon with it, so it could live and leave Ilyara alone. But it…it drained everything but my sea witchery, I think. I knew it would. A…a voice said so in my head, and told me I had to choose." That wasn't exactly right, but it was close enough, and he didn't know how else to explain it. "So of course I chose to save the dragon. I never wanted anything but to sail on the *Wafiya* anyway."

"Of course you did," Desimi muttered. "Of *course* you did, because…of course you did!" He threw his hands in the air, completely exasperated. "Why do you have to be so *good*, Sunburn?"

"But no!" Kisia's voice shot up in genuine distress. "No! You can't have done that! You can't be not a witchmaster! You have to be, because you're the heir to the throne!"

"*What?*" Rasim backed away from her and would have crawled up the throne room wall to escape the accusation, if he could have. The thought *had* crossed his mind during the battle, but he'd made himself not think about it. It was far too awful to contemplate. "I'm not! I don't want to be! I never wanted to be!"

"You've been working all our witcheries since all of this began!" Kisia protested. "I've been trying to tell you all along! I've been trying to tell you since Shenryal that you were the heir! Look at what you've done, Rasim! You got yourself out of the fire jail in the palace basement, you set the *Wafiya*'s ropes on fire—"

"I did not do that!"

"—you kept using sky witchery to make yourself heard during storms and fights, you made the—" She actually broke off, although Rasim knew what she'd been going to say. He had sculpted a memorial to the witches who had died in the Northlands, hidden from where anyone could see it. He was grateful she didn't mention it aloud, because he didn't want that to be known about, not unless someone discovered it accidentally.

The silence where she reworded her accusations barely lasted a moment, though. "—the shelter for Sesin on the stone roof in Hongrunn, and she said you shaped a window frame so she could fit through, too! And nobody ever *saw* the heir die, Rasim! He was lost in the fire, just like everybody else, but he wasn't lost! He's you! You're the heir to the Ilyaran throne!"

"I'm afraid he's not," Taishm said with rolling amusement in his voice. "I'm sorry, Kisia, but you're mistaken. Rasim isn't the heir to the Ilyaran throne." He paused. "Desimi is."

"What?"

Rasim didn't think he'd ever heard one word come out of so many mouths at the same time. Nasira, Asindo, Milu, Telun, Donnin, Adele: nearly everyone who had ever met Desimi blurted that *What?* all together, mostly in shock. Rasim's had been relief, he was sure of it, but Kisia's was pure outrage. Desimi himself barely whispered the word as he went grey with shock. Rasim grabbed for him, afraid the bigger boy would fall over. Desimi staggered and leaned, turning horrified eyes to Rasim, who immediately felt guilty at his own relief.

Behind them, around them, the throne room absolutely burst into sound, almost as loud as the Moranese arena. There were fewer people, to be sure, but there was a roof to hold the noise in as voices rose in excitement, bewilderment, anger, disbelief, even joy. Rasim, holding half of Desimi's weight, turned an incredulous look on Taishm, who had a tiny, tight grin, as if he'd enjoyed that very much indeed.

Sunmaster—*Guildmaster*—Endat was now at Taishm's side with a slightly bigger grin, his round face and dark eyes sparkling with delight. Dizziness swept Rasim as he realized that, given his gleeful expression, the Sunmaster must have known.

Even more astonishing, though, were the similar grins on Bayar and Bikat's faces. Bayar was beaming with smug elation, while Bikat was clearly trying very hard to look serene and knowledgeable, but completely failing. His own grin was nearly as big as his son's. *They* had known. Rasim, gaping at them, suddenly remembered the Shenryalan shaman sniffing Desimi repeatedly, and finally re-weaving her silks around her hands in some kind of acknowledgment. He said, "Siliaria's fins, Oyun knew," out loud, although in the cacophony, only Desimi and Kisia could hear him.

Kisia had come to support Desimi, too, although her expression was still one of pure outrage. Her jaw dropped, though, when Rasim spoke, and she hissed, "Siliaria's *teeth*, she *did* know!" in equal parts fury and amazement. "*You* knew!" she said across Desimi to Bayar and Bikat, whose huge smiles were completely unrepentant.

"I can't be royal," Desimi croaked. "I'd be terrible at it. Rasim should be. You're me," he told Rasim, wide-eyed. "You're Desimi. I've been Rasim all along, we got it backward. Or he did. He can't be right. This can't be right. I can't be *royal*."

"I can't *believe* I didn't see it." Kisia's outrage turned

on herself, suddenly. "Of *course* you are. You've been —*you* set the *Wafiya*'s ropes on fire!"

"I—" Desimi was far too dark to blush visibly, but Rasim, still supporting half his weight, was close enough to feel heat flare in the other boy's face before he slumped. "Yeah, I did. I knew it, too. Or I was afraid I knew it. But it seemed a lot more likely to be Rasim!"

Rasim mumbled, "I guess that's kind of fair," but Kisia was on a tear, frustrated with herself.

"I've been sure—I was sure for practically the whole last year—that it was you, Rasim! I *knew* it was you! I've been trying to tell you for weeks!" Her jaw set resolutely. "I will *never* make this kind of mistake again."

"Well." Rasim blinked at her neutrally. "Really, you're not very likely to ever have the chance to make this *particular* kind of mistake again."

Kisia's eyes narrowed. "Shut up."

Rasim, despite himself, grinned hugely at her, and Desimi wailed, "Stop being so *yourselves* when I'm not me anymore!"

Taishm, still grinning, rose and patted down the noise in the throne room. It quieted slowly, but once silence fell, Rasim thought it would hold tight. No one wanted to miss a word of what the king had to say. "In your defense, Kisia," Taishm began, "until very recently I thought you were right, myself."

Astonishment exploded across the throne room again, proving Rasim wrong. This was too big to keep quiet about, especially with a new revelation coming with every sentence. Because if Taishm had thought Kisia was right, that meant—

"I knew my nephew had survived."

Another roar went around the room. Taishm waited it out, with a steady, sympathetic smile for Desimi, who still couldn't stand up without Kisia and Rasim's help. "Not at first," the king was finally able to say. "Not for some years. Not until long after the Great Fire and Laishn's death. Sunmaster Endat was a counselor to Laishn and Annaken before the fire, and knew their son was extraordinarily gifted in sea witchery. And Annaken's rooms weren't far above the river."

Taishm closed his eyes, mouth working briefly as he pushed back old grief freshly remembered. Tears glittered in the corners when he opened them again, a broken smile on his lips. "So Endat hoped that perhaps she'd risked everything for her son, and given him to the Ilialio. He spent years watching the Seamasters' Guild, hoping there might be a child who showed the same potential as that lost little boy. Desimi did, obviously, but Desimi, I'm sorry, you really don't look very much like either of your parents. Now that I know it's you, you have the stamp of my grandfather so strongly on your features I can't believe I didn't see it, but until I knew…" The king made a rather helpless gesture. "Laishn and Annaken were both slightly built, and with her Northern blood, we thought the copper-skinned boy with less obvious talent was most likely to be the heir, if he'd survived at all."

Desimi spoke to his uncle for the first time, a trace of bitterness in his croaking voice. "Especially because Rasim is quick, and you wanted a clever heir."

"I have a clever heir," Taishm said wryly. "I've been

informed by any number of people in the past week, as they've related your adventures from their points of view, that you're maturing into an intelligent, thoughtful young man. You might not come by it quite as naturally as Rasim does, but gods help us all if you did. I don't think Ilyara could survive two Rasims."

A genuine laugh went through the throne room. Rasim ducked his head, and Desimi, for the first time in several minutes, gained the strength to stand up on his own. "Why did you leave—" He glanced at Rasim and made a face. "Us? There. If you thought one of us might be your heir?"

"Because the Sunmasters had no time for me." A smile touched Taishm's face with the same bitter trace Desimi's voice had shown. "Because in so far as I have a particular talent, it's skymastery, and while I was trained adequately, I was clearly not favored by my own counselors, even when I became king. I knew it then, and it's even more abundantly clear now. Leaving you—whichever of you it was—in the Seamasters' Guild was the only way I could think to allow you to grow into your talents."

"What if we hadn't been able to learn other witcheries later?" Desimi stared at Taishm, verging on offense. "You could have messed Ilyara up for generations! What were you thinking?"

"That it was worth the risk. Ilyara hasn't needed a major working *in* generations, Desimi, save for the Great Fire, and that was orchestrated in so many ways that it might not even count. Naisha was the last Ilyaran queen to channel a guild, and there is—no one left who remembers her, now." Taishm's expression broke as he recalled Isidri's death, and this time the rush that went through the gathering was one of sorrow and remembrance.

Desimi muttered, but gave a grudging shrug of acceptance that made Taishm grin. "Never lose that edge of challenge, Desimi. It'll make you a good king, someday."

Pure horror wiped the acceptance off Desimi's face again, but before he could speak, Rasim said, "How did you know? You said you just figured it out. When? How?"

Taishm chuckled. "Your silks, Desimi, the ones from Shenryal. Do you have them?"

"Uh." Desimi dug the beautifully braided bright strips of cloth from his belt pouch and offered them to the king, who spread them across his hands. "You showed these to me in the cellars under the city. The last time I'd seen anything like them was when Laishn returned from Shenryal. He cast them aside, as he did all the mantles of kingship, but he did say they were a gift given from one royal family to another, in Shenryal. And they had been given to you. My heir. And then, *knowing* you were my heir, I sent you into the teeth of danger again, because you three children have shown an astonishing ability to turn the world upside down. I am so very sorry," Taishm said unhappily. "And so very grateful."

"Well, you're welcome, but—why could Rasim do all that magic, if he's *not* the heir?" Kisia demanded. "Nobody else is supposed to be able to do that!"

"I don't know. There's no way for us to know who his parents were, but—"

"Oyun didn't sniff the royal in me," Rasim said. "Maybe it was just because I was unbalanced, Kees. She said—oh! Oh, it was right there and I never saw it. I'm a sun witch, Kisia. Or I was. Naturally. That's what Oyun said. And Pydasho told us days ago that the Ilyaran heir was a natural sea witch. It couldn't have been me, ever." Relief made him so dizzy he forgot how to talk for a moment, although Kisia glowered with frustration. "Um. But the Great Fire, it made me afraid of fire, and besides that, the Seamasters' Guild found me. So I was out of balance. Maybe that's all it ever was."

"Or perhaps Ilyaran blood and Northern mixed together makes good witchmasters," Taishm said. "We have proof of two such talents here. But given what we've learned—or re-learned—about the dangers of witchmastery, it's probably not something we should experiment with."

Another laugh rippled around the room, although this one was tinged with nervousness. Taishm came down off the throne's dais to put his hand on Desimi's shoulder. "I promise you, Desimi, I'll give you time to adjust to this. You won't take over an heir's duties and life overnight, and you can stay at the guildhall until you're ready to take up those duties. That said," he said with a glance over their heads at the tightly-packed throne room, "I'd like to suggest you stay here a few hours or even overnight, until this mob clears out and some of the city's excitement has calmed down, because it's going to be…fraught, for a little while."

Desimi, desperately, said, "Are you *sure* you didn't make a mistake?"

Taishm took his hands and placed the Shenryalan silks over them. "I'm afraid I'm very sure, nephew."

Rasim's heart clenched and Desimi, suddenly teary-eyed, bolted the single step forward into Taishm's arms at that word. "Nobody in the guild has aunts and uncles," he said hoarsely. "Not really. Nobody could ever call me nephew like that and mean it the same way you do."

The king curled his hand around Desimi's shoulders and lowered his head over the boy's. "Welcome to the family, Desi."

"*Daishimi,*" Kisia said with sudden delight. "They're going to call you *Daishimi* now, Desi. It's almost as good as Keesha becoming Kisia!"

Desimi raised his head, his eyes wet, and glared half-heartedly at her. "Keesha *decided* to be Kisia. It's not really the same. Do I have to be Daishimi?" He looked up at the king, who shrugged.

"The people will use it, even if you don't, because it's the royal styling of your name. Either way, you'd best get used to it."

Desimi slumped and gave Rasim a baleful look. "This is your fault."

Rasim grinned. "Probably. Just this one last time, though. After this, you're the prince and I'm just a Seamasters' journeyman, so anything else is definitely your fault."

"The worst part is that almost makes sense." Desimi glanced over his shoulder at the throng of loudly-chattering courtiers, who were mostly being kept back by a wall of Guildmasters and dignitaries. "Maybe we should get out of here before they roll Guildmaster Asindo over."

Kisia cackled. "I'd like to see them try!"

"*I*," Taishm said firmly, "would *not*, so yes, please, go hide a while and come to terms with this, children. And you may find yourself some new clothes, if you look."

Rasim and Kisia exchanged startled glances. "All of us? You must have known you were going to tell Desimi, but—"

"Actually, I had no intention of telling him in front of a crowd of hundreds. Kisia forced my hand. But I did hope to talk to him today, yes, and I'm not foolish enough to imagine that even at thirteen, my heir would want to be without his closest advisors."

"I knew it!" Kisia caroled triumphantly. "I knew you'd end up in the palace, Rasim!"

"Because you thought I was royalty!"

She waved a hand. "Details! I was still right!"

"Go!" Taishm pushed them toward the doorway he'd come in through, off behind the throne. Rasim went a little reluctantly. It held memories for Rasim that the others didn't share. Lorens had killed Roscord there, and seconds later, lied about it to Rasim's face. He wished that he had listened to his doubts about the Northern prince, but also knew that without the proof they'd finally gotten of Lorens's betrayal, no one would have wanted to believe him.

There *were* clothes laid out for them, but before they got to them, the door opened again and most of the sea witches who had been in the throne room followed them, as did Bayar and Bikat. Desimi immediately turned to Asindo, his hands clenched and his voice rough with worry. "Did you know?"

Asindo studied him a moment before answering. "No. But I think Isidri did. Maybe from the beginning, given that she seemed to know everything. But before her last battle? I'm almost certain of it. She wouldn't let you fight, remember? Perhaps not *just* because you were a journeyman and she was a master, Desimi. Perhaps she knew what she was preserving, in you."

"She did know," Rasim said abruptly. "Remember what she said, Desimi? When you were trying to figure out how to guide the whole guild's magic? She said you were born to this. She knew. She knew, Desi, and she was proud of you."

Desimi stared at him a moment, eyes gone terribly bright before he said, "I'm not cut out to be a prince, Guildmaster," to Asindo.

"No. Not yet. But you will be, Desimi. I'm confident of that," the Guildmaster said reassuringly

"*Why?*"

Kisia drew attention with a dramatic shrug. "Because if you didn't have it in you, they would have lied and said it was Rasim after all."

Everyone in the room, including Sunmaster—Guildmaster—Endat, who had just entered, focused on her, which didn't seem to bother her at all. It bothered Rasim quite a lot as their gazes bounced back and forth between him, Desimi, and Kisia while they tried the idea on for size. Eventually, Endat said, "What was that you said about ruthless, Nasira?" and the adults in the room broke out in chuckles. "We hadn't actually considered that," Endat told Kisia. "But I'm both admiring and alarmed that you did."

"How long have *you* known?" Desimi asked the new Guildmaster.

"Since Shenryal. Not because of the ribbons," Endat said with a lift of his eyebrows. "When you shaped earth witchery, though, I thought that was beyond an ordinary 'witchmaster' skill."

"But I shouldn't have been able to do that, either."

"Milu, an Ilyaran-trained stone witch, can shape earth, just as Isidri, a sea witch, could shape ice. There's some crossover, and, as I believe you said to Rasim, it was important." Endat smiled. "I'm sure we'll have a great deal of time to talk later, Desimi. I merely wanted to wish you good luck, and say congratulations."

Voices chimed in, agreeing, although Rasim thought Desimi looked like congratulations were the last thing he wanted, and that good luck had obviously passed him by when he was announced the heir to the throne. He still tolerated being jostled and embraced, at least mostly: when it came to be Bikat and Bayar's turns, he muttered, "I'm never forgiving you for this," into their hugs, which made Bayar laugh.

"I've lived with this kind of burden all my life. There are worse things, Desimi." The short young man put his hands on Desimi's shoulders, looking up at him with intense solemnity. "I believe you will do well by your people, Prince Daishimi. You listen, and you learn, and although you try to hide it behind a frown and a gruff exterior, you care. It will be the honor of the Horse Clans to welcome you to Shenryal once again, when you are grown."

Desimi nodded roughly. "I'd like that. I'd like it."

Within a minute or two, everyone else had slipped out of the room except the three journeymen. Kisia bounced toward the clothes, but Desimi said, "Wait!" in a shaky voice. Rasim looked at him, surprised and Kisia turned back with a worried frown between her eyebrows.

"Desi?"

"You're not going to—" Desimi's voice cracked and he cleared his throat, although the next attempt didn't come out much better. "You won't—I mean, you're not going to—"

"Leave you alone to deal with all of this?" Rasim asked in sudden understanding. Desimi barely managed a nod, his eyes huge with fear, and a little to his own surprise, Rasim went over to hug him tightly. Kisia squirmed into the hug, and Rasim mumbled, "No, of course not. Statue."

A burst of laughter rolled through all of them as Desimi bent his head over theirs. "Well, all right, then. I guess it'll be all right, then."

And it was.

Prince Daishimi, witchmaster and heir to the Ilyaran throne, still called Desi by his friends, stood on a very thin stretch of mountain shore on the great lake above the Northern city of Hongrunn, his arms folded across his broad chest in a hug. He had grown more in the past year, remaining a stubborn head in height above Rasim, although Rasim had finally shot up and was taller than Kisia, who resented it.

All three of them had cloaks on over their long-sleeved shirts, tunics, and warm trousers. Kisia was wearing fur-topped boots. Princess Inga laughed every time she saw them all bundled up, and Rasim shivered every time he saw her in a sleeveless tunic and light trousers. Northern summers were cold, no matter what Inga or Hassin, who seemed to have gotten used to it easily, said.

"It's beautiful, Rasim. You should let other people see it." Daishimi walked carefully beneath the shaped stone memorial that Rasim had worked nearly two years ago. It had never been meant to last: the spindly bewitched rock that rose up to make a partial dome above the memorial's human figures were too fragile for Northern winters. Rasim had known it at the time, but was still a little surprised that a couple of the dome sections had broken already.

None of the people had, though. The stoneworked memories of Stonemaster Lusa, of Journeyman Daka, of so very many others, were still whole, and that settled Rasim's heart a little. He didn't want them to fall away *that* fast. "I'd rather let someone discover it someday, if it's still here at all."

"Not likely," Kisia murmured. "They don't sail on this lake much, even though it's beautiful. I'd take a little coracle out all by myself and paddle around in all that blue. They'll probably never find it." The journeymen had used seamastery to carry them across the glacier-colored lake and around the juts of mountain that separated Rasim's memorial from the main shore.

"That's the point," Rasim said. "If they discover it, that's fine. But it should be a discovery. I don't know why. Because that's what I wanted when I shaped it." His voice had changed and still startled him sometimes, especially when he heard it bouncing back in echoes, deep and strange.

"I know. But I think you should let them know about it. At least other Ilyarans." Daishimi, with a glance at Rasim for permission, found a space beneath the broken dome a little distance away from the grouping of stone people.

Witchery lifted a new addition to the memorial

with smooth, confident ease. Daishimi didn't try to make his sculpture look like the thin, over-stretched people Rasim had shaped. His was a much more realistic rendition of Seamaster Usia, the guild's beloved healer, whom they had finally learned died the day of the slaver raid. "He was a healer," Daishimi said in a low voice. "He should last a long time."

"You've gotten really good at that," Kisia said just as quietly. She'd grown, too, and her hair, jaw-length now when straightened, was currently tucked under a hat she'd been given in Shenryal. "You could be a real artist, Desi."

"I'll leave that to Milu."

"Milu is an architect at heart, not an artist. He's still arguing with Taishm about whether Ilyara should be redesigned from the ground up."

"Ilyara's fine," Rasim said as they turned back to the water. "He should go to Moran."

"You're still on about that," Daishimi said impatiently. "I *did* talk to my uncle about it, you know."

"I know you haven't pushed him, because if you did, he'd agree." Rasim's own hair, always less curly than the other two's, wasn't safely under a hat, and blew into his face as wind swept off the water. It wasn't long enough to pull back yet, but was much too long to stay out of the way. If he couldn't start his journeyman's braid soon he thought he might lose his mind.

"I'll push him if you'll let me shape a trail out to this memorial."

Rasim glared at him. Not much had changed, really, since Daishimi had become the heir. His name, of course, but he was still annoying and pushy and getting smarter all the time. "That's playing dirty, *Statue.*"

Daishimi gave him a sunny smile. "Depends on how much you believe in your equality for everybody, including people who put you in slave chains, *Sunburn.*"

"You two are going to be seventy years old and still bickering like apprentices, aren't you?" Kisia said with a roll of her eyes. "People will say to me, 'Tell me, Guildmaster Kisia, were they always like this?' and I'll have to say 'Only as long as I've known them.'"

"Guildmaster!" Daishimi hooted. "Don't let Asindo hear you say that! He's got a lot of years left in him yet!"

"And I've got a lot of years of learning ahead of me. Go on, Rasi. Let him make the trail."

"*Fine,* but it has to be at least a little bit hidden, all right?"

"Fair, and I'll make it narrow enough that it's impassable in the winter. How's that?"

Rasim bared his teeth in a mockery of a grin. "Ugh, I hate it when you're all negotiate-y and reasonable. Yeah, that would be good." They ended up following Daishimi as he shaped a narrow passageway, wending it through the mountain until they came out on the lake's main beach. With a gesture, the young prince did something to the rock face that made the passage's entrance disappear even though Rasim was looking right at it. He stepped forward cautiously, hands lifted to find where the entryway had gone.

Kisia gave a sudden shrieking laugh. "You're in the mountain!"

"What?" Rasim looked to his right, finding granite

there, and to his left, where the passage bent away into the stone. "You made an illusion! That's perfect, Des!"

"Good." Desimi sounded satisfied. "Now come on, we'd better hurry. We're going to be late to the wedding, and Taishm says it's very rude for visiting royalty to be late to things."

"Oooh, well, if visiting royalty can't be late…!" Kisia's voice rose and fell teasingly before she bolted down the mountain, the boys on her tail. They didn't want to be late anyway: they'd only attended one royal wedding before, a few months earlier, when Taishm had finally done with they'd all suspected he'd wanted to for a while, and married Commander Yalonta. She was no longer Commander, of course, although she actually twitched any time someone called her 'Queen.' She and Daishimi had turned out to have a lot in common, starting with being unexpectedly royal.

But that had been a rather quiet wedding, all things considered. Taishm, who had never sought the throne, simply wanted to be happy with the woman he'd loved for years rather than make a fuss. He also preferred the title 'Regent' to 'King,' now, saying he was only holding the throne for his cousin's son. He and Yalonta didn't plan to have children, so the Ilyaran line of succession wouldn't be complicated.

Inga, on the other hand, was already four months pregnant and Hassin glowed like a thunder wolf every time he looked at her. After a great deal of debate among the Guildmasters, it had been decided that Hassin, who was already giving up the sea for love, didn't also need to give up sea witchery. There were discussions about Ilyaran-style guilds developing in the North, so magic might be brought back in safely. Hassin hoped to oversee that.

Almost no one had attended Taishm and Yalonta's wedding: just the three journeymen, all the Guildmasters, and a handful of city guard who were also the new queen regent's close friends. In contrast, Rasim was fairly certain all of Hongrunn, and possibly all of the Northlands, was at Inga and Hassin's. They were married on the longest day, an important date so far north where the length of days varied wildly, and the party went on for most of the next week. Lady Donnin of the Islands attended, and when she left, Captain Nasira went with her. No one suggested Nasira give up her witchery again, either.

There were faces Rasim missed, more than just those who had died. Bayar especially, of course; in fact, most of the people he missed were in Shenryal. As one of the late nights began to wind down—in a matter of speaking; the sun wouldn't set, no matter how long they waited for it to—he climbed the parapets of Hongrunn's castle alone, and sat on their edge, looking down at the blue-black harbor Kisia and Desimi once jumped into. It was still too high for his liking, but he was getting better about it.

He drew the horsehair braid Oyun had given him out of his belt pouch, winding its rough fibers into a circle in his palm. She had told him to come to the steppes again someday, and when he did, to burn the braid. It would bring riders from anywhere in the vast plains to escort him to her camp again, so he could study with the ancient Shenryalan spiritmaster. He looked forward to doing that someday, maybe even someday soon. It was important, he thought. There was still a lot to learn.

Because there, alone in the quiet evening on a Northern mountainside, Rasim opened his other palm, and called a glimmer of fire to life.

~ the end ~

ACKNOWLEDGMENTS

For the second time in a row, I owe editor KB Spangler my life and my sanity for this book. She went above and beyond on an appallingly short deadline, and saved me from myself roughly seven thousand times. Thank you, KB. You're a star.

I owe Aleksandar Sotirovski for the Guildmaster Saga's wonderful cover art, and am so grateful to cover designer Tara O'Shea, who also turned things around on a short deadline.

I cannot thank my Patreon enough, either. They *also* came through on that short deadline and read an early version of this book to help me find the errors that had snuck through. Thanks especially to SB Beasley, Sharon Corbet, Doreen Farrar, Vicki Greer, and Nichole, whose sharp eyes caught all kinds of things I just couldn't see.

And finally, thank you to my family, who basically didn't see me for six weeks while I got this finished and out the door. I love you all.

ABOUT THE AUTHOR

CE Murphy began writing around age six, when she submitted three poems to a school publication. The teacher producing the magazine selected (inevitably) the one she thought was by far the worst, but also told her–a six year old kid–to keep writing, which she has.

She has also held the usual grab-bag of jobs usually seen in an authorial biography, including public library volunteer (at ages 9 and 10; it's clear she was doomed to a career involving books), archival assistant, cannery worker, and web designer. Writing books is better.

She was born and raised in Alaska, and now lives with her family in her ancestral homeland of Ireland.

You can find her online at CatieMurphy.com.